Jeff Noon

MOON OVER BRENDLE

A NOVEL

ANGRY ROBOT

ANGRY ROBOT
An imprint of Watkins Media Ltd

Unit 11, Shepperton House
89-93 Shepperton Road
London N1 3DF
UK

angryrobotbooks.com
The *beautiful* puzzle.

An Angry Robot paperback original, 2026

Edited by Simon Spanton Walker and Andrew Hook
Cover by Sneha Alexander
Set in Meridien

ISBN 978 1 83673 030 9
Ebook ISBN 978 1 83673 031 6

Printed and bound in the United Kingdom by CPI Group (UK) Ltd, Croydon CR0 4YY

The manufacturer's authorised representative in the EU for product safety is eucomply OÜ - Pärnu mnt 139b-14, 11317 Tallinn, Estonia, hello@eucompliancepartner.com; www.eucompliancepartner.com

9 8 7 6 5 4 3 2 1

MIX
Paper | Supporting
responsible forestry
FSC
www.fsc.org   FSC® C013604

For
Bill Clarke and Mike Rooke

Teachers

My name is Joe Sutter. Under a pseudonym I have written a number of science fiction novels. If this current book, *Moon Over Brendle*, is accepted by my publishers and sent out into the world, it will be my twenty-first novel. Every word I have written in this and all my previous books, and in every published short story, all fifty-six of them, every single word has flowed from things that happened to me during the summer of 1968. I was eleven years old. Every word, every sentence, every idea, every image, every theme, every character trait, every plot and subplot, every twist and turn, every made-up world or beast or race, every hidden or not so hidden message, every beginning and every ending: not one would have been created unless I had visited a house called Pike View and met with the strange people who lived there. I am not exaggerating. Every single word.

PART ONE

SUTTER'S FANCY

1

The man was covered in dust. Thousands of particles of many colours, glittering. I couldn't see his face. Dust was crawling inside his nostrils, in his mouth, his ears. His eyes were grey with it. Grey twitching eyes. His hair was completely hidden behind a blue shimmer. The dust crept down inside his collar, it gloved his fingers in red. It was already heaped up around his lower half, his legs and hips. He was a shape on the ground, nothing more. But the shape was moving.

Denny said to me, "Look at him."

I looked. The man was lying at the bottom of Slew Hill, in a shallow ditch next to a dead-end railway track, near a set of rusted buffers.

"Look at him. Is he dying?"

"I don't know."

Neither of us moved. I was scared, and fascinated. I could feel the tension from Denny when he spoke. "Yeah, it's cool. He's on the way out."

I wasn't feeling too good, but I tried not to show it. "Who is it?" I asked.

"It's Tom Halfpenny. What's up, Joe, can't you see him?"

"No."

"Why not? You mean…?"

I nodded. Denny had turned to look at me. I kept my eyes forward. "Koag has taken him over. Head to foot. The dust. It's in his eyes, his mouth, everywhere."

Denny whistled. He went quiet then. I could hear him breathing.

I was one of the few people who could see the dust. Maybe that's why Denny wanted me to be his friend. I didn't mind that, I was glad of it.

"You can't see his face?"

"No. He's completely covered. Koag has him."

Denny spoke in awe. "*Koag*. Koag is strong, Koag is all powerful."

The proper name of the dust was Greot. Everyone called it that. You learnt it first of all from your mum and dad, and then at school. But we were different, we were special. We had our own name: *Koag*. We were the only two people in the entire world who called it that. Denny had sworn me to secrecy: "Never ever use that name with anyone else, do you hear me, Joe? Do you swear?" *Yes, Denny. I swear.* And so the Slew Hill club was formed.

The man groaned in pain. It made my stomach heave. But I held the puke down, so my friend wouldn't laugh at me. It was the first week of the summer holidays; endless days of heat lay ahead of us, and here we were, staring down at Tom Halfpenny as he writhed about for one last time. Then his body stopped moving, not a shiver. For a long moment neither of us could speak.

"Is he dead?" I whispered. "I think he's dead."

"It looks that way."

"*Pow! Boom!*"

I had a habit of adding sound effects to my life. It was nerves, I suppose. Denny and I loved superhero comics. Spider-Man, Daredevil, the Fantastic Four. I always put an explanation mark into my voice whenever I used these magic words: *Whaaam! Kerpow! Kraaaang!* Earlier that year Denny had surprised me by saying we should make up our own stories, with our own mighty heroes and evil villains and trusty sidekicks, drawing pictures, panels, speech balloons, writing it all down. This would never have occurred to me. But Denny was like that, always making up new games to play, riddles, puzzles, and fantastical stories. There was no stopping him.

A tatter of crows crossed the land, wanting to examine the corpse, maybe. They loved to hang around the old rail-yard. The Slew wasn't much of a hill, truth be told. Mrs Pierce, our teacher at junior school, called it a burial mound, and she spoke with a wistful look in her eyes of the Saxon king and queen who were buried there, arm in arm. She wanted it to be true. The hill was as high as a two-storey house, with a gentle slope covered in grass and weeds. It was easy to climb, and from its peak you could see the course of the Stubbs Canal and the chimneys of five different factories, and then the higher hills beyond the town, westwards, where Brendle Pike tower stood proudly, pointing up at the sky. Denny likened the chimneys to giant sentinels overseeing a dying world, and the tower as their leader. Closer by, you could follow the criss-crossing of the railway lines towards the locomotive shed, all empty now. No trains ran that way any more, not since they closed down Ormsley Vale station. There was a lone goods wagon parked up near the hill, which we used as a den. It was filthy and rusty and a home to beetles, but we loved it. Our secret headquarters. It was from the wagon, while sitting on the roof playing rock-paper-scissors, that we had first spotted the body in the ditch.

Sunflowers hung over the scene. They stank of summer rot. Denny moved closer to the dead man, a few steps at least. But I held him back, telling him to wait. The dust had stirred into life. Koag was rising, rising from the body. It floated in clusters, and now I saw its varied colours more clearly, ruby red, acid yellow, deep salmon blush, mottled tan and burnt orange. So many strands. Each grouping was separate, but they all flew off in the same general direction, high into the sky and drifting away towards the mill towers to the east. All except for one particular strand – rose-pink tinged with silver – which crept along low to the ground, vanishing into a patch of brier bush tangling the yard's fence. The face of the man was now revealed to me.

Tom Halfpenny was a character who hung around the door of the Weaver's Arms, singing and dancing, hoping to cadge dregs of beer and half-smoked cigarettes. But now his face was stretched tight in a final grin. I could not understand why Koag had shown such interest in him. But this was a brilliant story to tell, and it had to be told! Denny set off first, myself following. We raced across the goods yard, skipping the tracks with wild leaps, shouting our battle cries, along the canal bank, across the humpbacked bridge, running full pelt alongside Bradshaw's Mill, past the wasteground where Monty's caravan was parked, over the wall of the churchyard, back into town, and finally along the high street, where with breathless voices we told everyone who cared to listen of the poor twitching dying man we had found in the dry-earth ditch by Slew Hill.

2

I got home late for supper, after all the excitement. Chloe was upstairs in her bedroom, listening to records. Most probably "Do You Know the Way to San Jose" by Dionne Warwick, her favourite single of that year. She would play the same song over and over again, driving me nuts. Our mother worked hard at the factory, and most evenings she would just plonk herself down in front of the television, occupying herself with cigarettes and chocolates. She called out to me.

"Do you have to bang the door every time?"

"Sorry, Mum."

"The whole street can hear."

She often said this, and I never responded.

"Where have you been? Your supper's in the oven."

"Thanks, Mum."

"Sausages and mash. It'll be dried out by now."

I went to the living room doorway, lingering there. "I was out with Denny Portman."

"That layabout."

"We found a dead body."

"What?" Her eyes were fixed on the TV.

"It was Mr Halfpenny. The man who sings on the green."

"A dead body, you say?"

"The coppers are out there now. We had to show them where he was and everything."

"What did he die of?"

"I don't know. Probably old age or something." I didn't want to explain that we couldn't see any wounds or anything

9

like that on the body. And I certainly said nothing of the dust covering him head to foot. That fact was for Slew Hill club members only, Denny had insisted. We had a growing number of secrets, and it made me excited to think of them all.

"He was getting on a bit, I suppose," my mother said.

"Someone said it was a heart attack."

She looked over from the television screen for the first time. "Oh, that Dennis Portman, I always said he'd lead you astray."

"We both found him."

It seemed important to explain such a thing, a joint venture. But she tutted and told me off for being such a dirty wreck. It was true; I had grass stains on my shorts and scrapes on both knees, cuts on my hands, burrs stuck in my hair, smears of dirt on my face. She shooed me away and returned to *It's a Knockout!* and her box of Milk Tray. I was heading towards the kitchen when I noticed the handwritten "do not disturb" sign hanging on the door of the parlour. This could only mean one thing, that Grandma Sykes was conducting one of her viewing sessions. I crept along and nudged open the door, peering through a gap. The back parlour was a place all of its own, with its own mood, its own smell, a mix of furniture polish and talcum powder. Grandma had taken the room over. There was a single bed in the corner draped with a flowery eiderdown. Her clothes hung on a portable metal rail, of the kind she had once used on her haberdashery stall on the market. Pushing the door a little further open, I could see the table where Grandma was sitting with her visitor, someone I recognised, even though her back was to me. Her long straight blonde hair gave her away. It was May Harper from the next street along. May worked as a shop assistant in a boutique, and wore miniskirts, coloured tights, strings of beads around her neck, and jingle-jangle bangles on her wrists. She was a hippy. I knew this from looking at the photographs in the *News of the World* every Sunday. *Hippies are happening! Wild music, mind-expanding drugs, and orgies. We expose the outrageous lifestyle of the young.* I looked up the word *orgy* in the *Family Dictionary* but there was no entry for it. Denny told me it was "like a party, where people roll around on the floor and Koag lands on their bodies, tickling them all over."

"Really? Do they have any clothes on?"

"No, nothing at all. Totally starkers."

Denny knew everything. He learnt it all from his older brother, Michael. The hippy girls in the photographs all dressed and looked like May Harper did. She fascinated my young mind for reasons I could not work out.

Two women, one old, one young. A darkened room.

And myself, the peeper at the doorway.

Taken by a sudden boldness, I stepped into the room. Usually Grandma kept her consultations private, but this time she did not mind me. Perhaps she knew that something strange had happened that day. She had a knack of reading people's thoughts, one of her many gifts.

The earliest records say that all can see the dust. This is no longer the case. Nowadays, only a few of us can view Koag, or Greot, or whatever name you like to use, perhaps five percent of the populace. We are known as *witnesses*. I have that ability. Sometimes I can feel it on my skin, or I can move it with my breath. But mostly I just look at it, like watching dust motes in a sunbeam. My mother could not see the dust, nor could my father. But my grandma could see it. Such a talent can sometimes run in families, skipping generations. Growing up I knew of a few others in the towns of Lancashire who had the gift; they were featured in the local newspapers now and then. And of course there was Yvette Bishop on the BBC, the country's most popular witness. She spoke every evening after the weather forecast of the day's sightings, the local colours, the shapes and patterns of dust across the nation. My grandma was even more special than Mrs Bishop, however. Not only could she view Greot, she could also see *through* the eyes of Greot, and then share that vision. She was more than a witness, she was a *beholder*. Some likened beholders to mediums, or else to witches and wizards. Or to charlatans. Some refused to believe, while others wanted desperately to believe. And it was to those believers that Grandma directed her talents. So the back parlour of our house was now a "Chamber of Living Eyes". She advertised her wares on a card placed in the window of Cooper's corner shop: *With great foresight and wisdom, Mrs Dorothy Sykes (widow) will reveal your innermost secrets and desires. Visit the Chamber of Living Eyes today.* Below this was our address and a drawing (my own work) of a huge staring eye with magical energy rays coming out of it in wavy lines.

The curtains were closed, as was always the case when the Chamber was in session, day or night. Grandma's hair was fiery red. Her cheeks were shiny with rouge. She kept a stuffed animal under a glass dome; I could never tell what species it was, something her brother, Uncle Jud, had picked up on his travels as a merchant seaman. The creature's glass eyes would stare at me. Of course, I thought of Dotty Sykes as being incredibly old at the time, but in reality she would be in her late fifties, younger than I am now. She had only moved in with us recently, about a year ago. It made sense, as she was alone in life now, and Mum was thankful for the extra money, now that Dad had left home. Her customers came from all the nearby towns, from Ashton-under-Lyne, Oldham, Stalybridge, Droylsden, and even from Manchester, the nearest city. Dotty was famous. Bowls of Greot were lined up on a shelf, separated into their colour schemes. Coco the budgerigar was busy in his cage, pecking at his own reflection in a mirror. That was the only noise in the room. I held my breath. One of the glass bowls stood on the table. Dotty asked, "Are you sure now, dearest, this is your choice?" She always let the visitors choose the bowl they liked best, even though Greot was invisible to them. May Harper nodded. Grandma took up a handful of dust and poured it from her closed fist in a controlled sweep across the polished tabletop. The dust was air-force blue, a very common colour, mixed with the rarer mint green, the two strands separate from each other. Slowly, dramatically, Dotty moved her hands back and forth like a magician at work on a television show. She started to moan, to shiver and shake. Her chair rocked back and forth as the passion took her over. Her head reared back, revealing the tendons of her neck. The dust on the tabletop was animated by her jittery movements and started to rise up towards the hands which passed over, left to right and back again. The dust glowed with light. I never knew how she managed to control Greot in this way; it was something I could never do. But it responded to her as always, and quickly settled into a small cloud trembling in the air between the two women.

Dotty calmed herself. Her face took on a serene look. Her hands stirred the dust gently in the air, shaping it. Coco pecked at his bell. That sound, I hear it in my dreams. Any bright tiny tinkling noise like that always brings me back immediately to those days, the back parlour and its attendant smells and my grandmother going into her spiel. Her voice lowered. "To see not the world, but something beyond the world, that is our purpose." I suppose such words were never meant to be spoken in a thick Lancashire accent – *T'see not t'world, but summat beyond t'world* – but she had perfected the speech over the years, taking bits and pieces from various cheaply-printed pamphlets received through the post: *Dust to Dust; The All-Seeing Eye; The Watchers*; and so on. She was a member of the *International Society of Beholders*, whose international headquarters were contained within a back bedroom (I imagined) of number 12, Leatherhill Drive, Kirby Bridge, Birkenhead, the address printed in their magazine. Dotty went on with her patter: "Something beyond this petty world. Something that cannot be seen otherwise, only with the help of Greot. To see into the darkness that surrounds our pitiful ring of senses, the darkness encircling." She spoke with urgency. "Open your eyes, wider, wider!" May Harper did so, as wide as possible. Then Dotty puffed out her cheeks and blew upon the dust cloud, sending it towards May's face, into her stretched eyes.

"BEHOLD!"

Dotty's shouted instruction had its desired effect. May looked startled. Then she blinked a few times, and started to gently weep.

"Do you see?"

May nodded. "I see, I *do* see."

But what did she see, this eager young hippy woman? The basic idea was that Greot travelled everywhere, and saw everything, and so therefore knew all things, and a beholder could in some way transfer this vision into people's eyes. Grandma never allowed me to join her in this work, no matter how many times I asked. I was not old enough. *You're not ready, Joe. Not nearly enough.* And then sometimes, and even worse: *Who knows, perhaps it will never happen.* She would laugh, saying this. It maddened me. But still I loved to watch her ply her trade. And right now May Harper looked to be in ecstasy. Her hands reached out to grasp at some invisible object.

But then Dotty's voice changed again, becoming a rasp. I had never heard it reach such a tone before. The sound made me nervous, and I stepped closer to the table.

"In the dust, in the dark."

I caught my breath. Viewings didn't go like this. Usually the visitor reported what they saw, things like "a bird", or "a clock face", or "a stranger dressed in black". Grandma then interpreted these images, rather like other old ladies on the housing estate would read the future in tea leaves. But this time Grandma was seeing the vision. Her eyes were fixed and staring as she spoke: "In the dark of the dust, she is waiting." The words came from deep inside, a horrible thing to hear. "Little girl, poor little girl! Come to me." Grandma stood up, her body rocking to and fro over the table. "Come to me, my child."

May had broken out of her trance. She pressed back in her chair, unable to move. I was the same, frozen to the spot. "Grandma? Grandma, are you…" I could not finish the question. She was most certainly *not all right*. I watched in fright as a sudden stream of dust darted towards her open mouth. The vision of Tom Halfpenny's body came to me, with its shroud of many colours. I cried out. But then Dotty coughed, and came to her senses, falling back to her seat, but not quite making it and landing on the floor. I went to her. Her eyes were flinty green, sparkling. This time she whispered to me, not to May, that same phrase.

"In the dust, in the dark."

Mum and Chloe hurried into the parlour, roused by the commotion. May Harper slipped past them on her way to the front door; she had seen enough, more than enough. Mum knelt down at Grandma's side, rubbing her shoulder and asking what the trouble was. Then she glared at me, as though I were to blame. What could I say? That little bell rang on and on, needling at my head, my ears. It marks the day when my life started to change.

3

I woke up at three o'clock in the morning, as I sometimes did. For me personally there was no need at all for such a thing, but for other people it was a popular time to be awake, all across Britain. I would prefer to sleep through. The darkness of my room paled as house lights came on across the alley. There was noise below, voices speaking to each other quietly, but carrying easily in the warm night air. I got up from my bed and went to my window, which was already open. I looked out and saw a small family group in the alleyway at the back of our house. They had torches with them. It was four minutes past three. Only two minutes to go. What was I expecting, something different to the usual show? Something affected by the death of Tom Halfpenny, perhaps? I didn't know.

In the dark of the dust, she is waiting.

What in God's name did that mean? Who was waiting? Grandma had mentioned a little girl, in her vision. I could only think that the image of the girl had been carried along the strands of dust from some other place, perhaps a far-off place, a bit like how we can see actors and pop stars on the television. But really, I had no clue.

There was a cry from outside. I leaned over the window ledge to see that Mr and Mrs Powell from number 12 had their youngest boy with them. He was little more than a tot, and I'll bet this would be his first proper sight of Greot. He was excited, pointing at the streamers of red and gold dust that suddenly appeared above the houses. There wasn't much of it in evidence this particular night, a light drift only, but it shone with its own lovely phosphorescence. The youngster reached up with his little hands. The dust haloed his fingers, attracted by him. His father held him aloft, the better to partake of Greot's blessing, while the mother shone the torch this way and that, making the twirls and clusters of dust sparkle and shimmer.

At this exact time every morning of the year, six minutes past three, the dust was briefly revealed to all. During this short period, I was no longer special in any way. All across the land people would now be gathered as witnesses, scientific experiments would take place, collecting of samples would occur, monitoring stations would be on alert for any changes, photographs would be taken, watercolourists would try to capture the moment before it disappeared. People would revel in the dust as it tickled at their hands and faces. One minute, two minutes. But if Koag had any extra message for me, it was not shown, or not made obvious.

Koag, I whispered. *Koag, Koag, speak to me. Show me a sign.*

Two minutes and thirty-nine seconds. That was how long the public viewing lasted, each and every day, before Greot vanished from normal sight. The little Powell boy cried in dismay at losing the wondrous display of colours. For me, however, the dust remained as it was, drifting along the alleyway to join with other clouds of different shades.

But Koag was silent.

4

The front door bell rang right after breakfast, before I could make my escape into the wilds. It was a reporter and a photographer from the *Ormsley Chronicle* who wanted to interview me about finding the body of "poor Tom Halfpenny", as the reporter called him. Mum led them into the front room, while Chloe ran upstairs. She came back down in double-quick time wearing a snazzy minidress with wavy black-and-white lines on it, like an optical illusion; the kind of thing the girls on *Top of the Pops* wore. The reporter asked lots of questions, hardly giving me time to answer any one of them. I found myself saying *Yes*, or *No*, in response, or just shaking or nodding my head. I looked to Mum for help, receiving just a proud smile: "Go on, Joe, tell them everything!" And I looked to Grandma, who remained silent throughout, sitting in her favourite chair. The reporter kept talking and talking. She was very keen on my status as a young witness, during, as she said, "an era when so few seem to have the ability." The subject quickly turned to my going to secondary modern school in September, and not to a grammar school. "You know, I'm sure," the reporter explained, "there are many now calling for all witnesses to go to grammar school automatically, without having to take the eleven-plus, to make sure those chosen few do the best they can for the country's prospects."

What did all this mean? *Chosen few? The country's prospects?* Granted, the last but one prime minister had been a witness, Harold Macmillan; he could see the dust that swirled around and around the Houses of Parliament. But just a few months back, another witness had been revealed as the "Lake District Charmer", a murderer, claiming five victims before the police tracked him down to a cottage near Lake Windermere. So the talent was no guarantee of goodness, or success, or even happiness. You saw entertainers on the television, using the dust to read minds, or to predict football results. The famous magician Preston Heyes could make Greot visible to the audience in clouds of red, blue and white dust. Yes, there were a few well-known witnesses. But many were alone in life, by choice or by accident. The newspapers told their sad little stories: *She was found dead in her one-room flat, having taken an overdose of sleeping tablets. According to her neighbours, Susan was a quiet woman, a witness. Some say she was a beholder, as well. But she didn't like to show off. She kept herself to herself.* Oh yes, I had my fantasies, of using my powers to save people's lives, of one day becoming the Grand Beholder, of helping Manchester United win the FA Cup. But in reality, I would more likely end up unknown, hiding myself away like poor Susan in her bedsit. Or worse: coming in last on *Opportunity Knocks*.

The reporter moved onto the state of the corpse. "Is it true that Mr Halfpenny was covered in the dust?"

I was nervous of answering this, after Denny's urging for secrecy. I stuttered. Everyone was looking at me. The photographer took one photograph after another. Chloe managed to get herself in quite a few of them, showing off her fancy outfit.

"Your friend, Dennis Portman, told us."

"He did?" Now I was confused.

"That's right. Dennis said that–"

"Everyone calls him Denny."

"That's good to know. I'll make sure to call him that in the piece."

"He hates being called Dennis."

"Well, *Denny* said that you were very excited by what you'd seen. That the dust covered the body from head to foot. That it covered his face. That's very unusual, isn't it?"

Again, I hesitated.

She went on, "The dust wasn't hurting him, we know that now–"

"Ko–I mean, *Greot* would never hurt anyone."

"Of course not."

The reporter's head was haloed by a dust cloud of shocking pink. It sparkled around her hair. If only she could see, if only! In my nervousness I had almost revealed the secret name, *Koag*.

"Denny is your best friend, isn't that true?"

"Yeah, I guess he is, I think so, but…"

"Joe, why should the dust want to cover up a dying man like that? Do you have any idea?"

I didn't. But Chloe had her own thoughts: "I reckon it wanted to copy his features, at the moment he popped his clogs. Greot likes that kind of thing." She smiled at me and went on, "Greot wants to know everything."

"Shut up, Chloe," my mother said.

"But it's true! Greot is really good at copying things. All it has to do is land on something, for five seconds only, that's enough. A perfect copy! I know stuff, I do, just as much as Joe does."

"Oh, please, let your brother speak."

But I stopped then, saying no more. I was aware of a sudden darkening of the room, the dust drifting away from its chosen objects. It made for the door and the windows, seeping through the tiniest cracks in the walls. I looked over to my grandma. Dotty had noticed the change as well, the change in the air, in the light. She went over to the front window, looking out. The reporter was curious about our behaviour.

"Is something wrong? Have you seen something?"

Neither of us answered.

"Is it the dust?" She joined us at the window. "Is something happening to the dust?"

It was. A shadow crawled across the street, colouring the pavement and the front of the houses opposite. The sun was blotted out. This could only mean one thing. I ran into the hallway and out the front door. The sky was cloudy all over, the bright blue of the summer's morning dirtied with clumps of black and grey, mixed in with other colours, many colours in strands and blotches. The cloud quickly expanded as other, more colourful streams of Koag flew in from all directions.

It was a gathering, a Gathering of the Eyes.

I think the dust cloud covered Stoneybrook housing estate entirely, miles wide, miles long. The sun had disappeared behind it. All things were lit with a soft violet light.

The others had followed me out into the street.

"Can't you see?!" I cried. "Look. It's everywhere. The entire sky!"

But they couldn't see it, even when the dust was packed in so tightly, even when it hovered like a huge spaceship above the town, beckoning to us. The photographer raised his camera to the skies, taking as many pictures as he could. What was he hoping for? They would show only sky and sunlight, nothing more. The street was perfectly normal to all other residents. Mrs Turnbull chatted with Mrs Brown at the bus stop. Life went on. But, of course, my grandma was also an eyewitness. She was bent over backwards, her hands on her hips, her head raised up to best receive the sight, the blessing, the coming disaster, whatever it might be. She was lost in a reverie. Above us more and more of the dust arrived, multicoloured and varied in its patterns. The most prominent was a vast ribbon of dark blue, striped at the edges with orange, that undulated like a river across the sky. Some patches of dust fought with others for the privilege of occupying certain choice areas. Colours clashed with colours, and the daytime darkened further. Smaller clouds billowed against each other; they seemed to be in conflict. At least a dozen different colours were now taking part. It was the best ever psychedelic show. And all of this seen only by myself and my grandmother, unless other witnesses stood in those streets, as yet unknown to me. The cloud suddenly lowered itself in one layer, joined together, descending to just above my head. The entire street was now filled with the dust, this and other streets alongside. Then it lowered further until it covered my face, my neck, my shoulders. It was so dense I could not see more than a few inches in front of me. Usually the dust was no more substantial than a whispering breath, but now, gathered together like this, it felt like a hand, or a series of hands, pressing at me.

Koag, Koag.

Again, I called to it. And again there was no answer.

Grandma appeared before me, stepping forwards. The dust had settled on her face, masking her with green and gold stripes. She looked like a strange beast from a fairy tale. Her eyes glinted brightly. What was she seeing? Would I ever share in her visions?

Mum's voice pierced the gloom. "Joe, Joe! Come away now."

It wasn't often I disobeyed my mother, but this time I did. I pushed through the cloud layer, causing ripples to part around me, and to close again in my wake. I ran to the end of our street and then took a quick left onto Stoneybrook Road. When I think of myself in those days, often I am running, running at speed, sometimes with Denny alongside, other times alone, always hoping to get somewhere, or away from somewhere, or someone, some gang of bully boys perhaps, or an angry teacher, or my father when I'd done something wrong. It never ends. I was brimful of life. I was Roger Bannister running the four-minute mile. I was the Flash, Billy Whizz, Speedy Gonzalez, all of them combined! Along the canal path, skirting the factory. I knew where I was going without even thinking of it. The massive cloud of dust had risen a little, away from my shoulders, but was still there in the sky, above me. The air was powdery. And then on a sudden it took off on its further travels, with a swerve to the east. I stopped to catch my breath, watching as Koag flew away over the town, dispersing, vanishing into the heat haze of the sun. Only a few small clumps remained, settling on the trees and the factory wall.

Whooping with excitement, I ran on towards Slew Hill, and the goods wagon. This area had been our playground, our field of battle, our distant lands, our alien worlds. Over the years we had invested it with so many childish stories, they had taken residence here in dribs and drabs. I was expecting Denny to be around somewhere. I had so much to tell him. I heard music from the open door of the wagon, a transistor radio playing "Hurdy Gurdy Man" by Donovan. I loved that song, the looping melody, that brilliant electric guitar sound, the weird character of the title with his yearning call from a dream world. The sun was in the music, the summer air, the drift of dandelion clocks across the fields. I rushed forwards, eagerly. But then I stopped in my tracks.

I heard a voice over the music, and then a giggle.

Who was it?

A girl's voice. Then Denny's, laughing in turn. A funny feeling took over my stomach, I could not explain it. Something new in my life. I reached the doorway and peeped in. The girl was Eileen Barlow. What was she doing here? It didn't make sense.

The second rule of the club was very strict: *No girls allowed!*
Eileen had been in the same class as Denny and me in junior
school, but was going on to grammar school after the holidays.
The two of them were sitting on the floor of the wagon, cross-
legged on either side of the little radio. Neither of them noticed
me. The Hurdy Gurdy Man went on and on, singing his songs
of love. The shadows were deep in the interior, cut by a sharply
etched line of morning light. Then they saw me. Denny's eyes
held something I had never seen before, and as with so much
that day, something new. I could not work it out.

"Alright, Denny?" I said.

I didn't know what else to say. It was our standard greeting.
Alright, Denny? Or *Alright, Joe?* And then the other one had to
reply, *Yeah, not bad.* We always did this. But not this time, for
some reason. Instead, Denny just stared at me. I thought he
looked a bit miffed. I was tongue-tied. Eileen Barlow gazed
at me. She blew a bubble of pink gum until it popped. Then
she giggled some more and asked, "Sutter, is that your best
shirt?" It was, actually, a paisley pattern affair my mum had
bought me for the Whit walks that year. She had made me
wear it that morning for the interview and the photographs.
I thought it made me look a little like Steve Marriott of the
Small Faces, but now I wasn't so sure. I started to answer, but
again stuttered over my words. Eileen kept looking at me, her
wavy hair hanging over one eye. She was dressed in a summer
frock and ankle-socks and brown sandals. She looked, as she
always did, like a girl off the television, one of those goody-
two-shoes always telling the other kids what to do. She visited
me in dreams sometimes, a golden figure. Now she was sitting
in the secret den, *our* den, with my best friend. He must have
brought her here, to show off about finding Tom Halfpenny,
that was it.

Her bubblegum popped again. She asked with a sneer, "Seen
any good dust, lately?"

I couldn't help being enthusiastic. "Denny, a giant cloud
appeared over the town. I wish you could have seen it. It was
incredible!"

"Really?"

Now I had his attention. "Sure, the biggest ever! *Pow!
Kaboom!*"

Eileen shook her head. "What's he doing now? *Pow? Kaboom?* What is that?"

Denny looked embarrassed; yet another new expression. He flicked his hair from his eyes. He'd been growing his fringe, ready for the big school, but I imagined the headmaster would have strict rules for the allowed length of boys' hair. Denny was a few months older than me, tall for his age, good-looking. Often he would look away from you, onto other things. He might appear to be half-asleep. But he was awake, awake, awake!

Donovan gave way to Tommy James and the Shondells singing "Mony Mony". Eileen was on her feet in an instant, swinging around, the hem of her dress flying. She was doing the hitch-hiker dance. Denny, to my surprise, quickly followed her lead, jiving and jittering madly, flinging his legs and arms this way and that, singing along. This really wasn't his kind of music. Yet there he was. They disappeared into the shadows of the wagon. I felt awkward. What should I do now? Jump up and join them in the dance? No. No, absolutely not.

I walked over to the ditch where we had found the body. There was no sign of it now, not even an indentation or a broken weed stalk. I thought of that one strand of dust that had gone a separate way from the others, drifting into the undergrowth by the goods-yard fence. The colour of it, rosy pink dappled with silver; I had never seen such a combination before. There were no bowls of such a mixture in Grandma's collection. I wondered where it had gone, that dust, and for what purpose? Perhaps it was seeking some other object to cling to, even another victim, or something better than that, a treasure of some kind. The sunflowers drooped over my head. The sun dazzled me. Flies buzzed in the heat. I brushed one away from my face. Droplets of sweat were in my eyes. I could hear the transistor radio, playing softly, seemingly from the far distance, or even from another time: "King Midas in Reverse" by The Hollies. (My sister had that single.) The ominous dusklight of Koag had drifted away, revealing a sky brighter and bluer than ever, with not a cloud in sight. A kind of soft fuzziness covered everything, like a mirage seen in a war movie set in the desert. The music was blurred at the edges. Small clusters of dust floated by, visible only as a shimmer to the eye.

I set off walking, following the route I had seen that wayward strand take. I pushed through the brier bush at the fence, careful to unpluck my best shirt from the prickles before moving on. There was a gap in the fence. I climbed through onto a patch of land that belonged to one of the factory owners, but had not yet been used for any purpose. It was barren but for a few strong weeds, the soil as reddish brown as the large clay pool at its centre. We used to play here, sometimes, when we had nothing better to do. Lumps of rusty machinery were dotted about. I skirted the pool, wary of the giant blood-sucking leeches we were sure lurked in its depths, wondering where the special dust might have gone next, my eyes attentive for that distinctive glimmer of rose-pink and silver.

I found it trapped in tiny clusters of dew on a spider's web. I found it caked to the leaf of a rhubarb plant growing beside a gatepost. I climbed the gate and entered a narrow lane that went on between tall hedges. There was a sewage farm here, glimpsed through gaps in the foliage. This wasn't a place we went to much, because the lane ended in another gate, this one marked with a *PRIVATE PROPERTY* notice. I stopped here. I recalled a much earlier conversation, from a few years before, when Denny and I had pondered the exact meaning of the word *prosecute*. It was a mystery to us. In the end we'd decided on *electrocute*. "Trespassers will be electrocuted." We always went for the most dangerous option. Dust hovered about me. But the colour I sought was not there, only the common chalk-white. I climbed the fence and continued on the other side, along a dirt track.

Ormsley Vale was a small town in Lancashire. It lay on the lower slopes of the Pennine Hills, the streets, houses and factories quickly giving way to fields and small farm-holdings. I expected a man with a shotgun to appear at any moment, threatening me. But the way was quiet, empty. Trees bent over the track, their leaves filled with birdsong. Here and there I spotted my treasured dust on a branch or floating in the air, a few swirls only. I decided to name it, thinking myself the discoverer of something new and strange and beautiful. Something like *Silver Delight*, or *Rosy Blur*, or *The Gleam*, like the name of a pop group. I said various other names out loud, testing them, but none of them sounded right. Perhaps it should take after my own name? Because then people in the future would know I was the first discoverer. Something like *Joe's Special Powder*. No, that sounded like a medicine. Maybe it was better to use my surname. *Sutter's Chance*. Or *Sutter's Fancy*. I needed Denny here with me, to make up a really good name.

Such thoughts were cast aside as I nearly tripped over a railway track, its lustre already reddened and weed-covered. No locomotives would ever come this way again. I followed the branch line for a while, seeing that Sutter's Fancy marbled the wooden sleepers, one after another. Then I veered away from the track, following my quarry deeper into the woods. I would soon be lost, a common occurrence. We were all latch-key kids back then, happy to roam, unsupervised. I thought of Denny, of what he was doing right now, with that girl, Eileen Barlow. Probably holding hands, or kissing, or something horrible like that. Dancing arm in arm. Or even worse, he was telling her stories. Stories that should be mine to hear. I'll just bet he was using the name Koag. Oh, forget them both! I had a new game to play. I was a super sleuth, like Sherlock Holmes, or Batman (The World's Greatest Detective), following a clue. But where would Sutter's Fancy lead me? And then I stopped dead still. I crouched behind a tree trunk, peering out at what I had seen. A mass of the pink and silver dust hung from the branch of an elm, mixed in with another strand, this one ultramarine in colour. Together they formed into a thickened clump about the size of a wasps' nest. The thing was oozing a syrupy whitish fluid, which dripped to the ground below. It happened rarely, or at least was viewed rarely, this peculiar activity. I had only seen it on the television before now. Mum told me that Greot was crying, when it took on this form, but I suspected she had made that up. Denny announced that Koag never cried, he was too powerful. It would be like Mick McManus crying, on the Saturday afternoon wrestling. In fact, according to Denny's older brother this clumping effect was actually called "The Multiplication of the Species". Here I was, a lone spectator, and it filled me with a kind of sick dread. I felt queasy, and yet excited at the same time. I was aware of the sweat on my palms. Perhaps this was King and Queen Koag going about their married business?

I snuck out from my hiding place and crept forwards.

The stink was high, and sweet, like rotting leaves mixed with washing-up liquid.

The sap oozed and dripped. It formed into a sticky pool on the ground.

Bluebottles hovered around the pool, sucking at it.

I was tempted to place my open hand under the dripping fluid and lick at my fingers. But of course that would be horrid, and nasty. So instead I skirted around the clump of dust. I had visions of describing all this to Denny, of bringing him here, to show him, or at least to point out where the action was taking place. I would describe it in great detail, as I always did. That would win him back, surely. Smiling at this thought, I walked on further until I came to the edge of the woods. I could see Weeping Cross Lane and then the slopes of a hill. Now I knew where I was. Perched on the hill's summit was Brendle Pike. I crossed the lane and walked up towards the tower. Denny and I often visited this place, bringing orange pop and crisps with us, but we always came here by a different pathway. I had made a semicircular route from the town. At the peak of the hill I rested. I lay flat on my back in the grass. I had scratched my forearm on a thorn and I wet the cut with my tongue, tasting blood. My best shirt was already dirty, but there was nothing I could do about that. I closed my eyes. The sunlight remained as a dance of red blotches behind my eyelids. I tried to make out shapes, faces, aeroplanes, but the blotches kept changing all the time. A grasshopper made its clicking song. Drowsy, drowsy days.

The first tower on this hilltop had been built by the Roman invaders, as a lookout post. Other towers had been built here over time, but the current stone-built one, from the Victorian era, was now bricked up. On a clear day you could see four counties: Lancashire, Cheshire, Yorkshire and Derbyshire, and on the far horizon, a smudgy glimpse of the Welsh hills. I sat up. This day wasn't so clear, as the sun was too bright and hazy, but I could easily see Hyde, Oldham, Dukinfield, a few other towns. Further on was the city of Manchester, with its thick black-grey pall of dust.

I stood up and walked around the tower, taking in all four shires. We had come here with Mrs Pierce, and she had pointed them all out to us, before moving onto the subject of Greot.

She talked in a romantic manner, like she was praising a lover. "There is no real explanation for the dust," she said to us that day. "It is a part of the world, like sunlight and birdsong and autumn leaves on the wind. It has always been with us, and we pray, always will be." Denny joked: "Like Morecambe and Wise on the tele, miss." And that got a good laugh. But Mrs Pierce soon returned to her subject: "You can see Greot in the Stone Age cave drawings, in France, in Spain, and at Creswell Crags in Derbyshire. It floats above the woolly mammoths." She spread her arms wide, worshipping the landscape. "Greot watches over us. It moves with purpose. It darts forwards and back, and hovers and dives and swoops." During all this I was made to indicate where Greot was seen in the sky, and in what colours and shapes it was formed. I hated doing this kind of thing because the other kids felt I was showing off. Mrs Pierce went on, "Thank you, Joe. Most enlightening. Picture it, children. Let Joe here be your eyes!" (No, no, no, please no!) There was no stopping her now. "Greot migrates, on occasion taking off in giant formations across the land, seeking out other climes, other lands, but who knows for sure what it is looking for?" She left this question open. I was then asked to point out where Greot was resting on the surrounding fields and towns. Mrs Pierce called this the "Coagulation Effect", a big new word for us. (In the last few weeks of the term she had introduced us to quite a few big words like this: she was getting us ready for secondary school, I think. She was a good teacher.) The dust, she told us, was attracted to certain locations more than others, certain cities and towns, like Ormsley Vale, and other places, "Such as ruined castles, old bridges, river crossings, sacred woodlands, stone circles. Nobody knows why this is." She sighed. "We live at the centre of a mystery that we have long forgotten to view as mysterious." Mrs Pierce often grew wistful. It was later that same day, when we got back to the classroom, that Denny came up with his new improved name for Greot. *Coag.* Taken from the new word, coagulation. But then he changed it to *Koag*. "It sounds better with a *K*," he whispered, not wanting the other kids to hear.

"It sounds the same, doesn't it?"

"But it looks better, when you write it down. Look."

He wrote the name out in his exercise book, using capitals.

KOAG.

It did look good, I had to admit. More powerful, more magical.

INCREDIBLE KOAG.

He borrowed this from *The Incredible Hulk*, a comic we both loved to read.

"And it looks a bit like Kong, doesn't it?" I noticed. "King Kong."

"That's it, Joe!"

"Only one letter different."

So then it was King Koag. Before then, I had never thought of the dust having a personality, it had always been an *it*, rather than a *he* or a *she*. Now it took on power, like a hero or a villain in a story, if only in our own heads.

INCREDIBLE KOAG, THE KING WITH A TRILLION EYES!

Koag was certainly plentiful, from my current vantage point at Brendle Pike. I saw its various strands and clusters below me, dotted about the hills and fields, gathering at wells and stiles and crossing places. England lay at peace under a veil of many colours. A thin horizontal rectangle of dust, sandy orange in colour, covered the entirety of the cricket ground at Fossett Moss. The dust above Ashton-Under-Lyne rose in vertical columns, so unlike any other town's display. Ormsley was covered in a dome of lemon and indigo. Stubbs Canal was a long straight line of amber, while the church spire of St Matilda's was hidden behind a purple cloud, as it nearly always was. The sight of it made me hum the guitar riff to "Purple Haze", and to sing the opening lines to myself. I then moved on to "Space Oddity", only to forget the lyrics after verse one. So instead I started to count all the mill chimneys in view, each with its plume of smoke. One, two, three, four... Until a kestrel drew me away from the task. It lingered high above the field, its body perfectly stilled. Then on a sudden it dived. *WHOOSH!* Some poor field mouse was about to meet its end. I followed the bird's plummeting shape until it reached the ground, when something even more interesting caught my eye. It was that kind of day, when one thing led to another, on and on.

The dive of the kestrel had directed me to a long meandering line of pink and silver dust that was creeping across the field. Perhaps from any other place it would have been invisible, but from this high up the flowing shape was set out as clearly as a stream flowing down the hill, or a line on a map. I walked down to meet it, and then followed alongside. The dust stream was a hand-span across. It floated at knee-level. The silver streaks sparkled in the sunlight, while the rose-pink body had a matte effect, a very pleasing contrast. It was leading me towards a house, a place I had not taken much notice of before this day. There were a few such buildings dotted about the lower slopes of the Pennines, separate from each other, fed by single-track lanes. But as I drew closer I saw that the house was a bit run-down, perhaps even empty. It had probably been a farmhouse at one point, but now the roof was in disrepair, and the walls were crumbling beneath the crawling vines. A sign next to the open gate told me the house was called *Pike View*. There were no vehicles parked in the front yard, other than a pushbike leaning against the wall, a lady's bicycle with a wire pannier on the front. All was quiet. But once again I acted like Sherlock Holmes, noticing a series of tyre-tracks in the powdery dirt of the front yard. A car had definitely been here, and not too long ago. Sutter's Fancy was heading down a side alley, between the house and a large shed. I followed it to the rear of the building. The back door was ajar and the trail of dust flitted inside through the narrow gap, the long tail following. I watched its progress. By my Timex Military Commando wristwatch it took fifty-seven seconds for the whole thing to disappear inside the house. I knew that I should follow, even if I didn't know why. But I was scared. If Denny had been here, it would be different. We would spur each other on. Or even better, my dad; he was always urging me to be courageous. On the day he left home he took me aside and told me I was now "the man of the house", and that I had to be strong and brave, for the sake of the family. I took it all in, with tears in my eyes.

Oh, I missed him. I missed him dearly.

Often, when he came home from work at Bradshaw's Mill, he would bring a comic for me, sometimes *The Dandy* or *The Beano*, and later on when I was older, *Valiant*, featuring the adventures of Captain Hurricane in the Second World War. I also liked Dan Dare in *Eagle*. But then came that special day when he brought me a very different kind of comic: *The Amazing Spider-Man*, issue number 14. I was seven years old

at the time, so I didn't understand all of it, but it excited me
more than anything I had ever seen. The issue was titled on the
cover, "The Bizarre Mystery of the Green Goblin!". Beneath
this it said, "The most twisted villain Spidey's ever battled!"
And then, "Look Out! Special guest star, the Incredible Hulk!"
Altogether there were eight exclamation marks on the cover.
Eight! I showed this new treasure to Denny Portman the
next day, during playtime at school. I always mark that as the
beginning of our friendship, and our adventures together.

I thought of all this as I stood at the door to the farm house,
hesitating. My father gave me some really important advice
that day, just before he left: whenever I faced some difficult
task, such as taking a penalty kick against a rival school, or
fighting back against a bully, or leaping over the clay pool
without getting drenched, I had to ask myself this question:
What would Spider-Man do? So I whispered the words aloud to
myself, lowering my voice as much as I could to mimic his gruff
smoky tone. "What would Spider-Man do, lad? Eh, Joe? Think
on it." And of course, there was only one answer. I pushed the
door a little more open and slipped inside.

5

I entered first of all a small room with a wooden tub and a mangle, a wash room. Then the kitchen. There was no sign of Koag, not a tinge, not a single eye to watch over me, or to spy on me. That long meander of silver and pink had scarpered into some deeper part of the farmhouse. The kitchen was untidy: unwashed pots in the sink, food left out on a table, the stone floor unbrushed. I got the impression there was definitely more than one occupant. But the place was quiet. All evidence of the outside world seemed to have vanished away. The house had a certain quality, a way of cutting off the light of day, even with the curtains wide open. I took notice of a pair of dog bowls, one filled with water, the other with a few scraps of dried meat. This wasn't good. A dog. It was probably a bull terrier, or something German like an Alsatian, or even a Rottweiler. The Nazis used Rottweilers to attack British soldiers in the war, I'd read about it in *Valiant*. But then I saw the name written around the edge of each bowl: *Nipper*. Now then, did that mean it was a creature who liked to nip at ankles? Or did it mean a small dog? Or a large dog, even? Because sometimes pet owners liked to use a joke name. Grandma's dog was called Princess. She was a huge, smelly, slobbering lurcher. Dead now, poor thing. But further from a princess you could not get. No, it was definitely worrying, this dog bowl situation.

But on I went, Spider-Man style. A corridor led off the kitchen, ending in the front door. A grandfather clock ticked. I realised then that I really should have walked around to the front door, and rung the bell, or rapped on the knocker, rather than enter like a burglar through the open back door. What was I thinking of? Well, it was too late now, I was inside. I halted where I was, just a few steps along the corridor, and listened intently. I could hear music, the sound of a piano playing. Classical music, it sounded like, although I knew little of that at the time. I was shaking with fear, and wanted desperately to retreat, to leave the house. But Koag had led me here, I had to believe that. It all seemed so deliberate. The Gathering of the Eyes had caused me to run to Slew Hill, which linked me to the dust that once inhabited the ditch, whose visible route led to Pike Hill and the tower. Even that kestrel had played its part, directing my viewpoint down to the final trail of Sutter's Fancy.

I called out, far too softly to be heard, "Hello." My throat closed on the word. I tried again, a little louder this time. "Hello, is anybody in?" There was no reply.

A door led to a dining room, empty, and yet one more to a living room, also empty. The music was coming from there. Looking through the open doorway, I noticed a piano, an upright model, the kind you still saw in pubs back in those days. Strangely, it was playing the melody all by itself. I thought it must be a mechanical piano. Either that, or someone invisible was playing it. I imagined the hands of a ghost on the keys. But then the music stopped and a presenter's voice told me I had been listening to "Nocturne in B-flat minor, Op. 9, No. 1", by Frederic Chopin. "Performed there by Artur Rubinstein, and recorded in 1936." (That tune, that particular recording in fact, will forever be burned into my soul as an indicator of the day's importance.) I realised the voice was coming from a radio gramophone, and a little of my fear left me. I was seeing, and hearing, spooks everywhere. I turned to examine a large bookcase. I had never seen so many books outside of Ormsley Vale Public Library. All of them, I would later learn, were of the science fiction genre. But right now the titles and authors on view were unknown to me, for I had not yet progressed much beyond kid's adventure stories and superhero comics. One of the books was resting on a side-table next to an armchair. Someone had been sitting there, listening to the radio, and reading. The book was called *The Stars My Destination* by a writer named Alfred Bester. The cover illustration was amazing. It showed the head of a man, or more likely an alien being, floating in space against a red and yellow background. He had a strangely elongated head, as though a larger than normal brain resided in his skull. But he was terrified, his eyes wide in horror, his mouth twisted in torment. Below, flying towards this vast interplanetary head, was a silver spaceship. I was held by the image in a very weird way, hypnotised almost. The silver ship glided through space, the alien's features became even more anguished. Surely, a war between the galaxies was about to begin! For a good few moments I was many light-years away, a traveller among the stars. The book trembled in my hand. But then the spell was broken, and I returned to Earth with a bump, to the room in the farmhouse. The title of the novel and the colours and imagery of its cover contrasted markedly with my current surroundings, which were dark and shivery, despite the heat outside. The furniture was old, antique probably. The rug in front of the fireplace was threadbare. A vase on a sideboard held a bunch of wilting flowers.

I left the room and peered up the staircase, happy to see traces of Sutter's Fancy on each step, little pools of dust sticking to the carpet. I imagined them as a set of footprints leading upwards. The staircase wall was decorated with a series of moulded translucent masks, all of the same man's face, each one made from a thin layer of wax. They were blank, colourless, with small openings for the mouth and the nostrils. But, very disturbingly, there were no eyeholes. The man's face got older and more wrinkled the higher I climbed, telling the story of a life.

The stairs creaked under my heel. It seemed very loud. I stopped.

After a moment a man's voice from above called out, "Margery! Is that you? Margery!" The sound was high and strained. I didn't answer. How could I? He called again. "Margery! God damn you!" He seemed to be in pain. He called a third time, but now his voice was muffled, as though he were being smothered. It was terrible. I stood frozen.

I was wearing short trousers. And a paisley shirt tucked into them. Plimsolls, blue socks. My hair was little more than a pudding-bowl cut. I wasn't sure at the time why all this struck me as odd, but looking back I realise that I was performing an adult action, perhaps the first true one of my life. And I was woefully unprepared, a child still. What exactly was I doing here?

Trespassers will be electrocuted.

Koag drifted around in little clouds, hardly moving at all. The radio downstairs was playing another piano piece, I have no idea which one, but its bittersweet tones held a spell. I thought to call out, to answer the voice from above, but he had fallen silent now. Instead I carried on up the stairs. I summoned up not the strength and agility of Spider-Man, but the "radar-sense" of Daredevil; after all, Daredevil was known as The Man Without Fear. I had to become The Boy Without Fear. Four doors led off the landing, two at the front, two at the rear. The first door on the right was open, revealing a woman's bedroom from the look of it, clean and neat, a well-made bed, a pair of fluffy slippers on the carpet. The door opposite was closed. I looked down and saw a strand of silvery-rose dust creeping under the door, entering the room. This was it, the end of the trail. I rapped gently, receiving no answer, so I pushed the door open.

Another bedroom, larger, dirtier, darker, the curtains closed.

A strange light came from the bed.

I could not make it out properly, but I recognised the colours instantly. Sutter's Fancy. But I had never seen it glow brightly before now. This was far more powerful than anything my grandma had managed to conjure into shape. The dust billowed in a large heap all across the bed. I felt sure that every last speck had been pulled here from all over Lancashire, and who knows, beyond that, from Derbyshire and Yorkshire, from the rivers and valleys and mines, from the towns, the villages, the nearby big cities, from the depths of vacuum-cleaner bags, from the lungs of pedestrians, from the graveyards, shops and cotton mills, from the windows of bedrooms where it whispered each night, *let me in, let me in*, from churches, schoolrooms and public houses, from the dreams of those just awakening, uncurling through startled eyes, from the golden flowing hair of pop stars and movie actresses; from wherever it might be in the furthest reaches of the land, Sutter's Fancy had gathered here in this room, on this bed. I was entranced. Everything else had been forgotten: the old man's voice, the classical music on the radio, Mum, Dad, Denny and his new friend, everything.

My one thought was this: I had found a nest of Koag.

I stepped forwards. The mound of dust reacted to me. It changed shape, taking on a form, that of a sleeping person. The body was rose-pink from head to foot, webbed through with silver, like veins through an organism. It breathed, like a man would breathe, the chest rising and falling. The hair was silver, and long and ragged over the pillow, the face all crinkly. The lips moved as though to speak, the eyelids fluttered. But the figure remained silent. Every detail was perfected, each one fashioned by a tiny and continuous shifting of dust. It was incredible. My young mind reeled with it, and gloried in it, even as my flesh crawled. I was freezing cold, and trembling.

The figure lying on the bed was Tom Halfpenny, the dead man of Slew Hill.

I could not understand it. Did he live here? Or more likely, did his family live here, in Pike View, and was his body returned here, to lie at rest before he was buried? And then Sutter's Fancy had taken up residence on his body, just as it had yesterday, when he lay in the ditch. That was the only possible explanation. But it seemed too little a time for the body to be returned. I thought of the ballads Tom used to sing for pennies outside the Weaver's Arms, songs of the old folk, such as "Jack O'Bower", and "Fair Maid of Farthingdale", and "The Witch's Knot", lyrics telling of merry ploughboys and fallen maidens, love potions and magic charms. He had a sweet voice, even when drunk on the dregs. And then, as I looked on, Tom Halfpenny came alive. He moved, raising his hand. His fingers spread apart. The dust sifted from him as he sat up. It fell away from his upper body, from his face, taking his features with it. And another man was revealed, a living man, an old man with a bald head. He had been lying on the bed, and the dust had formed over him, covering him completely, giving him the form and face and hair of Tom Halfpenny. It had carried the likeness here, all the way from the Slew Hill ditch. "Greot likes that kind of thing," as my sister had said that morning. Watching, learning, recording, remembering.

Greot wants to know everything.

The man in the bed was agitated. His face, his real face, was covered by a waxen mask, of the kind I had seen on the stairs. It was thin and clear and white enough that his features could be made out through the layer, at least to a degree. But surely he could not see clearly through that mask, nor speak easily. The eyes were blank. Yet he turned to look at me, and he did speak, his words muffled as they had been before when I had heard them on the stairs.

"Who's there? Answer me!"

I was petrified. I could not say a word. He stared at me with those missing eyes.

"Who in the blazes are you?"

His hands moved in front of his chest, pushing waves of dust aside. They responded gladly to his commands, which meant only one thing: he could see Greot, Koag, Sutter's Fancy. The old man was a witness, perhaps even a beholder. He started to choke, and to call out repeatedly, "Margery, Margery, help me!" The dust rose up in an angry cloud around the bed. It spun this way and that, whirling about. "Margery!" he roared. "We have an intruder. Help me!" He pounded on the bedside table with his fist.

I ran. Out the bedroom door, down the stairs, clattering. Along the hall to the front door. Not even thinking well enough to head for the back door. Was the front door locked? I prayed to God the latch would work! I don't know how I managed it. I was outside, but not free yet. I pictured the masked madman shaking his fist, and cursing, and calling the police. I saw in my mind's eye Sutter's Fancy chasing me across the field, through the woods, down the high street of Ormsley Vale, a great seething, cloaking, choking, writhing cloud of it, smothering me.

And so I kept on running.

PART TWO

THE ANTI-BOREDOM MACHINE

6

My father owned a pair of binoculars, which he handed on to me as a gift. They were old, from the war days, and very scuffed. But I loved them. They had cross-hairs, like a rifle sight. I used them mainly for birdwatching, and for Koagwatching, but I was currently putting them to a very different use. I was lying on the grass near a gap in a drystone wall. It was a good spying position, well concealed, with a clear view down the hill to Pike View. I adjusted the focus until the front door came into vision. It was closed. A vehicle was parked outside the house, a dilapidated Land Rover, its green paint streaked with dried mud. No sign of the old man, or any other occupants.

It was half past ten in the morning, a Thursday. Two days had passed since my first visit to the house. The day before, I had to go into Ashton with my mum, to buy my new school uniform. The badge on the breast-pocket of the jacket was a shield crossed with a pikestaff and a cricket bat. I had no idea what it meant; Fairfields was a secondary modern, a direct route into a factory or a coal mine, and what use was a pikestaff or a cricket bat in a cotton mill, or down a mineshaft? But I liked the uniform. It was smart. The neck-tie was dark grey with blue and white diagonal stripes. The blue stripe showed that I would be a member of Defoe house. The four houses were Austen, Chaucer, Defoe, and Gaskell. Mum also bought a briefcase for me, another item on the list of requirements. It was made out of brown leather, and had a lock and key.

Back home from the shopping trip, I kept expecting the doorbell to ring. A policeman would be standing there, wanting a word with me, talking to my mother. "Excuse me, madam,

but does a Joseph Sutter live here? A boy of eleven years? He's
wanted for trespassing." Something like that. But could the
man in the farmhouse possibly know where I lived, and what
my name was? I felt safe, or fairly safe. And then I thought of
him sending out Sutter's Fancy and other strands of Koag to
find me. It would be easy. Greot knows everything! The eyes
never close, they just get replaced with other eyes, millions of
them.

Luckily, I had not yet been arrested.

There was no activity at the farmhouse, so I turned the
binoculars onto other sights. Koag was going crazy above
Dukinfield; the poor old town looked as though it were being
attacked by a swarm of giant foggy bees. Swinging round I saw
a flock of sheep nuzzling at the grass, their white coats speckled
with purple dust. Beyond the sheep I spotted a figure walking
up the hill towards me. I focussed the binoculars a little more
until his face became clear. It was Denny. My heart did a flip.
Our friendship worked on a share-and-share-alike system: I
would give him exciting news of Koag, he would protect me
from various dangers; this would be especially helpful when
I started at the big school. I had already told him about the
man in the mask, asking if he wanted to join in on the spying
expedition. He'd been non-committal. He had to do this, he
had to do that. But now here he was, climbing over a stile,
giving me a single wave of his arm. And then I saw the figure
behind him, the girl, Eileen Barlow. Oh no, what's she doing
here? Her face filled the binoculars' field of vision, caught in
the cross-hairs. I took careful aim. *PEW*, *PEW*, *PEW.* Bullseye!
Her head exploded in a great gout of blood and...

"Alright, Joe?"

"Yeah, not bad."

They joined me at the wall, both of them flopping down on
the grass. I saw that Denny had put some Brylcreem in his hair,
another new addition. He would have taken a dab of it from
his father's jar. He was wearing a blue shirt with red buttons,
and white shorts (already grass-stained), with a penknife in
a holster fitted to his belt. His legs were covered in scratches.
Eileen had pulled her hair back with a blue band. I noticed it
was the exact same shade as Denny's shirt.

"What are you doing here, Sutter?" she asked.

"Nothing much. *Barlow.*"

She gave me another of her practised sneers. "Denny told me you'd seen some weirdo, or something, some old codger wearing a mask."

Suddenly, this girl was in on all our secrets. It made me mad.

"Yeah, that's right. A waxen mask."

"Really? Wax?"

"Yeah."

"I don't think you can make a mask out of wax, can you? It wouldn't be strong enough."

She had made me doubtful. "Well, it looked like wax."

"More likely rubber, or plastic."

Eileen was lying on her stomach next to me, Denny on the other side. We were all looking down towards the farmhouse, but nothing much was happening, it had to be said.

"How come he wears a mask, then?" she asked.

"Probably got badly burned in the war," Denny offered.

I said, "Nah, he's too old for that, I think. From what I saw."

Eileen made a dismissive noise. "Why, how old is he?"

"Really old. He was bald."

"First World War then?" said Denny. "Maybe that's where he got his wounded face?"

"Aye, maybe."

"The Germans threw hand-grenades from their biplanes, I know that. He might have got hit by one of those. Maybe a big chunk of shrapnel caught him in the face."

We all contemplated such things for a while, in silence.

"I think he's a commie," said Eileen. "He's an undercover agent, must be. If he's in disguise."

"It's not a disguise. The mask is see-through, well, almost."

"Well, what's the point of it, then?"

She took the binoculars off me and looked through them.

"Anything?" Denny asked.

"It's just a house, a boring old house. Oh, wait..." She adjusted the focus.

"What is it?" I asked. "Is it the masked man?"

"No, it's a woman, right there, at the bedroom window."

Denny whistled. But I had an inkling. "I know what you're going to say next," I told her.

"Oh, you reckon, do you?"

"I do reckon."

"You think you might, but you'd be wrong."

"You're going to tell us she's taking her clothes off."

"No. No, I wasn't–"

"I think so."

"As if."

Denny interrupted, "He's got you there, Eileen."

"Oh, you two. You think you're so clever, don't you?" She rolled onto her back. "God, this is boring. Silly Sutter. Peeking in at windows."

"His name's Joe. Why don't you call him that?"

"Aye, if you like. I don't mind." She sat up. "Come on, Denny, let's run along the ridge. I'll race you."

And off they went together, past Brendle Pike, and onwards. I thought to myself: *They'll probably be married by the time they're seventeen.* And where would that leave me? I went back to my position on the grass and gave the house a sweep with the binoculars, left to right and back again. Still nothing. And, of course, there was nobody at the bedroom window, naked or otherwise. Perhaps Eileen was right, this was all a waste of time. I hadn't even seen Sutter's Fancy in the days since, not a wisp of it.

My mind strayed to Daniel Defoe. As a member of Defoe house I would have to compete against the other three houses, for prizes in rugby, cricket and football, and in exam results. The whole school would be a nest of boa constrictors, trying to out-strangle each other. And yet there was Daniel Defoe with his story of *Robinson Crusoe*, a man alone. I had read an *Illustrated Classics* comic-book version of the tale. I really liked that Crusoe had no one to bother him. His life was his own. Until the day he spotted the footprints in the sand and imagined that Greot had taken on a more solid form, the ghost of the island...

The front door of the farmhouse opened.

I gave the focus a nudge, to get the best possible sight.

Yes, it was the old man. He appeared thin and frail out in the sunlight. The cross-hairs moved up to his head. Flipping heck, he still had the mask on, I couldn't believe it. Even outside. The wax face caught the slant of sunlight. He looked like a visitor from outer space. God, his face must be really badly damaged.

He stretched out his arms and thrust out his chest. I imagined him breathing deeply of the morning air, sucking it in through the tiny nostril holes. What a palaver that was, he should just take it off. Then his chest started to heave. I couldn't hear him, but I knew he was coughing. He wasn't that far away from kicking the bucket himself, never mind Tom Halfpenny.

Oh, this was amazing. I was the star of my own story. "I have you in my sights, Doctor Mask, evil genius and the sworn nemesis of all that is good. People might think of me as Joe Sutter, mild-mannered schoolboy, but in reality I am Kid Koag! Nothing escapes me. Oh yes, I see everything, every little thing that you do–"

A dog barked behind me, close by, and then a woman said, "What are you up to?"

I rolled over. The sun was behind the figure, making her a silhouette. The dog yapped, straining at the leash.

"Well, then? Answer me, boy!"

"Nothing, miss."

I was automatically addressing her as a teacher. It was her tone, the clipped words. Then she stepped forwards, allowing the dog access to my ankles. It snapped at them as I pulled them in, and quickly I tried to stand up, failing miserably. I was a jumble of limbs.

"That's right, get him, Nipper! Get him!"

Luckily, the fabled Nipper was no Nazi Rottweiler, but a Jack Russell. Still, he had teeth, he had a strong jaw, and he wanted his meat. His body seemed to be one long muscle covered in white fur. You could see pink flesh beneath in places, like he had suffered an over-eager crew-cut. But I saw that the woman was holding the dog back from the final half-inch of attack. She was taunting me, and I knew I was at her mercy.

"Here, Nipper, good dog! Heel!"

The beast followed her orders. It was panting, its tongue lolloping out.

"What's your name, boy?"

I looked along the ridge past Brendle Pike, hoping to see Denny and Eileen, to call to them for help. Two dots, too far away.

"Quickly, I haven't got all day!"

"Joe, miss."

"Surname?"

"Sutter."

"What's that, Sutton?"

"*Sutter*. It means *shoemaker*, miss. An old word for it." Why was I talking in this way? It was madness! But I carried straight on: "My grandma told me."

"Joe Sutter. So your family makes shoes, does it, cobbling, and all that?"

"No, miss."

"Oh, do stop calling me *miss*."

I shut up. Best job. Just keep quiet, say nothing. Keep still. Watch.

The woman had a stylish look, like one of those characters in an Agatha Christie drama, the kind who smokes a cigarette through a long ivory cigarette-holder. She was dressed in a purple velvet jacket, a blouse poking out at the collar, and a skirt reaching to just above her knees. Her hair was short but stylish. Nowhere near as short as Nipper's, of course, but more like Twiggy's, a bob. There was an angle to the fringe. She had a ruddy complexion; her cheeks glowed with health. But her mouth was narrow, which added to the sternness.

"What are you up to, spying, is that it?"

"No." I stopped myself just in time from calling her *miss*, yet again.

"What, then?"

"Birdwatching." It was the first thing that came to mind. And then, flowing easily on: "I saw a kestrel a few days ago, catching a mouse, and I thought I might be able to find its nest."

"You're an egg stealer, are you? A nasty habit."

"I just like to watch them, that's all."

She grinned at me, shaking her head. The dog had planted itself flat on the ground with its limbs splayed out at front and back. Seeing him like this, I relaxed a little. I was still sitting down, my back against the wall, the sharp ragged stones pressing into me. I was hoping she'd bought the birdwatching ruse.

But then she said, "I know what your little game is."

I blurted out, "I have to go home now, miss. My mum will be worried about me."

She didn't bother telling me off for using the title. That grin was still in place, a little twist of the lips at each end, nothing more.

"Are you the boy who broke in, the other day?"

I had been dreading this question.

"Well, are you?!"

"No. Please, miss. No. I swear."

"You've been spying on us."

This time it wasn't a question. Just a fact. And I have to be honest, I was on the edge of tears. I was scared. I knew I'd done a bad thing, and that I was about to be punished for it. I stood up, keeping my eyes on the dog the whole time. But I think Nipper was bored of me. He was licking his paws. Could I trust his boredom?

"Sit down."

I shook my head. I was edging along the wall, getting ready to run.

"Come on, I'm not going to hurt you."

Oh, a change of mood. I was used to this from teachers at school. Cruel one minute, and then nice – *This is going to hurt me more than it hurts you* – and then all nasty again.

"Stay!"

This to the dog. But it worked on me, as well. I stayed. Then she reached out a hand. I realised that she wanted the binoculars. I gave them to her. Then she placed herself behind the wall and peered down at the house, at her own house; at least I assumed she was part of the household. What was she playing at?

She tutted. "There he is. The old *bastard*. Out and about."

The swearword shocked me. You never heard a lot of swearing in those days, certainly not in front of children.

"Look at the state of him."

I bent down beside her, looking through the gap. The man was sitting on an iron bench next to the front door. That's about all I could make out without the binoculars.

"He's got the mask on," the woman said. "Oh, it angers me, it does." All this was said in a hush, which I took as an offer to join in.

"I know. It's spooky." I kept my voice as low as hers.

"You don't know the half of it, Joe Sutter. If I told you the real reason he wears that thing… Well, you wouldn't believe me, so it's best that I not bother."

She had a Yorkshire accent, but it had been softened a little, perhaps by being away from the county, far from the North of England even.

"Are you Margery, then?"

"How do you know that, eh?"

"The old man called that name out, when I saw him."

"He's always shouting for something or other, it never ends. But I was out that day, see, when you came a-calling. I was out shopping. Stocking up on his nose-bag. God, he can eat! Can he! Lamb chops, that's his favourite. Two of them, mind, never one. 'I can't taste one,' he says, 'I need two!' Spuds, tinned peas, gravy. He's happy then, but he always wants seconds, and then a big dessert, spotted dick or roly-poly, and he never puts an ounce on him. Brrrr. Nasty skin and bones."

"My favourite is egg and chips."

"Aye, that's nice enough, with some ketchup."

"And bread and butter."

"Lovely."

Margery gave me back the binoculars, saying, "He likes to wear the mask outside because it's more exciting for him, that way. Much more. But I always warn him about it, in case someone sees him, and thinks him... well, mad, or something. Do you think he's mad?"

This took some careful answering. "I don't know. I don't know anything about him."

"Oh, the bother he causes me."

Now we were both sitting with our backs against the wall. "Look," I said. "High up. There's that kestrel."

"Oh aye. I've seen him before. A handsome creature."

We both sat there, staring at the bird as it surveyed its terrain. Below the bird was a layer of violet dust, which drifted upwards to meet the kestrel, becoming a companion in flight.

Margery laughed. "You gave the old boy a right shock, you did, breaking in like that."

"I didn't break in, honest. The door was open, the back door."

"Still, it's not nice, is it?"

I decided to tell the truth. "I was following Sutter's Fancy."

"And what might that be?"

"A strand of Greot. A pink and silver dust."

She looked at me. "Oh, you're one of that sort, are you? Like his Lordship. Well, well. More trouble, I shouldn't wonder."

"I'm not trouble, honest, I'm not."

"I beg to differ. He was in a right mood after you'd broken in. Margery this, Margery that, all the day long." She sighed. "Oh, he worries me so. I do wish he'd take care of himself."

The kestrel had disappeared from the sky. Koag lingered.

"Are you his daughter?" I asked.

That set her off, laughing like mad. "His daughter! Could you imagine?!"

She got to her feet and called for Nipper to come running, which he did. I could still hear her laughter as the two of them descended the hill towards Pike View. I watched their progress through the binoculars until they reached the yard. It looked like Margery was telling the old man off, which I could easily imagine, having experienced it myself only a few minutes before. The white mask nodded and gleamed. And then Mysterious Margery bundled him into the house and the door closed behind them.

I rolled onto my back and tried to make sense of everything I had learned.

7

I was having a very nice dream that starred Twiggy and May Harper dancing with Pan's People on *Top of the Pops*. They were jiggling about to "Hurdy Gurdy Man". The melody lasted for a moment after my eyes opened. I checked my alarm clock. Four minutes to three. Oh, not again! I'd slept straight through the last two nights, no problem, but now here I was, awake for the second time this week. If Koag had something to say to me, he should say it. Otherwise, let me sleep.

I got up, not even bothering to look out of the window this time. Instead I turned on my light and looked at the drawings I had been working on that evening, a new idea from Denny for a comic. I had trouble with spelling, I could not do multiplication, my stories of derring-do usually got a *D* or a very occasional *C-* from Mrs Pierce. For the life of me, I could not hold a tune on the recorder or the xylophone. But I had a passable skill at drawing, as long as I avoided faces, and drawing superheroes was perfect for that, because they always wore masks. Our comics were always one page long, and told in six panels. We kept it simple. Denny had invented a hero called Nowhere Man, named after the track on the *Rubber Soul* album. But our version of Nowhere Man wasn't anything like The Beatles' version. His superpowers meant that he never appeared on the page, but was only ever seen by his effect on the other characters. Nowhere Man was a series of sound effects without any visible cause: *KERBLAM! THWIK! ZZZZT! KRUMP! SPLOOOOOM! PING, PING, PING!* He was certainly easy to draw. *HA HA HA!* Easier even than Invisible Girl of the Fantastic

Four, who had dotted outlines around her disappearing shape. Nowhere Man was never seen. Only his sound effects gave any clue as to his current location.

After my adventure that day with Margery and the binoculars, I had introduced Doctor Mask as a new arch-enemy for the hero. I drew the mask carefully, mindful of what Eileen had said about the possible material. I now thought of it as a kind of transparent rubber that clung to the man's face. I had no alter-ego for him, no secret identity, because I didn't yet know the old man's name. (I should have asked Margery. There was so much I should have asked!) But the mask looked cool, especially when it filled an entire panel. Speech bubble: *Blast you, Nowhere Man. I shall have my revenge!*

I made my way downstairs to get a glass of milk. I could hear the television from the living room. It was Grandma. She too had woken up, a very unusual occurrence. But there she was, glued to the screen. She was dressed in a linen nightie under a dressing gown, her reddened waves kept in place under a hairnet. I took my place in the big armchair, where Dad used to sit every evening, and which Chloe and I now fought over whenever a favourite programme was on. Grandma nodded at me. The *Three O Six Show* began at half past two every morning. The first half-hour contained a lot of boring chatter, all leading up to that special daily moment, when the public witnessing began. And then our screens would fill with marvellous images, each location around the country hoping to show the most dramatic or most beautiful examples of the dust. They aired from Land's End, from Cardiff, from the wilds of the Outer Hebrides, a housing estate in Birmingham, the gardens of Kent. The whole of Britain was represented, in some way or other, different towns and cities each night. It was enjoyable to sit there with Grandma, to view the sights as others saw them; a shared experience. After the public witnessing was over, the presenters and the guests talked about the various Gatherings of the Eyes that had been seen these last days in Aberdeen, in North London, Crewe, and of course, our own little Ormsley Vale. Not so many had been experienced all at once, not since 1930, according to the programme's resident Greotologist. Everyone was in agreement, it all had to mean something, but none of them could agree on what. The Grand Beholder came on, her wrinkled face filmed in close-up. She said a prayer for the nation, reminding us of the holy covenant that exists between ourselves and Greot. "The dust is the dust is the dust, and so it shall be, now and for evermore. It offers guidance. Without its presence, our darker spirits would reign supreme." At the end of the sermon, the Grand Beholder put on her scary voice, saying that the giant dust clouds were a warning: "The all-seeing Eyes of Greot are looking down upon the world, and into people's hearts and minds. Beware!" Grandma was irritated by this remark.

"Oh, turn off the sound, Joe," she said.

I did so. The flickering screen was the only light in the room. I wondered if I should speak, perhaps to talk about what had been happening the last few days, the sense I had of things changing around me. But I could not make it all add up, even to myself. Then she asked, "Do you know why people are so fixated with Greot and its comings and goings?" I shook my head and she went on, "Because it's a mystery, and it always will be. Everything else about life can be explained away, but the dust… No. It just is."

"What about the Grand Beholder? She must know."

Grandma scoffed. "That decrepit old thing? She knows as much as the rest of us do: next to nothing." Her eyes glistened in the television's light. "People live in fear of the dust, and in love with it, both at the same time. Because… Oh, I don't suppose you know what I mean, you're too young."

There it was again, that reminder of my not being ready.

"Joe, dear, come and help your Grandma. There's something I want to show you."

She got up and led the way into the parlour. I wasn't sure what help she needed exactly, as she walked with a sprightly enough step. But once we were in her bedroom, her mood changed again. She looked around at her little set of belongings, the results of her marriage, and her years and years of hard work on the market stall selling buttons and ribbons, needles and thread, and yards of cloth. Her hands were trembling. I knew that she had not opened up the Chamber of Living Eyes since the incident with May Harper, and that fit of nerves that had come over her.

"What is it, Grandma?"

"Stand on that chair for me, that's it, and look on top of the wardrobe. There should be a tin box there, can you see it?"

"Yeah."

"Bring it down for me, there's a good boy."

The box was decorated with a portrait of George VI on the occasion of his coronation, his face surrounded by banners and flags of various nations, and a drum and a shield. Grandma opened it up and pulled out, of all things, a neatly folded handkerchief. It was the only thing in there. But I knew she had a whole collection of these already, each one embroidered by her own hand with her initials in blue thread: *D.S.* She turned to look at a framed photograph of herself and her husband Leonard when they were young, perhaps newly weds. And she smiled wistfully.

We both stood in silence. Coco's cage was covered in a cloth. Nearby, the stuffed animal sat rigid in its glass dome, staring at me. Koag roamed the room in strands of vermilion and purple.

"I was carrying your mother at the time, but only just. Nothing more than a stirring within. I was a few months married."

This startled me, I must say.

"I was still but a lass, nineteen years old. My Leonard came with me that first time, for my comfort, and because he had his doubts about the whole shenanigans. Poor dear, he could hardly understand what was going on."

She sighed. Her eyes had that flinty green look as she sat on the edge of her bed and told the story. "There were a few more of us in my day, a few more witnesses and beholders than now. But we were not well liked. Times change. We would meet in back rooms and cellars, with the windows blacked out. We conducted experiments on Greot. I was young, and I barely knew what I was doing, nor why." She looked at me intensely. "But I had to do it, that was the thing. I wanted to learn."

I focussed on the one thing she'd said that excited me: "What do you mean, *experiments*?"

"There was an older man, Walter Dunham. He ran a local group called the Ashen Society. It was a bit like a witches' coven, or at least that's how I saw it the first few times I went. He was a beholder, you see, and a very powerful one. Mr Dunham taught me how to see, how to see through the eyes of Greot. We all fell under his spell."

She looked at the handkerchief, unfolding and refolding it, but with careful movements so as not to crease it. It looked very small and dainty.

"Before that group," she continued, "I had no one to talk to about my talents."

I sat down on a chair at her table, where she conducted her sessions. "But you have me now, Grandma, don't you?"

I got a smile for this, but there wasn't much warmth to it. She went on: "We met in his house in Failsworth. Every Tuesday evening, this was. Mr Dunham recruited us from all over the county. After tea and biscuits he would introduce some topic for discussion."

"You mean about the dust?"

"That's right. We talked about Greot, the various colours and shapes and what they all meant, and the history of the dust, the true history, that is. But you see, I was the youngest in the group, and I thought it was all a bit of poppycock really, that Mr Dunham was just making up new stories to replace the old ones. But I was all fired up. I think that's why I dragged your granddad along with me, a few times at least, so he could understand just what he'd married into. He was a coalman by trade, and the only dust that bothered him was the one that billowed up from a sackful of coal, all of which settled on his lungs, it did, oh, the coughing at the end, dreadful it was. Bless him."

She raised the handkerchief to her face, I thought at first to wipe away tears, but instead she very delicately sniffed at the scent it must have held. Her eyes closed. We both sat in the quiet of the room. I knew best not to disturb her. Her little mantel clock ticked away. Then, Dotty opened her eyes and stared at me, saying, "Come and sit close, while I talk to you."

I went over to the bed. Now I could look down at the handkerchief and see it as she saw it, a relic of another time, small enough to belong to a child. Perhaps Grandma had kept it from her own childhood days? But then I saw that the embroidered initials were in green thread, not the blue she always used, and that they spelled out *H.T.*, not *D.S.* It was another puzzle for the puzzle box, which was already full to bursting.

"Leonard was with me that last time, when it all went wrong."

"Why, Grandma, what happened?"

"I'm getting to it, don't worry yourself. So, after the tea and biscuits and after the discussion we always went on to practical exercises. How best to connect with Greot, how better to see through the eyes of dust, how to focus our minds and get in the right mood, and so on. Over the weeks we went deeper and deeper into this. It was a time like now, when many Gatherings of the Eyes were reported up and down the land. Mr Dunham took this as a sign. We performed rituals, summonings, in the parlour of his house this was, but a room much larger than this one."

Now I was bewildered. It sounded like something you would read in the Sunday newspapers: *Witches at work behind the net curtains. We reveal all!*

"Our final meeting, we sat in a circle of chairs, and held hands and chanted in praise of Greot. The dust was clouding the air, all orange and lemony and dashed about with scarlet, so lovely, and the scent of it, oh my, it was as flowery as a meadow. I was giddy with it. Leonard was standing against the wall along with a few other bystanders. But only beholders were included in the circle. Seven of us, all told, which Mr Dunham proclaimed as a number of mystical import. He was holding my left hand. I was his star pupil, I like to think."

She allowed herself another smile at this memory.

"What were you trying to do?"

"I didn't rightly know. I could hardly understand a lot of the talk, especially when they got into the esoterics of it all."

My grandma learnt words like this, *esoterics*, from her collection of pamphlets, a tottering pile of which occupied one corner of the room. Of course, I had no idea what the word meant, and decided it best not to ask. I let her carry on.

"We all concentrated on the dust, trying our best to form it into a shape. It was a joint effort. At first Mr Dunham whispered instructions to us all, but after a while he shut up and just let us get on with it. He wanted us to work together, to see if our combined powers might improve the results. However, there was little progress. Greot does not take kindly to being told what to do, and so we failed in our set task. Mr Dunham was angry with us, and with himself, no doubt, and disappointed, so much so that he left the room. There were six of us remaining in the circle. I don't know what happened, but as soon as Mr Dunham went out, there was a change in the mood. There was me, there was Mrs Goode, a greengrocer's wife, mother of five. And there was Bill Arkwright, he was a gentlemen's outfitter, passed away now, I suppose. And there was... Now let me think, I can see them all like it were yesterday. Yes, there was Olivia Carr, twenty-nine, unmarried, the shy retiring type. Then there was Jonah Stapleton, a man of means. He always wore a cravat. And last but not least, Tom Watson. Or Tom Halfpenny, as people later called him, after he fell down on his luck."

The name surprised me. "Tom Halfpenny?"

"Oh yes."

"I didn't know he was a beholder."

"No, not many did, and he was always troubled by his gift. And then one day, just like that, *poof*, his gift left him."

"He could no longer see the dust?"

"Not a speck, poor thing. And it never came back to him."

She shook her head at this part of the tale. Now I understood a little more about old Tom and why he behaved as he did, dancing and begging, and singing all those ballads of lost love and spells gone wrong. And also why the dust had settled on his body at the end of his life. Perhaps it was one last viewing at the moment of death.

Grandma went on: "Three men and three women remained. Maybe that was significant, who can tell? But suddenly the circle came alive. I could feel a sort of electrical current in my hands, coming from Tom Watson on my left and passing on to Jonah Stapleton on my right. Anti-clockwise it moved, this energy, around and around. Greot started to glow, brightening still more in the orange and lemony parts, while the scarlet flecks flickered here and there like, like... Why, like little thoughts and feelings floating around inside your head."

The idea of this took her over. I looked at her face. She was sitting forwards, her eyes staring. And I knew she was back there again, with her younger self as company.

"None of us were doing anything, but all of us were doing something. The dust formed itself into a dense cluster at the centre of the circle. Some of it reached out to me in long spindly tendrils, touching at my face, my hands."

I shivered a little, hearing this. "What happened next, Grandma?"

"Well. Not one of us could dare speak, seeing how Greot was behaving. And then..." The handkerchief twisted and twisted in her hands. "And then she appeared to us."

"Who did?"

"A child, a girl. Young, seven or eight. A sweet little thing. We saw her from a distance at first, and then she came closer, and closer, and closer, you know, like how Omar Sharif appears out of the mirage in *Lawrence of Arabia*?" I didn't know, I had no clue. She went on: "There was a soft fuzzy patch of orange and lemon dust, and then a darker shape, and then the child's dress, her limbs and then her head, and finally her face. But her features were blurred, not yet clear. The only sound was a gasp from Olivia, across the circle."

I had never heard of such a thing. "You mean the dust created a film for you?"

"More than that, much more. We all saw the girl, all of us. I mean, the beholders, of course. My Leonard and the other bystanders, they knew something strange was going on. We talked about it afterwards, when we got back home. But none of them saw, not like we did. The six of us. That's me, and Olivia, and Bill Arkwright, and–"

"Yes, Grandma. But what happened next?"

"She was struggling madly, the child, as though... as though... Well, like she was trying to get through some wall or barrier, struggling to be born."

"Struggling to get through to you?"

"Yes, that's it. Struggling to get through, into the room. The little girl wanted to join us there." Dotty's eyes were full of life as she said this. "But she never quite made it. Almost, almost... Close enough for us to see her, if not to touch. She was dressed in old-fashioned clothing, like someone from the Victorian age. If I'd been alone, I would think her a fancy of my mind only. But the other beholders saw her, Joe. They saw her! She was facing towards me, and her little hands reached out. Oh, she might have been reaching across Ormsley Vale, from one side to the other, so distant it was! Yet she tried her very best, the poor thing. And then the dust took her back into itself, and she, well, she just drifted apart, like threads of candy floss on a breezy day."

Grandma unfolded the handkerchief completely. She traced the embroidered letters.

"The child did not last for long in our sight."

I thought for a moment, trying for an explanation: "It was a young girl Greot had copied somewhere, and then sent her picture along the dust clouds."

"If so, I've never seen it done as well before, or since."

"I can't think what else it could be."

"Here's another puzzle for you. Why was she dressed like she was? I mean to say, who walks around like a Victorian child in today's age? Nobody, that's who."

"An actress? Someone from a television programme?" But even as I said it, I felt the weakness of my argument.

"Mr Dunham came in just as the girl was fading away, back into the dust. He was more angry than ever that he'd missed out on such an event, a *visitation*, as he called it. And that was our last meeting. The Ashen Society split up. Some of us were scared by what had happened, myself included. But over the years... Well, I have often wondered."

"About what, Grandma? That it might happen again? Is that what you saw the other day?"

"Which day? What are you talking about?"

"Monday evening, when you did the viewing for May Harper."

"Oh, I don't know, I can't just remember things whenever you ask me to."

"You said, *In the dust, in the dark.*"

"I said what?"

"*In the dark of the dust, she is waiting.*"

"I never said any such thing."

"You did, I'm sure of it. You said, *Poor little girl, come to me.* You were nearly crying."

"Oh, shut up!"

"It's true."

She sighed then, as though finally remembering. "The thing is, Joe, my lad, our little visitor left something behind her." She held out the handkerchief.

I took it from her. It was a square of white cloth with a lacy trim, nothing more. But it was unlike any other object I had ever held. It was perfectly formed in all its details. And then

I realised, it was made from the dust, and the dust only, but made solid in some special way, the many strands of dust so tightly wound together that it resembled a real object, a real handkerchief. But it wasn't, it wasn't real. Or at least, not quite real. It was *almost* real. Now, Koag was famous for its ability to copy things, to make models of them, but these items always drifted apart when you touched them, or tried to pick them up. But this object remained as it was in my grasp. I could turn it over, I could fold it in two, and unfold it again. Only a few wisps escaped the edges of the lace, and even these were quickly recaptured.

"It just floated in the air in front of me," Grandma explained. "I thought it an afterglow of the dust, but no, the thing fell to the floor. I got up from my chair to pick it up. At first it wasn't real, it nearly crumbled in my hands. But then it was real. And that's when Mr Dunham started his ranting and raving. Leonard got me out of there, forbidding any return. And I was very happy to comply, let me tell you. Especially with my condition." I must have looked puzzled. "With a bun in the oven," she explained with a grin.

"So *H.T.*, those are the girl's initials?" I asked.

Grandma nodded. "I spent many an hour coming up with names. Harriet Taylor, that was my first favourite. Then Helena Tavistock. I was thinking of names for what she looked like, the straw-coloured hair in ringlets, that lovely dark-blue gown with the white ruffles at the neck and sleeves, and the handkerchief with such nicely embroidered initials."

"Henrietta Tudor?" I tried.

"Oh, that's good! I like *Tudor*, sounds like she might be related to royalty. How about Hannah Tomkins?"

"Or Heather Truman."

"Hermione Todd."

"Holly Toppingham."

"Heidi Trebleclef."

I had to think quickly to keep up with her. "Hayley, Hayley, Hayley… Tablecloth!"

Then we were laughing together, quietly though, as suited the early morning hour. As it was, we quickly ran out of names.

"Well. I like Henrietta Tudor the best," Grandma said.

"Yes, me too."

"But you know, after a while I had another idea, that the initials might not actually stand for a girl's name at all."

"What else could it be?"

She took a moment and then asked, "Have you ever heard of Sir Robert Helme?"

"Of course. Mrs Pierce taught us about him, at school. He was a scientist." I remembered one detail from the lesson. "He had a fight with Isaac Newton."

"Did he? How rum."

"Yeah, because Newton thought Greot was just a big pile of dust, whilst Sir Robert thought it to be alive. And they came to fisticuffs over it. *WALLOP!*"

Grandma nodded at this. "Pay attention, Joe, and I'll teach you something. It's very important. It might just explain the mystery of the handkerchief." After a breath, she said, "Most of the time the dust cannot be seen. It keeps itself invisible, hidden away."

I nodded.

"But sometimes, just sometimes, mind, it appears before us. Greot can then be seen, at least by some people, people like you and me, Joe, witnesses and beholders. And also to everyone else, at six minutes past three in the morning. Now then, according to my pamphlets, this point, when Greot suddenly becomes visible, well, that's known as 'Helme's Threshold'."

"Because Sir Robert worked it out?"

"That's right. Now then, do you see what I'm saying?"

"No, I can't say I do."

"I thought you were good at puzzles? Go on, have a go."

It took me a while, I'll admit. I was still holding the handkerchief, folding it and unfolding it. And that's when I noticed the initials again, and it clicked.

"So *H.T.* stands for Helme's Threshold?"

"Yes, why not? After all, the girl was invisible at first, and then we saw her. Little by little, she came into view. That was her crossing the threshold, don't you see?"

"But what does *threshold* mean?"

"It's like a doorway, or a boundary line. A crossing place."

I shook my head in wonder.

Grandma took back the handkerchief. "Time to get some kip, I think, my lad."

I nodded. It was past four by then.

"Now, all of this is a secret, just between the two of us. About the girl. Do you hear me?"

"Yes, Grandma."

"I've never even told your mother, so mind, now."

I went back upstairs to my bedroom. I had so much to think about, now that Dotty Sykes had let me into her world a little. That handkerchief: *At first it wasn't real. But then it was.* Those words would serve as a prayer, or a magic spell, for that whole summer.

8

From my grandparents and from Princess Slobber I knew about dog owners and their pets, and how they both liked to keep to a regular schedule. So the next morning I got to Brendle Pike as early as I could, binoculars at the ready around my neck, hoping to catch Margery and Nipper on the way out. I had the idea that I might walk with them for a while. But there was no sign of anyone at home, nor of the Land Rover in the yard. Maybe they had all gone out for a drive, Nipper included? It was a colder day than usual, with a few dark grey clouds marring the blue. Koag was present in the fields and mills and towns as a flitting ghost. But no kestrel today to keep me company. Right then, Joe Sutter, enough dilly-dallying! I walked down to Pike View, throwing a few stones along the way, scaring a thrush from its perch on a fence post.

The bicycle was parked against the wall of the house, as before. At the front door my heroic spirit of adventure took over and I rapped the knocker, which was in the shape of a ram's head. No answer, and no yapping of a Jack Russell, which proved the house was empty. I walked down the side alley, peering in at the windows of the shed as I went, seeing only dirt, spider's webs and dead flies on the glass, nothing beyond. I turned my attention to one of the house windows. There was a wooden crate next to the wall, so I used that as a step to give me a good height. There was a gap in the net curtains. I was looking into an office. There was a desk with a typewriter sitting on it, and a set of bookshelves. But most of all, I noticed

the air of the room moving in waves. It was Sutter's Fancy.
The office was full of the special dust. The colours were muted
because of the glass and the netting, but I definitely saw glints
of silver amid a drift of rosy pink. I felt the tingle of excitement.
My nose pressed itself against the glass. Then a figure came into
view, getting up from a chair.

Doctor Mask! Yes, his face was still covered. So he'd been
there all along, ignoring me when I knocked on the door. Oh,
he was clever. He was a crooked soul. He was a scoundrel,
beyond a doubt. A sneak, a Russian spy (just like Eileen had
said), a dirty old codger, a monster in disguise. A Pied Piper
of children, a snipper at the threads of life. A murderer, a
vampire, the Wolf Man waiting for the full moon to shine,
Mr Hyde with no Dr Jekyll to hide inside, Doctor Doom, the
Red Skull, the Green Goblin, all rolled into one! The masked
man turned to the window, his fist raised; he staggered
forwards and I took an involuntary step back, falling off the
crate, down to the paving of the alleyway. The net curtains
were torn aside and there was that hideous white waxen face,
peering down at me. He was shouting, I knew, I could hear
the muffled sound: the words were a garbled noise. His fist
was banging on the glass.

I ran down the slope of the hill without stopping. So much
for being a superhero. I had to stop running one day, I had to!
But I didn't, not then, not until I'd entered the safety of the
woods, only slowing down when I found the old railway track,
following it for a while. I came to the place where I had spotted
King and Queen Koag snuggling up together in the branches,
producing their sticky fluids. But the coagulated dusts had
gone on their way and the fluid had soaked into the ground. A
few bits of colour floated around the clearing, but not Sutter's
Fancy, not my favourite. I thought briefly of what Grandma
had told me, how Koag was normally invisible, until it crossed
that special barrier, what had she called it? A *threshold*. I felt
closer than ever to the dust. In fact, sometimes I felt closer to
the dust than I did to people.

Joe Sutter lived alone in a one-room flat. His neighbours said he
was a strange man, always muttering to himself about the Human
Torch and Daredevil, and the great dust clouds of yesteryear. Such a
poor old thing.

The air was heavy, darkening. I was shivery, and could taste metal on my tongue. That feeling you get just before a thunderstorm. I blamed Doctor Mask. He was a wicked hoarder of magic, of magic that I had followed to the source, that I had named! And now, that, that, that… (I reached for the word Margery had used to describe him) …that *bastard* had stolen all of Sutter's Fancy for himself, for his own use, every last speck and twirl and wisp and flutter. The swearword gave me a thrill. I said it to myself, quietly. "Bastard." What a delight. Set free, I shouted the word at the top of my voice, into the trees, disturbing a bird from its hidden perch. Flap, flap, crackle of twigs.

"Bastard!!!"

Well, I had fantasised about being a castaway on an island, and now here I was, Robinson Sutter, stranded in everyday life, swearing like a low-down bruiser.

"Bloody, bloody bastard!"

A sound answered me. It was a dog barking. No, not barking, but yapping. I knew that sound, it was stored in my brain from yesterday's savage, near-fatal attack. *Nipper*. I followed the noise, coming out onto a narrow tarmacked lane that ran through the woods. The terrier was tied to a fence post by its lead. Beyond that, parked under a tree, was the Land Rover. I put a finger to my lips in some attempt to hush the dog. It worked. I couldn't believe it. Nipper fell quiet, sitting down on his haunches, wagging his tail. He had already grown used to me. So now I turned my attention to the vehicle. I had a view of the back door, and the two rear windows. I looked all around. There was no sign of Margery anywhere among the trees. What was she up to out here, I wondered? Why leave the dog tied up, if she was going off for a stroll? Also, why use the van to get here, when it was in walking distance of Pike View? None of it made sense.

And then the back door of the Land Rover opened. Margery climbed out.

I instinctively backed into the undergrowth near a tree trunk, where I could observe without being seen. I saw that Margery's skirt was on sideways, and she was fastening the zipper. She then spun the skirt around her hips a quarter-circle, so the zip was now at the back. There was a man with her. He had long hair, centre-parted, and was a bit younger than her.

A hippy. All those newspaper exposés I had read came back to me. He was buttoning up his shirt, which was tight-fitting, a soft lilac colour with penny-round collars. I remember it all so clearly, every detail. He looked a little like Ray Davies, the singer with the Kinks, but seen from an awkward angle.

Now they were kissing.

Oh my God.

But there was something awkward about their movements, as though they could no longer touch each other easily, or completely. The kissing done, the young man walked off down the long, shaded lane towards Ormsley. I had no idea who he was. But this was my golden treasure, I knew that. Margery was doing something forbidden, something Doctor Mask didn't approve of, otherwise why do it in the woods, in the van of all places? Mysterious Margery had a little secret. And now I had it too. Perhaps this would be useful to me, in the future?

My young mind was having adult thoughts.

Margery was patting her hair into shape. She released Nipper from captivity and he leapt into the back of the Land Rover. She got into the cab and a moment later the vehicle drove away in the opposite direction to the man. I came out from my hiding place and watched until it disappeared around a bend in the lane. The trees settled into place around me, into silence at first, and then into the various tiny sounds of nature: chirruping, clicking, ticking, scurrying, slithering. It sounded like an orchestra tuning up, and never quite finding a common key. And yet it all sounded perfectly in harmony. And then a sudden hush. A moment unlike any other. The rain began. A summer's rain, gentle to begin with, large droplets hot on the palms of my hands, on my upturned face; they fell on the leaves and dripped down to the ground.

There was a single crack of thunder, a distant rumble.

The loneliness returned, yet now I revelled in it. I took power from it.

The shower was over in a few minutes, and the animals and birds came back to life. Koag was left on the branches and leaves in spots of muted orange and brown and purple and gold and pink and ruby red, deposited here by the rain, made heavy, turned into a smear of thin paste. It would dry out quickly enough and then float free, away on its criss-crossing journeys across the county.

I would follow, I would follow!

Ormsley Woods holds powerful memories for me, not least that it was here that I first became aware of desire, of secret desires. I had no real idea of what had taken place inside the Land Rover. Sex Education, or "The Facts of Life" as it was then known, wasn't taught until the first year of secondary school. And my mother was entirely silent on the subject. So I had what I could glean from *The News of the World*, and what Michael Portman passed down to his brother, Denny. All of it, from both sources, was muffled and hinted at, fed by our imaginations, which often got things wrong. But I knew for sure that Margery and her friend had been doing something naughty in the back of the van. The idea was mixed in with the smell of the dank earth, the humid air, the dripping of the leaves, the worms that the rain had brought wriggling to the surface. An entire world lay in wait, on the edge of being known.

I walked along in the same direction as Margery's lover, climbing one fence then another, until I came to the goods wagon. Denny and Eileen were there.

"Alright, Denny?"

"Yeah, not bad."

"Eileen?"

"Yeah, not bad, Joe, not bad."

Oh, she was learning, she was weaving her way in. But this time I was glad to see them both, even if the pair of them were having a good laugh at my expense. The *Ormsley Chronicle* came out every Friday, and they had a copy with them. I was featured on the front cover, looking like a right idiot in my paisley shirt, stupid grin plastered across my face. Inside was a photograph of Denny (much nicer), and of the ditch at Slew Hill where the body had been found. Another page featured an artist's impression of the Gathering of the Eyes that had covered Stoneybrook Estate. I actually didn't mind the laughter. I was getting used to Eileen's presence, and she was now calling me by my first name, so that was all right. Every so often my mind would flit back to the Land Rover and its two occupants. If Eileen hadn't been with us, I would have asked Denny for his thoughts. Instead we played knockout whist and talked about the article and how famous I was going to be. I wasn't sure I wanted that. We did learn that the official cause of Tom Halfpenny's death was a heart attack, and that he had "a history of drink-related problems". I was glad that Koag wasn't to blame for his death. In fact, the reporter hinted the opposite: "The body was covered in dust at the end, perhaps in a final blessing from Greot." Then we walked back into town, the three of us talking rubbish to each other. I did see some people staring at us on the high street. Was this good or bad? I couldn't decide. Two young kids laughed and pointed. More people than ever would now know of my talent. That evening, my family went crazy over the article, cooing at the photographs, ruffling my hair and calling me silly names. "Oh, doesn't he look handsome, Dotty?" Grandma Sykes had to agree with my mother at this statement. Meanwhile, Chloe was looking peeved; she was missing from every single photograph. I retreated to my room. I fell onto my bed and thought about Margery and her skirt, the way she had swivelled it around her hips after fastening the zip, the slight struggle it caused her. And then the kiss from her hippy friend. I fell into a daydream.

My sister woke me. Only half an hour had passed since my eyes had closed, but the images still tumbled over and over each other, a constant parade of nature's bounties: the birds and the bees and the worms and the barking dog and the clumps of dust clinging to the branch, dripping, dripping...

A letter had arrived for me.

"A letter?" I didn't understand.

"Yeah, someone pushed it through the letterbox."

This was weird. I mean, who would send me such a thing?

"I reckon it's a love letter," Chloe said. "What else could it be?"

"How do they know where I live?"

"That reporter put our address in the paper, didn't she? Well, open it then!"

I couldn't, not with her sitting there on the edge of the bed. I ordered her to leave, which she did, reluctantly. Then I examined the envelope. It was white and crisp. No postage stamp, my name and address nicely written by hand. I broke the seal. Inside was a single sheet of paper. The message on it was typewritten.

Mr G.K. Holbrook & Miss Margery Adams
request the attendance of
JOSEPH SUTTER
(plus guest)
for tea and cakes
at 4 pm on Saturday, 3rd August
at Pike View
Informal dress

So much information! Margery's second name was Adams. And Doctor Mask's secret identity was G.K. Holbrook. But what did the *G* and the *K* stand for? Why not spell out his full name? The third of August was tomorrow, not long to wait. But what on earth did *informal dress* mean? I went downstairs to look at the *Family Dictionary*. Mum, Grandma and Chloe were all staring at me.

"Well then," Mum asked, "What does your letter say?"

"Nothing."

"Oh, I can't believe that."

"It's from someone who read the newspaper."

Chloe insisted on her original idea: "It's a love letter."

"No it isn't! It's from a person who's interested in Greot."

I looked up the word *informal* in the dictionary. *Casual. Without ceremony. Of behaviour or speech: relaxed and friendly. Of clothing: suitable for everyday wear.* Phew, that was a relief. Everyday wear. Chloe wanted to know what I was looking up: "A dirty word, I'll bet! So he can write to his lovey-dove." She came to stand near me, but I managed to close the book in time, and hurried back upstairs. One further thing troubled me. After twice sending me away with a shout and a raised fist, Doctor Mask had now invited me into his home. Why the change of heart? Was it something to do with the article in the *Chronicle*? And then there was that mysterious *plus guest,* in brackets. Was that an order, meaning that I wouldn't be let in the house without a guest alongside? But who could I ask? Mum? No. Grandma? Not really. Chloe? God forbid! Denny? Maybe. But the Portman family always went out on a Saturday, usually to Belle View Amusement Park. I couldn't think of anyone else. Until… well, until Eileen's name popped into my head.

Now, where did that come from? I do not know. But once in place, that single quick thought sent a shiver all the way through me, head to toe. Eileen Barlow and me, going to a tea and cakes party together! Could you imagine? It was a perfect picture to hold in my mind: the two of us walking up Pike Hill together, her in her nicest frock, me in… (informal outfit not yet decided on), the both of us looking very smart and yet extraordinarily casual. The sun was shining, the kestrel was high in the sky, while Sutter's Fancy danced around us in shimmering swathes of colour.

I knew where she lived. Denny had pointed the house out to me one time, and it wasn't too far away. And so Saturday morning found me standing outside 26 Heather Avenue. It was a very nice looking bungalow, recently built, with a garden, and the woods not too far away at the back. Eileen was no housing-estate girl, that was a fact. I thought about ringing the bell, but then worried about who would open the door. It might be her father, and he would look me up and down like I was a scruffy urchin. Maybe if I waited around she would come out of the house and I could accidentally bump into her. Yes, that was a much better idea. I waited there for at least three-quarters of an hour, sometimes walking up and down the road, so as not to look suspicious (I looked very suspicious). And then, finally, I went home. I could not pluck up the courage. But also, the thought of Denny made me leave, that he might not like me inviting Eileen for tea and cakes, for some reason. The feelings were too complicated to work out.

I have no recollection of how the rest of the day passed, only of arriving at Pike View on the dot of four o'clock. I was wearing long trousers (corduroy), with a polo shirt (tucked in). To hold the trousers up I wore a purple and cream striped elasticated belt with a snake buckle. My hair was combed, but not too neatly. I had to hope Mr Holbrook and Miss Adams didn't mind me being on my own. I waited until the second hand on my wristwatch reached the hour before rapping the ram's head against the panelling. Nipper started up at this noise, but was quickly hushed by Margery's yell of command. A moment later, the front door opened and I was welcomed inside.

9

The house had a different atmosphere compared to my first visit. It was homelier, cleaner, brighter. They had had a good tidy up. Was this all on my behalf? Nipper was joining in with the new mood, friendlier than ever, rubbing at my ankles. "He likes you," Margery said. "I knew he would." She was smiling. Her hair was neat, her clothes more subdued that yesterday's frilly blouse and fitted skirt. She wore those for her boyfriend, I supposed. I could smell her perfume, a dark musky scent.

There was no sign of G.K. Holbrook.

Margery led me along the corridor towards the dining room, placed next to the kitchen at the back of the house. A table was laid with a white tablecloth, and on this were a selection of tea things: plates of triangular sandwiches, little cakes, cups and saucers. She directed me to a chair, which I took. "I'll just get the teapot." And she left me there, alone. I had not yet said a word. My corduroys felt uncomfortable, too warm for the weather. I regretted my decision. Should I take a sandwich? I was hungry. I was always hungry. Probably best to wait until I was told to begin, that was polite behaviour. Mrs Pierce was always telling us about such things. I could hear footsteps upstairs. That must be the mysterious G.K. Holbrook getting himself ready. Yet I'd arrived at the exact time. My eye was drawn to a large oil painting on the wall. I knew little of abstract art, thinking it only a pattern, but I couldn't help imagining Koag in the great swirls of ochre and violet and gold that moved over the green swathe at the bottom of the canvas.

I reached out for a sandwich, but then pulled back as Margery came in. "Isn't he down yet?" she asked.

"No. Not yet."

"I'll give him a shout." She placed the teapot on the table and went out of the room. I heard her calling up the stairs. "George! George, our guest is here!"

George. George K. Holbrook. Only the *K* remained a puzzle.

I could not hear a reply from above.

Margery came in. "He'll be down shortly." She eyed the table. "Have you taken a sandwich?"

"No, Miss Adams. I swear."

"Call me Margery, please. We're all friends here."

Were we?

"What shall I call him?" I gestured with my head to the ceiling.

She sat down. "*Mr Holbrook* is fine for now."

"Will Mr Holbrook be wearing the mask?"

She looked at me. It was a quizzical look, as though I'd asked a really stupid question that she couldn't quite understand. "Dear God, I hope not. Not at the dinner table. There are limits." She sighed. "You know, he's only supposed to wear it for four days at the most, in any one period. And he put it on, when? Monday, was it, when you disturbed him?"

"Yes, Monday."

"So, Tuesday is one day of wearing it, Wednesday is two, Thursday three, and Friday four. So I was strict with him last night, I was, very strict, that he had to take it off."

"Why does he wear it?"

"Shush, now. Here he is."

I heard footsteps descending the stairs. He was taking his time. I truly had no idea what to expect. I had seen him three times in a mask. Now I would see him properly for the first time. I was a little scared, wondering how his face would look, how badly injured it was. Clawed by a wild animal, burned by acid, or slashed into pulp by a German bayonet?

He entered the room and stood at the doorway.

Margery got to her feet. Following her lead, I did the same.

Mr Holbrook walked to the table. He had a slight limp and he was awfully thin. I still didn't know his age. He was definitely older than Grandma, but not, you know, *super* old. There was, thankfully, no damage to his face. He was dressed in a suit and tie, grey pinstripe, a bit ragged and shiny, but definitely not *informal dress*. Margery also was very smartly dressed. I felt cheated, and was suddenly very aware that my polo shirt (mauve) did not match my trousers (brown). I should have worn my school uniform with my Daniel Defoe tie. A cloud of Koag (lime and indigo blend) followed Mr Holbrook into the room, but sadly, not Sutter's Fancy. He was still keeping that one to himself. He took his seat, and then Margery did the same, and then myself. We sat in silence for a moment.

"Well, George, this is Joe," she said. "Our guest for tea."

He grunted.

She went on, "We usually have a little something around this time, but not this elaborate. I'll be mother, shall I?" She poured tea into our cups. "Well, tuck in, Joe. Eat your fill."

I started on a sandwich. Ham and cheese, very nice. But there were no crusts on the bread. I thought that strange, as though I'd been short-changed. And the sandwich was so small I needed another one straight away. Mr Holbrook was wolfing them down as fast as I was. Margery had not been lying about his appetite. I thought it best to keep up with him.

He had not yet spoken.

Noticing the empty chair at the opposite side of the table, I said, "I'm sorry about not bringing a guest."

"That's fine, Joe," Margery said. "We never expected you to, not really."

"I had someone in mind, but I didn't get round to asking them."

"A friend, was it?"

"Yes."

"Did you hear that, George? He wanted to bring a friend."

I turned to look at Mr Holbrook. He was staring at me intently, a sandwich half-digested in his mouth. His cheeks were shiny, very closely shaved, and because he was so perfectly bald it looked like he'd shaved the entirety of his head, from under the chin to the back of his neck. His nose was thin and long, but crooked to one side, broken. (I imagined a brawl with ruffians.) His eyes reminded me of the glass marbles Denny and I used to play with, a cold blue and grey mixture. He had a lot of little wrinkles and marks all over, but most prominent were the three deep crevices on his forehead, each one the same length. Age had fiercely attacked him at that point more than any other. But his hands were worse off than his face, marked with liver spots, and quite trembly. Because of this affliction, he kept spilling tea into his saucer. But he supped it up from the rim with a loud slurping noise.

"George, really, must you?" Margery put on a posh voice, but in a jokey manner. Then she turned to me. "The thing is, Joe, I'm glad you didn't bring a guest."

"Oh?"

"I only put that on the invite so as not to arouse suspicion."

"I don't know what you mean."

"We wondered if your parents might think it funny, you being invited to a stranger's house, on your own."

"It's only my mum these days. And Grandma. And my sister. I'm the Man of the House."

"And what about your father?"

"He left home."

"What was the trouble? Too much arguing?"

I did not like this question. It reminded me of sitting at the top of the stairs, Chloe at my side with her arm around my shoulders, as we listened to the ranting and raving from the living room. Best to ignore the whole thing. I put on my best manners.

"No, he had to leave on important business. He lives in London now, in a fancy house, three storeys tall, with gardens front and back, and a huge garage at the side for his E-Type Jaguar. Paul McCartney lives on the same street, but of course Paul's house is much bigger."

Margery smiled at this. "And your mother's okay, is she, with you coming round?"

Mr Holbrook started on the cakes, so I did the same, matching him step by step. "I never told her." Crumbs fell onto my polo shirt.

"Right. I see."

"Nobody minds what I do, really. Mum and Chloe work during the day, and Grandma spends most of her time alone in the parlour looking at her budgerigar. See, I have a key around my neck." I showed them both the house key threaded on a shoelace.

"You should let your mother know, in future. Just so everything's above board. You could even ask her round, if you wanted to."

I had no idea why she was so worried.

She went on, "George was very keen on making your acquaintance, after reading the article about you in the *Chronicle*. Yes, very interesting, it was. We both thought so."

I drank more tea to wash down the cake. It was sticky. It needed cream, and maybe a dollop of strawberry jam, but neither were on offer.

Mr Holbrook burped.

I did the same.

Margery's fake posh voice came out again: "I must say, you gentlemen are free to express yourselves, aren't you?"

There was a lull in the conversation. Margery ate daintily. Mr Holbrook was on his second cup of tea. I wondered if he was going to speak at all, or whether he would stay quiet for the whole meal. It was a possibility. I tried to think of something to say. I had earlier that day prepared a list of subjects to talk about, but the piece of paper was in my pocket, and what's more, I could not remember a single item listed. I couldn't very well take it out in front of them and consult it. Perhaps I should go to the toilet, and memorise the subjects that way? But that would mean asking to be excused, and what would I say, what would I call it? *Please may I go to the toilet*, or *the loo*, or *the little boy's room*, or *the gents*, or *the lavatory?* No, best to stay here. If nobody spoke, then nobody spoke, and that was that, and there was nothing I could do about it. Oh, wait, yes, of course! Now I remembered one of my listed subjects.

"I went to the pictures last week, the ABC in Ashton, my mum and my sister and me. We saw *Yellow Submarine*. Have you seen it?" Neither of them replied, so I hurried on. "It's by the Beatles, but it's a cartoon. The Beatles star in it, but only their voices, their bodies are drawn in. Like Walt Disney." I was running out of words. "There are songs in it." Nothing, nothing more? I started to sing the title song, but stopped after two lines.

Mr Holbrook looked unimpressed. He finished off the last cake on the plate. Then he spoke for the first time.

"Do you read?"

His voice startled me. It was clear, a bit reedy, but pleasant. Bird-like, I might call it.

"Well, do you?"

I looked from him to Margery and back again. They were both waiting for an answer.

"Yes, sir, I mean... Mr Holbrook."

"And what do you read?"

"Comics."

"What kind of comics? *Beano*? *Eagle*?"

"Superhero comics."

"I see. And which are your favourite heroes?"

I reeled them off. "Batman, Spider-Man, Daredevil, the Flash." The list would be very long if I listed them all, so I stopped there.

"George likes to read them, on occasion," Margery said.

This news astonished me. So I went gladly on, "Cyclops, the Fantastic Four. The Hulk."

"Which is your favourite of the Fantastic Four?" he asked.

"The Thing. No, the Human Torch. Do I have to choose? I like them all."

"The Invisible Girl?"

"Oh yeah, Sue Storm, she's cool." (I sounded like Denny, now.)

Mr Holbrook's mind seemed to wander, but his eyes soon clicked back into focus. "Have you noticed, how, when the Invisible Girl turns invisible, she still has dotted lines to show her outline?"

"Yes! I was only thinking about that just the other night."

"Were you? Very good."

"My friend, Denny... Denny Portman, he found the dead man with me... Denny, he makes up superheroes all of his own, completely new ones, like, like, like Zigzag Woman."

"And what does she do?"

"She jumps from one place to another, at a really fast speed."

"As does the Flash."

"Yeah, but the Flash runs in straight lines, while Zigzag Woman jumps about, in..."

"In zigzags?" Margery asked with a smile.

"That's right." Were they laughing at me? Well, never mind, I would show them. "Then we have Spellcaster, a wizard who fights evil villains with his powerful magic."

"A bit like Doctor Strange, then?" Mr Holbrook said.

"Yes, but, but different, completely different!" I was floundering. "And there is no other hero anything like Nowhere Man."

"Is that so?"

"Oh, you bet! Nowhere Man is extra special because he can only be seen by the sounds he makes. Like… POW! and SMASH! and KRUMPH! and SCREEEEE!" I forgot myself completely in my excitement and was miming each sound effect with my hands and face. I did about half a dozen of them altogether. Margery was smiling and nodding along. Mr Holbrook was gleeful as well; he was tapping on his saucer with a teaspoon.

"How exciting," Margery said.

Mr Holbrook agreed. "He's a live-wire."

I settled down, containing myself. But I was happy to have entertained them.

"Shall we have that jelly and cream now, Margery, eh?"

"Yes, why not?"

She went through the door connecting the dining room to the kitchen, leaving me alone with the old man. I had so much to ask him, but I didn't know where to start, or even if I was allowed to. Again, I thought of the list of items in my pocket; if only I could access it! But there was one thing I absolutely needed to say.

"I'm very sorry, Mr Holbrook. For creeping into your house on Monday, and scaring you like I did."

He shrugged at this, as though the incident meant nothing at all. Instead he went back to the interrupted subject of a few minutes before, this being far more important.

"Joe, I want you to think about the Invisible Girl, and those dotted outlines."

"What about them?"

"I'm asking you to think, not to be told."

His voice was raised. It worried me a little. "I don't know, what do you want me to do?"

"Think!"

"About the dotted lines?"

"As I said." He was glaring at me. "The very thing."

My mind was a blank, completely so, blanker than Nowhere Man in a sound-proof booth. I tried to speak, but instead began to stutter. This angered him further. His fist hit the tabletop with as much force as he could muster, as he cried out in his reedy tone: "Think, boy, for pity's sake!"

Koag fluttered upwards. The dust formed into waves of unrest that crossed the ceiling like the patterns Mrs Pierce had shown us with a magnet and a pile of iron filings.

Margery came in carrying dessert on a tray. "What is going on in here?" she said. "George? Are you upsetting our guest? I am so sorry, Joe. He has the manners of a pig sometimes. A pig!" The tray clattered down on the table.

"Mr Holbrook was…"

"Yes, what?" Her eyes stared down at the three bowls of jelly and cream.

"He was teaching me about the Invisible Girl. About her–"

"Look at the state of you." She had come round to Mr Holbrook's side and was now wiping at his chin with a napkin, brushing the cake crumbs away.

"Get off me!" He pushed her hands aside. "Leave me alone."

She did so. "Oh, gladly, gladly." Then she burst into laughter, a sort of wild laughter.

I was too young to understand the mixed emotions on view.

Margery went back to her seat. "You must forgive us, Joe. We're meant to be having a nice tea party. Not pretending like we're in *Coronation Street*, arguing all the time."

"That's all right," I answered. "I don't mind."

"We've been together for too long, that's the trouble. We're like an old married couple."

Mr Holbrook grunted and sniggered at this. Then he laughed. And Margery laughed as well, a genuine laughter this time.

"A married couple," she repeated. "Well, I say. Imagine!"

So, what were they to each other? It was still a mystery.

I said to her, "Mr Holbrook was asking me about the dotted lines."

Margery was confused, I could see. She poured cream onto the jellies. It was evaporated milk, actually, which I loved even more.

"Sue Storm has dotted lines around her body," I explained. "When she's invisible."

"Well, she would need them, I suppose, otherwise how would the reader know where she is?"

Mr Holbrook nodded vigorously. "That's it. Exactly so! Do you see, Joe? Do you understand what is so very strange about those dotted lines?"

"Strange? No, not really."

His fists clenched on the tabletop. Oh God, I'd set him off again. What now?

"Can the characters see the dotted lines?"

"The characters?"

His eyes were screwed shut. The three frown lines scrunched together to form a deep crinkled valley. His voice screeched. "The other people in the comic book story, the Human Torch, the Thing, Mr Fantastic… can *they* see the dotted lines around Sue Storm?"

"Of course they can."

"Can they?"

"I said it already. They can see the lines. The lines are there."

"No."

"What?"

"No, they cannot see the dotted lines."

"Really?"

"Think about it."

Mr Holbrook was smiling at me. Margery was nodding encouragement. So I set myself to the task. *The characters in the comic cannot see the dotted lines of Invisible Girl*. This was the claim. It was ridiculous, of course it was. Yet, now the idea had come up, I couldn't stop thinking about it.

I exclaimed, "I feel like a bomb is about to go off inside my head."

Mr Holbrook grinned. "That's good."

Margery sipped at her tea. "Yes, that's very good, Joe."

"Let it explode!"

So I did. I pictured Doctor Doom sitting inside my head, setting off a dastardly device.

KERBOOM!!!

And among the scattered pieces of my brain, I saw myself reading a comic. It was a *Fantastic Four* comic. Not one I had read before, more a general idea of a *Fantastic Four* comic. And there was the Invisible Girl, Sue Storm, sometimes solid, sometimes transparent, sometimes dotted, but rarely completely invisible. I could see her. Doctor Doom could not see her. I could see her.

Mr Fantastic could not see her. I could see her. The Human Torch could not see her. But I could see her. And not just me, but all the other readers as well… Because of the dotted lines.

I was staring straight ahead. The giant oil painting on the wall came into focus. I spotted a single tiny black smudge in the shape of a tower, and realised the picture was actually a depiction of Brendle Pike from the distance, with the sky and the fields above and below, and the dust clouds streaming by. It was amazing.

The two other diners at the table were looking at me.

Putting the thoughts together one at a time, I said, "The characters inside the comic can't see the dotted lines… but I can." A pause to gather the idea. "The *reader* can."

"Good, very good. And?" Mr Holbrook leaned forward, eagerly. "What does that mean? What follows?"

Oh, he kept pushing at me. Just when I thought my homework was done, it began again. And in the end all I could do was shake my head. He leaned back, sighing. But this time he did not look angry, merely disappointed. He steepled his hands together and rested his pointed chin on the apex of the church. Then he said, "The artist drawing the *Fantastic Four* comic has one major problem, namely, how to show an invisible person to the reader." He raised his arms and cried out at the top of his voice, "We have to make the invisible, visible!"

I was startled. But he was not finished yet. Moving his hands in an enticing manner, he drew Koag away from the corners of the ceiling, back towards his head. The dust was under his control, down to the last little swirl. Blimey, how I wished I had such power.

He carried on, "So, let us consider the Invisible Girl. The readers can see her dotted outline, while the other characters around her can't. What does that imply?"

I must have frowned, grimaced, something like that, for his anger returned.

"There are two worlds!"

I focussed on the black smudge of Brendle Pike in the painting, almost lost in the violence of the sky and the dust.

"Two worlds. One real, the other unreal." Now his voice had a spell-like quality. "In the real world, you, Joe, are sitting at a table, reading a comic, and *you* can see the dotted lines around Invisible Girl. But in the unreal world, the fictional world that exists *inside* the comic, the dotted lines do not exist." He took a breath. "The two worlds are separate from one another, and have different rules." Then he just seemed to collapse, folding up his arms around his head, hiding himself. He went on in a kind of sobbing moan, "But they are joined... they are joined at the page, at the *page*..." He was crying. "And the page is... the page is a borderline." His tears continued.

How could this be? What had tipped him over into such misery?

Margery came around the table, to whisper to him. "Don't go upsetting yourself, George. You know it's not good for you."

I was at a loss. I felt embarrassed.

She explained, "I think he's tired. He's been working too hard. And wearing that mask all the hours. Help me, Joe, would you?"

We got him to his feet, and then steered him along the corridor. The two of them climbed the stairs step by step, while I watched from the bottom. Over her shoulder, Margery said, "Don't go just yet. I'd like a word with you." I nodded. They disappeared onto the landing and I heard a bedroom door opening. Not wanting to just stand there like an idiot, I went into the living room, with its upright piano, and the radiogram, and the bookshelves filled with novels. My eyes darted here and there. Ray Bradbury, Arthur C. Clarke, Isaac Asimov, John Wyndham, and so many others. There were a lot of books by someone called Robert A. Heinlein: *Have Space Suit, Will Travel*; *The Puppet Masters*; *Starship Troopers*; *Stranger in a Strange Land*. Next to Heinlein was Frank Herbert, with fewer books on offer: *Destination Void; Dune; The Green Brain*. And next to Herbert on the shelf... G.K. Holbrook. I could not believe it. My fingers moved along the spines as I read each title in turn, nine of them altogether: *Lost Among the Stars; Gods of Chaos; A Game Without Players; The Human Experiment; Prisoners of Nimbus; The Inside-Out Man; Morgue Planet; Dreams of Brendle; The Space Chrysalis*. The second-to-last title stood out the most to me, because I had never seen the word *Brendle* used for anything other than the tower on the hill. But as I reached for the book, Margery entered the room.

"Well, that's him asleep for a while."

I turned. She was pouring herself a drink from a whisky bottle. "You've found his collection, have you?"

"Yes. I didn't know he was a writer. He's written a lot of books."

"You don't know the half of it. Here, let me show you." She pointed to different areas of the bookshelves, indicating different writers. "Ken Brookholme, Arnold S. Holdforth, Kenneth West, Roland J. Dyer, Kenneth Samson. These are all our George, in his different disguises. He is a man of many masks." She laughed at her own joke.

"Is Kenneth his middle name?"

"It is, well guessed." She took a drink. "He told me once he'd written more than a hundred books. I think he's forgotten some of them himself." She sat down in an armchair.

"I'd like to borrow one of his books, to take home and read."

"Well, I'm not sure." But something in my look must have gotten through to her. "I'll tell you what, Joe, I'll have a word with his Lordship when he stirs, and then maybe the next time you visit, maybe then you can take one. Is that all right for you?"

"Yes, thank you."

I was encouraged by this mention of a second visit, because I wasn't at all sure the tea party had gone well, and that maybe I was to blame for it all, my presence there.

"What does he want of me?" I asked.

"How do you mean?"

"Why did you invite me here? It was very nice, and I enjoyed the cakes and the jelly. But you hardly know me. I'm just a boy, a schoolboy."

"You haven't worked it out yet?"

"No."

"I will say this plainly, as it's best that way. George does not have long to live." She stared at me as I struggled to find a word to say. "He's being eaten up from within."

It was horrible, I didn't want to think about it.

"In this, his last year of life, he wishes to pass on his knowledge."

"To me, you mean?"

"Yes, Joe. He wants to teach you how to write."

I truly did not know how to respond to this. My stutter made its dreaded appearance. "Ah, ah, ah, ah, ah... I can't write!"

"What about that story you made up?"

"Which story?"

"Is your daddy rich?"

"What? No, but--"

"Does he live in London?"

"No."

"In a big house?"

"No."

"Does he drive a Jag?"

"No."

"Is he neighbours with John Lennon?"

"Ah! It's Paul McCartney, actually. But, no."

"There you are, then, story, story, story."

I was flabbergasted.

"You have the wrong boy. You need Denny, that's who, my friend Denny, he's really good at making things up, not me. Denny invented Nowhere Man. He's going to be a writer one day, I know it. But no, not me! I just can't do it. Mrs Pierce says so. She gives me terrible marks for my stories!"

Margery let me ramble on, drinking her whisky in a few gulps. Her face took on a shiny glow, and she looked more relaxed. With a quiver in her voice, she said, "Still, that's his plan."

She was soon lost in herself, rambling on about this and that. I decided it best to leave. I stood outside the front door of the house, looking up the hill at Brendle Pike. It appeared to be the same view as the one depicted in the oil painting in the dining room. As I walked up the slope, I felt I was actually walking into the painting, through the canvas to the other side, into the real world. Leaving the house was like leaving a fantasy realm behind, where all the rules were different.

Two worlds.

One real, the other unreal.

They are joined at the page.

My mind was awhirl with ideas. None of which I really understood.

But they excited me!

There were two benches at the summit, one each side of the tower. I chose the one on the far side, out of sight of the house. Here I sat, contemplating the afternoon's events. I was happy to see Koag in his full regalia. The King of Dust pranced about the trees. There was a carpet of pink above Dukinfield, and a purplish veil across Ormsley. The chimney of Bradshaw's Mill was ribboned top to bottom in red and gold strands, like a May pole. It was fantastic to look at. I took the list out of my pocket and checked each item, seeing how many had been dealt with.

Things To Talk About at the Tea Party

1. *Why wear the special mask?*
2. *Cricket, football or rugby. Your favourite?*
3. *What does G.K. stand for?*
4. *Denny and I make our own comics.*
5. *Why steal Tom Halfpenny's dead face, using Sutter's Fancy?*
6. *Have you seen Yellow Submarine film?*
7. *Grandma is a beholder. Talk about her customers.*
8. *Favourite pop group? And why?*

I decided to rework the list when I got home, removing items already talked about and adding some new questions, such as the most puzzling of them all: "Why has Mr Holbrook chosen me to be a writer?" There really was no good answer, unless it had something to do with Koag. Nothing else connected us, as far as I could see. And even then, why should an ability to see a fancy cloud of dust lead to the ability to write stories? Poor Mr Holbrook. Perhaps his illness was making him lose his mind? But I had the feeling that Margery was also in on this scheme, that both residents of Pike View, working together, had come up with the crazy plan.

I gave in to the need to have a pee. I'd been holding it in. Nobody was around for miles, so I stained the old stones of the tower, seeing how high I could leave a mark. Denny and I had played this game many a time. I remember his tale of how Roman soldiers must have done exactly the same thing, at the time of the invasion of Britain, against the very first look out post. "Joe, we are peeing where centurions have peed!" Then his imagination ran riot, painting a picture of a warrior dampening the tower not with piss, but with blood, his own, and that of his enemy. I added the sound effects, the clash of swords, the shriek of the fallen. It all sounded true enough, the way my friend told it. But soon, Mr Holbrook would tell me far stranger stories of the tower, its true history, and the fifth county it looked out over, as yet invisible to my eye.

10

The lights darkened until only the giant clock was clearly visible, showing the time, the current time in the evening: eight o'clock. Preston Heyes narrowed his eyes, concentrating fiercely, moving the hands of the clock by the power of his mind alone. The big hand crept towards three and the little hand towards six, until the time became six minutes past three. He called out in his deepest voice, "Arise, Greot, show yourself to the nation!" On his command a cloud of red, white and blue dust appeared from nowhere. This was the famous magician's gimmick, that by making Greot believe it was the time of the early morning revelation, it would put itself on view to the general public and allow itself to be manipulated. My mother and sister were always impressed by this act, but now, suddenly, I saw it as trickery. Sure, Heyes was a beholder, absolutely, but all this hocus-pocus seemed a bit square after spending the afternoon at Pike View. Although I had seen little in the way of actual magic from Mr Holbrook, still he gave off an intense aura of power. I felt certain that he could make Koag do anything he wanted.

"It's not really Greot," I said. "It's just coloured dust."

My sister answered back, "That's what Greot is, stupid, *coloured dust.*"

"No it isn't."

"Yes it is."

"It really isn't, and I should know."

"Oh, you think you're so special, just because–"

"It's alive."

Our mother shushed us both. "Let me watch my programme, please."

I had not yet told anyone about the tea party. Over supper, Mum wanted to know why I was picking at my food, but I just couldn't bring myself to admit, "I've stuffed my face with ham and cheese sandwiches, and cakes and jelly and cream." Despite my promise to Margery, I wanted to keep the visit secret, for now.

Preston Heyes's lovely assistant, Topaz, stepped inside a wooden cabinet. The coloured dust floated in alongside her, and the door was closed. Much frowning and concentrating ensued, on the magician's part, with suitable dramatic gestures, until suddenly all four walls and the ceiling of the cabinet flew away into the wings, leaving the cloud of dust alone on stage, no longer red, white and blue, but now gold and bright green (very impressive, actually). The dust drifted away, again under the magician's control, revealing an empty space. Topaz had vanished. Poor Topaz. Over the past year we had seen her stabbed with knives, skewered by swords, sawn in two, sliced into quarters; she had floated six feet in the air, and been nearly drowned several times. But she always survived, every time with a big smile on her lips, as now, when she appeared at the back of the television studio, walking down the aisle to much applause from the audience.

My mum oohed and aahed. "Well, I didn't know how he did that, I must say."

"She went through a trap door," I answered, "in the stage floor."

"A trap door? Oh, don't talk rot, Joe. Honestly, the things you come up with."

"And what about the dust, though?" my sister asked. "How come the dust changed colour like that, eh, Mr Know-It-All?"

I couldn't answer that one. I tried, but soon ran out of words, and that was that. Chloe laughed triumphantly. I just wanted to make my exit. I wanted to join Grandma in the back parlour and watch her bring visions to the eyes of her current visitors, two leather-jacketed lads from Mossley. Thankfully, since our chat about ghostly girls and mysterious handkerchiefs, she had returned to her Living Eye sessions. But even more than watching Dotty Sykes at her craft, I wanted to rush up to

Brendle Pike and run around the tower, laughing out loud, and then walk down as cool as you like to the farmhouse and join in with whatever pastimes Mr Holbrook and Margery might be enjoying. Maybe one of them was playing the piano, and the other singing. Even listening to them bicker and rant would be better than this, glued to the goggle box for a Saturday night's entertainment. So I went upstairs to my room, put a Kinks single on my Dansette record player and read some of my comics, the latest *X-Men* and an old *Green Lantern*. I watched Koag crawling across the walls in at least five different shades of red. Were the grains making a secret pattern just for me? I could not tell the difference between what I wanted to happen, and what was actually happening. When the record came to an end, I raised my hands, trying to entice Koag towards me, like Preston Heyes in his magic show, and also like Mr Holbrook during the tea party. I crooked my fingers and concentrated so hard my ears started to pop. I willed it to happen. I said aloud, "Koag, come to me now, do as I command."

Nothing. Not a quiver.

"Koag, you will obey me, I am your master!"

But no, apparently not.

That night I slept soundly, right through the public witnessing, no trouble. Sunday morning saw me out and about nice and early. I ran down the high street, I scaled the wall of the churchyard. I ran along the canal and across the bridge, trailing electric-blue strands of Koag in my wake like Superman's cape when he's flying into action. I stopped to have a look at Monty's caravan on the patch of wasteground next to Bradshaw's Mill. They say Alfred Montgomery lived there for six years, all alone, living off God knows what. Some people suggested he was a criminal on the run, and that he had a stash of banknotes hidden under his fold-out bed. Others claimed he was a deserter from the army, or a man doomed in love, jilted at the altar. How could one man have so many stories? There were rumours as well that he was a beholder. But nobody knew the truth. I only remembered him a little, from my youngest years, because Monty simply walked away from Ormsley Vale one night, without a word of explanation. He left his caravan behind. It stayed on the site for a year, gathering dirt and leaves and rust. Pigeons used it as a target. Letters were written to the

Chronicle. Some rocker boys broke in, in search of the fabled stash of money, but nothing was found. Finally a council truck pulled up and towed the "eyesore" away. The wasteground was empty, and it stayed that way for a few days, until, one unseen night the caravan reappeared on the exact same spot, but not in substance, only in dust. I was seven years old at the time, and this was the best recreation by Koag I had ever seen: every detail of the outside of the vehicle was captured, and every inner detail as well, as it was on the day of Monty's leaving. Yes, Koag loved to mimic things, but it was rare to see the phenomenon on this kind of scale. It caused quite a commotion, and was a story of national interest. Spectators arrived, most often in the early hours for the six minutes past three witnessing. The BBC sent their presenter Yvette Bishop to our little town, to be filmed in front of the caravan. But the spot-lit, black-and-white footage did not capture the sheer magical beauty of the thing. Rain might pelt down, turning the vehicle into paste; gales might blow it away; frost might transform it into a brittle ice palace. No matter, every single time the dust returned to make the caravan anew. For a while it was my favourite place to visit, especially when I was feeling a bit sad over my dad's departure. All those romantic notions attached to Monty seemed to reside there still; if anything, they were now intensified.

I stepped up onto the first of the wooden crates I had put in place last year. These enabled the visitor to raise themselves up to the floor level of the caravan. The caravan had no proper solidity, so you couldn't actually climb the steps to the door. But you could walk right through the door like a ghost through a wall in a horror film, and then the door would re-form around you, remaking itself whenever it was disturbed. It was the same for any item of interest; whatever you passed through was always remade by the dust, instantly. It gave me a shiver to see Koag in action like this, so brilliant in its varied aspects and skills. I moved from one box to the next as I studied the items Monty had left behind: a shaving bowl and brush; a book beside the bed (*You Only Live Twice*), the title delicately picked out in patterns of dust; a girlie mag called *Mayfair*. (I longed to pick this up and examine the pictures, but the magazine fell into its constituent parts whenever I tried, and then reformed). There was a portable typewriter on a small table, its metal parts modelled in dust. Alfred Montgomery had been at work on a letter, on the day of his leaving; the dust-made paper was still in the roller of the machine. The words could be made out in wispy lines and curls that trembled ever so slightly under my breath as I stooped to reread them now: *Dear Harry, I beg you to reconsider. I made a mistake that day, a terrible mistake. But I am working on a new plan of action.* That was all, the letter was unfinished. This was the ghost of a caravan. There was even a half-drunk cup of tea on the tabletop, the liquid perfectly recreated. The entirety of a man's life, abandoned in a moment, had been preserved for future viewing by any witness who might pass this way. But why? What on earth was Koag up to, in games such as this? I swept my hand across the tabletop, through the typewriter, through the abandoned letter, the tea cup, scattering them all. Within a few seconds they began to drift back into place, the words slowly reappearing on the sheet of paper: *Dear Harry, I beg you to reconsider.* I loved to watch the magic at work. The talk of Monty being a beholder must be true. Otherwise, why would he attract such dusty attention?

I moved to the next box, walking through a shirt hanging on a hook, through a shaving mirror, into a framed photograph of a woman and child, through a spider's web complete with a tiny dusty occupant, each thing parting about me, each re-forming. A newspaper lay on the seat, a perfect copy of the *Daily Mirror* dated 13th August, 1964. The headline read, "Train Robber Escapes Prison". It was this headline, carefully preserved by Koag, which led to the rumours that Monty was in some way associated with the gang who pulled off the Great Train Robbery, and that the escape of gang member Charlie Wilson from a prison in Birmingham had caused Monty to make a run for parts unknown. But whatever the truth of its former occupant's life, this cloudy caravan would remain here, in this place, for as long as Koag deemed it so. I let strands of dust blend across my skin. My mind was filled with little splinters of images, of stories.

I jumped down onto solid ground, quickly making my way to the goods wagon at Slew Hill. I saw her legs first, dangling over the lip of the entrance. Red sandals today, white socks with little ruffles on the top. No voices this time, no music. Was Denny there as well? He had to be, surely. But no. It was Eileen on her own.

I made the usual greeting. "Alright, Eileen?"

But this time, instead of saying "Not bad, not bad", she answered, "Oh, it's you, is it?" Her face was hidden in the shadows.

"It is me. Who else would it be?"

"Well, I was just wondering whether it might be someone exciting or not. But then I saw it was you."

I looked around, as though the remark meant nothing to me. "No Denny, then?"

"What does it look like?"

I considered my options for a quick escape. Then I climbed up to sit beside her. It was all right here, half of your body cool, the other half warmed by the sun. We both had bare legs, as I'd gone back to my shorts after yesterday's disastrous corduroy experiment. I started thinking of how I had waited outside her bungalow for nearly an hour, like a stupid lump. But I wasn't going to admit it to her, not ever. And then I thought, what if she noticed me there, what if she saw me through the window? Is that why she was grinning to herself? I had to think of something to say. If I'd known we'd be meeting like this, I would have made a list of interesting subjects to discuss. But I had nothing. I could tell her about the tea party, but where would I start? The silence went on and on. I had to prove to her that I was exciting in some way, any way.

Finally I said, "I'm going to be a writer." It just came out. "When I leave school."

"Really?"

"You bet! Writers get to make things up."

"Like what?"

"Stuff, you know. Like adventures in space, and alien invasions, and mysterious–"

She blurted out, "Oh, did you see Preston Heyes last night?"

"Sure."

"The way he made that woman vanish."

"Topaz."

"What?"

"That's her name. Topaz."

She looked peeved. "I know that. But it's not her real name, is it?"

"I guess not, who knows?"

"It sounds a bit funny. A bit fancy, like."

"That's why she chose it, probably."

"Aye, probably. But do you know the secret of Preston Heyes's name?"

I shook my head. "There's a secret?"

"If you change the two names around, you get Heyes Preston."

"So?"

"Then take some letters away from the end of each word... and... what's left? Go on, work it out, let's see you!"

"I'm trying to, give me a chance—"

"Hey Presto!" Oh, she laughed and laughed.

I nodded. *Preston Heyes. Hey Presto.* Why hadn't I seen that for myself? We sat there side by side, Eileen still laughing, me grinning, but I'm not sure why. I liked it here. Koag formed into a perfect sphere of yellow dust above her head. Her face was brightened by it. Her legs swung back and forth, and so did mine. But then I stopped, as I realised I was copying her rhythm exactly. But then she stopped as well. What now? Should I start swinging again? Then I noticed that our legs were only an inch apart. That tiny gap; the more I thought about it, the more charged with electricity it seemed. I could imagine sparks crossing between us, across the gap. What would happen, I wondered, if our legs should touch, just a little bit, almost, like, accidentally? The idea thrilled me. Would she even notice? Perhaps her leg would move away. Or perhaps it would stay where it was, pressing against mine. And then what? I started to fidget about and my eyes were hazy with dust, like Koag had got inside my head somehow and was making me act all funny.

"You live on Stoneybroke Estate, don't you?" Her voice startled me.

"It's not called that. It's *Stoneybrook.*"

"I know, but everyone calls it Stoneybroke, because you're all so poor."

"We're not poor, we're not! And anyway, even if we are... so what?"

"If you were rich, what would you spend it on?"

"A millionaire?"

"Yeah."

"I'd buy a great big mansion for my mum, with a butler to serve her cups of tea, and a maid to do all the cleaning. And I'd have a room just for my comics collection, which would be massive, the biggest collection of superhero comics in the world."

"Is it true that your dad's in prison?"

"What? No! Who said that?"

"Stephanie Marsh."

"Stephanie Marsh? What does she know?"

"She said he'd stolen lead off the roof of St Matilda's."

"That's a lie, a stinking lie!"

"Where is he then?"

I thought of repeating the story I'd told Margery, of my dad driving his Jag around London, but decided against it. Instead, I told her, "I don't know." My voice was all quiet, like.

"You don't know? You must know–"

"Well, I don't. I just don't!"

"All right, Joe, don't get your knickers in a twist."

She was looking at me, her eyes unblinking. This was dreadful. I could feel myself going red. But luckily, Eileen had already found something else of interest. She picked at a scab on her knee. Then she announced, "I'd like to be a magician's assistant, when I leave school."

"Why?" It sounded like a crazy job for anyone to choose.

"Because then you get to vanish. Like Topaz."

"Oh. Right."

"It must feel amazing, don't you think, Joe... to just *vanish* like that, from inside the cabinet, with Greot swirling all around you?"

Should I mention the trap door in the stage? No, best not. After all, I was only guessing. It was probably much more complicated than that. And Eileen was so enamoured of the idea that her eyes had a sparkly look to them.

"And then you just... disappear."

"It's like that man," I said, "who invented that threshold thingy."

"The what? Threshold?"

"It's a new word I learnt. My grandma taught it me. It means doorway, or something like that. Anyway, it's all about Greot, and how it suddenly becomes visible." I remembered to use the common name, because I didn't yet know what Denny had told her. "The dust is invisible until it comes through that doorway, that *threshold*, and then…"

"Joe, what are you babbling on about?"

"And then it becomes visible, don't you see?"

"I can't say I do."

"It was discovered by Sir Robert Helme."

"That old scientist bloke?"

"Yeah."

"He punched Isaac Newton on the nose."

"I know!"

"Mrs Pierce was always going on about him. So boring."

"Yeah, boring."

"What's this got to do with Preston Heyes and Topaz?"

I stuttered, and then stopped myself from speaking. I had to think carefully now, to get it right. "When Topaz vanishes into the dust, that's like the threshold working, only backwards."

Eileen was staring at me.

"Working backwards, not forwards."

Staring and staring.

"Instead of appearing out of the dust, she disappears *into* the dust."

Staring. God, if only she would take her eyes off me! I could not look away. The urge to make sound effect noises took me over, but Eileen put a stop to that by jumping down from the wagon. I'd messed up. Why had I said all that? Helme's stinking threshold! It was stupid.

"Well, if Denny's not coming along, I guess I might get going."

"Aye, I suppose."

She walked away, back towards town. I watched her. Would she turn around? If she did, I'd give her a wave, but casual like, *informal*, not really meaning much by it. But she didn't turn around. Koag came dancing in towards me, in various colours, all of them accusing. "Don't look at me like that. I tried my best!" I ran along to Weeping Cross Lane and from there to Pike Hill, avoiding the woods this time. When the farmhouse came into view I veered towards it. There was no Land Rover in the yard. I knocked on the door. No answer, and no dog barking, but this time I bent down and shouted through the letterbox.

"Mr Holbrook, sir, it's me. It's Joe. Joe Sutter, from yesterday."

It took a while, but eventually the door opened. He was dressed in an anorak and a flat cap, holding a walking stick in one hand. No mask.

"I'm going up to the tower," he said. "Will you come?"

"Try and stop me!"

We set off, me racing ahead all the time so that I had to backtrack every so often; him huffing and puffing and digging into the dirt with his stick, using it as a lever. It wasn't that far of a climb, and not too steep from house to tower, but he was soon sweating and I was worried about him, especially after what Margery had told me, about his illness, and that he probably didn't have long to live.

I said, "It's too warm for an anorak, isn't it? And the cap."

"No, I'll get a chill otherwise."

He had to stop moving to answer me, catching his breath. It sounded a bit like a bicycle tyre with a puncture in it, that wheezing sound. Then we went on, and the last few steps were a chore, that was obvious. I put a hand on his arm and steadied him, pushing him up the steeper part. He was happy to let it happen, and I was happy to make it happen.

Then we were there, at the summit.

He leaned against the stonework of the tower, supporting himself with one hand. He looked like he'd run a marathon.

"Do you want to sit down, Mr Holbrook?" I indicated the nearby bench.

"Not yet, lad, not yet. I want to take it in."

He did so, breathing deeply now, and looking out over the land. Koag had come out in force for his arrival, painting the sky with purple and grey streaks and dropping tiny explosions of red, gold and blue on each of the towns. He was smiling at the sight. Then he coughed and I heard the phlegm rattling in his throat. God, it was a horrible sound.

"What about that Margery, eh?" he said.

"What about her?"

"Do you know where she is, do you?"

I didn't know how to answer. "Shopping?" I tried. "Walking the dog?"

"No. She's got some lover boy on the go. What do you say to that?"

I didn't dare say anything.

"She thinks she can fool me, but she can't. Greot sees everything. And Greot speaks to me."

"Do you know everything about Greot, Mr Holbrook?"

"Me? No, not all. No one can know everything. But I know a fair bit."

"Do you know Greot's real name?"

That got his attention. So I went straight on: "Its real name is Koag. With a *K*. King Koag. But see, it's meant to be a secret. A secret name."

He stared at me. I could not work out what he was thinking. He probably thought me an idiot.

"Take me to that bench now."

I took his hand (it was like cradling a bird's skeleton) and led him to the seat. His knees cracked as he sat down. I took my place beside him. In silence we watched the patterns of dust move across the land. Then he spoke. "Koag, eh? You made that up yourself, did you?"

"No, it was Denny's invention."

"Denny, Denny?"

"I told you about him, the boy who makes up superhero stories. It wasn't my idea."

His eyes were shadowed by the peak of his cap. He sighed. "Have you ever made anything up for yourself?" I shook my head. "Nothing at all? Not one thing that's unusual, or special, or startling?"

"No. Not really."

He sighed again, even more deeply. "Listen close, lad."

"I am doing. Very close."

"Human beings have only two goals in life, and the first of them is to astonish other people." I could hear his teeth tapping together. "And you, my boy, you are a long way off from astonishing me, or anybody else." His hands trembled around the head of the walking stick. "Well then, we begin from zero. How very interesting."

Was I the zero? Nought. Nowt. It didn't sound good.

He went quiet then, contemplating the fields and the towns in the mid-distance. The kestrel was back, hovering above the land. Then it dived. Mr Holbrook laughed with joy to see it, and he said, "Look at that, a noun becoming a verb."

"I don't know what that means."

"What do they teach you at that school?"

"Oh, lots of things–"

"A noun! A naming word. You know about those, don't you?"

"Oh yes."

"And a verb is a doing word. Right?"

"Right." My head started to spin. Was this meant to be a lesson? Was he already teaching me how to write?

"So when the bird suddenly dives, he's a *thing* becoming an *action*. Are you following me?"

I had to get back in his good books, so this time I said, "Yes, sir!"

"You do?"

"Absolutely. It's like when… when… when…"

"Come on, come on!"

I don't know where it came from, I really don't, but I found myself saying, "Like Geoff Hurst, when he scored in the final moments of the World Cup final."

"There you go, lad, there you go."

"Really?"

"Noun, the footballer. Verb, the kick. One into the other, fused in the moment of action."

I leapt up onto the bench in my excitement, punching the air. *"WALLOP! WHOOSH! GOAL!"*

He was laughing. Then he told me to get down. "Quickly now, before you make me dizzy."

I did as he asked. God, it was great to speak with him like this.

"Tell me… Joe, is it?"

"Yes sir. Joseph Andrew Sutter."

"Why did you come to my house that first time?"

"I followed Sutter's Fancy… I mean, the pink-and-rose-coloured dust."

"You made that name up as well, did you? Like Koag?"

"Yes, that was mine, not Denny's. *Sutter's Fancy*. That's special, isn't it, Mr Holbrook? That's astonishing, just like you asked." I launched into further comic book action. "I am Astonishing Man! With my astonishing powers of astonishment, I will astonish all–"

"No. Not really."

"No?"

"It's not astonishing."

"But why not, Mr Holbrook?"

He took a moment, letting his eyes glaze over. Then he said, "Because there are four levels of invention. Shared ideas, unique ideas, crazy ideas. And right at the top, genius ideas. And your made-up name, *Sutter's Fancy*, it occupies level one, the lowest level."

This was too much to take in all at once.

"That's not fair, Mr Holbrook! Because… because… Because I didn't even know there were any other levels."

"It's just your surname, *Sutter*, with another word stuck on the end, *Fancy*, a word meaning, what, *beauty*, or else the fantastical, as in a *fancy* of the mind, or something that you 'fancy', some petty desire, or something of momentary worth, a passing *fancy*. Whichever meaning you choose, you, Sutter, are possessing *Fancy*, as if Fancy could be possessed! Bah!"

That shut me up, I must say. It shut him up as well. So now we were both just sitting there, saying nothing. I had to keep him talking.

"Mr Holbrook?"

He muttered away to himself. But I kept on.

"Margery said to me, yesterday, after the tea party, that you wanted to teach me how to be a writer, a writer like yourself." He didn't reply. "I saw your books on the shelves, so many of them. It was amazing."

"Aye, I've written a few."

"Why do you use so many different names? Kenneth this, Arnold that."

"Well, each name writes a different kind of story."

"How many kinds of story are there?"

"Space Opera, Murder Mysteries, Horror Stories, Westerns, Romances."

"You've written all of these?"

"For my sins, so many pence per word."

"You must be very rich, then."

He smiled at this. "All the different types of stories, they each need a different pseudonym." He looked at me. "Joe, do you know that word, *pseudonym*?"

"No, sir."

"From the Ancient Greek *pseudo*, meaning 'false'. And then *onoma*, meaning 'name'. 'False name', do you see?"

I nodded eagerly. Even though I didn't have a clue what he was saying, I just wanted him to keep on saying it.

"If you know why and how a word was born, you have a spell at the ready."

I nodded some more. Was he teaching me how to be a writer, or a magician?

Then he sighed with pleasure. "*Koag*. Well, well. Now there's a thing."

His eyelids flickered. His head lolled deep into his chest. Was he sleeping? Oh God, he wasn't dead, was he? No. I could see his back rising and falling under the anorak. He roused himself into speech.

"I have known Greot by its various pseudonyms. Specklesoft, Summer Soot, Smutter, Grista, Krista, Mickle Meck, and Frickle Freck."

"Specklesoft? I like that one. But I didn't know it had so many names."

"Oh aye, down the ages people have called it many things, before they settled on Greot."

"Mrs Pierce did tell us it was once called Gilifrag."

"Gilifrag, yes, a fine name."

"But that was before 1066 and the Battle of Hastings. William the Conqueror banned the word, he had it scrubbed out from the Domesday Book."

"Not only that, my boy, in the past they had different names for it in different parts of Britain, things like Nolly Nu, Grickle, Iotum, Millimog, and many more. And all across the world, in other countries, they call it things like Magli Strom, Juetta, Flu-Flu, Hrikka, Polvo, and Malomamo. And then there's its real name, so-called, its scientific name, but that is a very long and unpronounceable word, not worth our bother." He paused. His voice lowered: "Until this day I knew it as others knew it, as Greot the Many-Coloured. But now…"

"Yes?"

"From this day on, I shall call it Koag."

I sprang to my feet again, I could not help myself. "Koag, King of the Skies!"

We both looked out over the world as Koag painted it for us, with sparkles of gold and rosy blush, and clouds of pearly shimmer, and gilifragious motes of sapphire and scarlet red.

Then I asked him, "Mr Holbrook, what is the second goal of life?"

He did not answer. He was too busy following the dust through the air.

"You said the first goal of life was to astonish other people. But you also said there were two goals. What is the second goal?"

He looked at me. "Why, to solve the puzzle of yourself, of course. And, further to this... Now listen carefully, my lad, take it all in."

"Wait, let me concentrate." I pulled my face into a frown. "Right, I'm ready."

And so he began. "There are two things necessary. One: Astonish other people. Two: Solve the puzzle of yourself. Not the problem of yourself, no, but the *puzzle*, the beautiful puzzle. Do this every day. And further: If you can solve the puzzle of yourself whilst astonishing people with the solving of the puzzle, then you can be a writer, or an artist of any kind." A great passion took him over. "Further: If you can solve the puzzle of yourself whilst astonishing other people with the solving, whilst at the same having them think they are solving, for themselves, the beautiful puzzle of their own lives, without them even knowing it, even though they are, and then meanwhile, at the very same time you're astonishing them, and yourself, astonishing yourself, well then, you'll be a number-one-bestselling author. Ha ha! Or just as likely, in fact more than likely, you'll end up in a flea-pit hotel, eating tinned sardines with your fingers."

I was in a daze. But worse was to come.

"Now, say it back to me, come on. What I just taught you."

"What? But Mr Holbrook–"

"Repeat, repeat!"

I tried, I really did. "First goal. Astonish other people."

"Yes, excellent work. Go on."

That was the easy bit over with. "Okay. Next up was... Solve the puzzle of yourself?"

"What kind of puzzle?"

"A difficult puzzle?"

"Ah, no. No, no, no. The *beautiful* puzzle. And the rest?"

"I can't remember."

"Try!"

"Astonish the puzzle of yourself so that the puzzle is astonishing?"

He shook his head in despair at my attempts.

"But, Mr Holbrook, sir, you said it too quickly. I couldn't keep up."

"Here's me, a man of seventy-one, and there's you, a boy. Yet I'm the poor bugger who's going too fast?"

He made to say more, but his passion came to a sudden end in a coughing fit, which bent him in two. I made to pat his back, but then stopped myself. He produced a large handkerchief from a pocket and proceeded to decorate it with spots of blood. The sight of this was very shocking to me, far worse even than watching Tom Halfpenny's final moments. But at last Mr Holbrook calmed himself. He drew some small clusters of Koag to him, for the comfort.

"Are you all right now, Mr Holbrook?"

"Shush!" He held up a hand to quieten me. "Look at Brendle Woods."

I followed his gaze, down to the woods at the edge of town. "Brendle Woods? Why do you call it that?"

"I call it by its real name. Just as this tower here is Brendle Pike. Look now at the way Koag gathers over the trees."

I looked. I saw that a canopy of green dust had flown in from the west, matching the green of the leaves, but of a brighter hue, a more vibrant expression of nature. As the leaves rustled gently, so Koag rustled, mimicking every pattern.

"It's called Ormsley Woods," I told him. "Mrs Pierce told us."

"It might be known as that today. But the oldest maps of the area name it Brendle."

"*Brendle Woods.*" I revelled in the idea of the place's first name, perhaps made up by Stone Age people.

"This Mrs Pierce, she's your teacher?"

"Aye. I mean, she was, last year. But after the holidays I'll be at another school."

"She brought you up here, did she, to the Pike?"

"Oh yes, the whole class. She pointed out the four counties for us."

"Can you name them for me." It wasn't a question, just a simple request.

"Of course." I pointed out each one with my raised arm. "Lancashire, Derbyshire, Cheshire, Yorkshire."

"And the fifth?"

"There are no more, not close by, anyway. You can see Wales in the far distance, is that what you mean?"

"No. I refer to Brendleshire." He stamped his foot, to make the point plain. "The fifth county cannot be seen, not easily, but Brendle Pike here..." He put a hand on the stonework. "The tower remains, the only thing with its old and proper name made known to us."

"It was first built by the Romans, as a lookout post."

"Before those times even, a marker has stood here, I am certain of it. Imagine the Pike is the pin in a pin-wheel; the centre, around which Brendleshire spreads out, in field and town and vale and hill, unseen to the eye, as yet untold."

"Have you ever visited there?"

He shook his head. "Brendle cannot be visited, only written about. In that special place all the ages coexist, sharing their stories back and forth, and all the names, both old and new, intermingle." His eyes widened in delight. "Why, you could walk from one era to another, if only you knew the way."

"Like time travel?"

"Yes, but only in the head, and on the page."

I thought about all this. Then I told him, "This is awesome, Mr Holbrook."

He nodded. "I invented Brendleshire as a name for this shared region, where the history of the country folds in upon itself."

"*Brendleshire*," I repeated, delighting in the sound of it.

He went on, "And dear old Koag, as you see it, the dust... The dust connects everything, all the ages into one age. Imagine Koag as the ink that writes the stories on the pages of the land. We can but reach out, as authors, and capture one now and then."

I stared and stared at the nearest clouds of dust, squinting, concentrating, hoping to catch a glimpse of these special stories.

Sunlight dazzled me. The trees swayed, a sheep was resting in the shade of a wall. Nothing more. The stories were hidden from me.

Mr Holbrook spoke again. Of all the things told to me that summer, none competes with this in my memory:

"I have read the skies, I have read the river. I have read the birdsong, and the fall of leaves. I have read the factories and the shadow of the walking man. I have read the soldiers who died here, in several wars, separated by centuries. I have read the blood, and the ploughing of the fields." After a pause, and in a deeper voice, he added, "But now, alas, I struggle to see. The words are fading."

There was nothing I could say in reply.

He was getting tired and he leaned back on the bench. "I've forgotten my cigarettes, Joe. Will you run and get them for me? Be quick, before Margery comes back. The door's open."

"On my own?"

"I can't make it there and back. Embassy Red, and my lighter. They're in a chest of drawers in my bedroom. You know where that is already, eh, you cheeky sod."

He was right on that one.

"Margery doesn't like me smoking, see, so I have to wait until she's out."

I nodded, and set off back down the hill, running at a steady pace. What I most wanted to do was to lie in the grass and think about all the things he had said. This wasn't at all like how Mrs Pierce taught us, with picture books and diagrams on the blackboard, and everything laid out in the correct order, nice and neat. *Brazil is a country in South America. Its chief export is the coffee bean.* Rather, Mr Holbrook kept flitting from one subject to the next. And worse than that, he seemed to pay no mind to how young I was. I felt like a high-jumper looking up at a bar set a good two feet out of my normal range. At the gate of the house I glanced back to check he hadn't wandered off, or pulled a Preston Heyes vanishing act on me. It was fine, there he was on the nearside bench, staring at the sky. The kestrel was keeping him company.

The door of Pike View opened at my touch. It was cool inside. I walked up the stairs, thinking of my first visit, how I had climbed these same stairs in utter fear and excitement.

The row of masks stared at me, each one in turn as I ascended. It was a portrayal of G.K. Holbrook through the last ten years or so, the cheeks sinking in, the lips thinning, the lines on his brow deepening. The mask I had seen him wearing this last week was now in its allotted place, at the very top of the stairs. I had an urge to take the thing down from its hook and place it on my face, to feel for a moment what he must feel. But a single touch persuaded me otherwise; the waxy surface was clammy, and slightly soft. I could not imagine wearing it for a minute, never mind days on end.

On the landing I pushed at the door of Mr Holbrook's bedroom and stepped inside. A window was open, letting in clean air. The bed was made. There was no sign of Sutter's Fancy. I searched through the socks and underpants in the top drawer of the chest, finding his cigarettes and a silver lighter tucked away. As I walked back onto the landing, curiosity got the better of me. There were two doors I had not yet opened, both at the rear of the house. The first led to the bathroom (the tub had brass feet in the shape of a tiger's claws), but the last door, at the far end of the corridor, led me to the most amazing treasures.

The room was filled with paintings, some of them stacked against the walls, others on easels. Most were landscapes, in a similar style to the one of Brendle Pike in the dining room. They were powerful, wild, full of the furies of nature, whether blasted by a storm, or blinded by sunlight. The smell of turpentine made me feel giddy. A workbench was scattered with dirty rags, brushes, and a palette encrusted with dried splotches of colour. Every painting was signed in the bottom right-hand corner with the name *Margery Adams*. She was a painter! I was so lost in the fierce overpowering images that I barely heard the noise behind me. I turned, fearing to see Margery standing there, expecting her to shout at me for invading her studio. But the room, the doorway, the corridor, all were empty. I was alone. Yet the far end of the landing seemed to shimmer, just before the stairwell. A ray of sunlight came in through a side window, not bright, but with enough of a glow to make my sight hazy. Koag swirled about. I heard footsteps descending the stairs. I had turned a little too late to spot the person, whoever it was. I moved more quickly to the head of the stairs and looked down, seeing a pale shadow dusting the wall. Somebody had just left the hallway, entering the living room. I walked downstairs, but halfway only. Here I waited. I called out, "Margery, is that you?" It came out strangled. Mr Holbrook had already told me she was out, and the Land Rover was missing from the yard. I knew all this. I knew it wasn't Margery Adams.

Then the piano started to play.

I walked downstairs to the hallway and stood at the doorway, looking into the living room. There was a child sitting at the piano, a girl, her fingers moving over the keys. It was so delicate a touch that the melody hardly sounded, but was more *sensed* in the air, a wisp of notes. It was a song, the kind of tune they give to a nursery rhyme, but the melody kept drifting apart. I listened. I could see only the back and shoulders of the girl, her fair hair in ringlets, her dark blue gown with ruffles at the neck and wrists in white. I thought of Grandma's words, how the ghostly child had looked, what she had worn, how she might be seven or eight years old. Yes, all this matched the girl before me. A light mist of Koag surrounded her, orange and lemon in colour, dotted with ruby. The dust moved in and out of her body, making her, unmaking her, over and over again.

Henrietta Tudor.

I knew then that a third person lived in that house.

And that she was not entirely of this world.

I spoke aloud the name: "Henrietta."

She stopped her playing momentarily, whether at the name being called, or more likely at the sound of a voice, a boy's voice, in the room. But she did not turn around. She began to play again, at the same low volume. I took a step closer. Her playing quietened further, and her figure started to fade away. Another step had a similar effect, and I realised that my approach was making her leave this realm, and vanish back into the world of the dust, which drifted about her in three-coloured splendour. A final step on my part was enough to reduce the girl to a mere shadow in the air. The music was a breath on the keys. I stepped back, and she darkened and took on a little solidity, and the melody rose again above the level of silence. I stepped back further still, and further, until the girl appeared almost human, almost in place, and the playing was at its low but delicate volume, as before. I turned and slowly walked from the room.

I was not scared. I simply wanted to leave little Henrietta Tudor to her music.

If my approach made her fade away, then quite simply I had to retreat, in order that she might live on, and finish her song.

11

I did not go back to Mr Holbrook at the tower. Instead I took a route downhill, one that kept me out of his sight as much as possible. Perhaps he saw me, perhaps not. And it was only when I got home that I realised I still had his cigarettes and lighter in my pockets. I had to hide them in my safest, most secret hiding place, for fear of my mum finding them. I could not imagine the commotion she would make. Then I had to decide about Grandma; should I tell her about the girl at the piano? No, for now I would keep it all to myself. I wanted to know as much as I could, before sharing my secret. So, that evening I wrote down everything I could remember of what Mr Holbrook had told me at Brendle Pike. It was a mess, a jumble of words, but at least I had made a start. It took me a good hour or more to capture all I could. At bedtime I lay half-asleep and heard again the soft strains of the piano, and that elusive melody Henrietta Tudor had played. I so wanted to be a part of the lives of Mr Holbrook and Margery. They were easily the most exciting people I had ever met. But their strangeness, and the strangeness of their home, worried me, and teased me, and repelled me, and tempted me.

I woke up late the next morning, an unusual occurrence for me. Mum and Chloe had already left for work. Grandma made me a proper breakfast, eggs, bacon, and baked beans, very nice. Then she said, "Oh, by the way, you've had another letter." She handed it to me. "I must say, the woman who delivered it looked a bit funny."

"You saw her?"

"I did. I went out and she was just riding off, a lady on a bicycle."

Dotty looked suspicious. But I said nothing, and just ran upstairs to my room. The letter was exactly the same as the previous one, the same type of envelope, same lack of a stamp, same neatly handwritten address. (Margery's handwriting, I would learn; Mr Holbrook's was spidery and jittery.) But I was worried now. After I had failed the Astonishing Puzzle test, this had to be a letter telling me I was no longer a pupil of the Pike View School of Science Fiction Writing, that I had severely disappointed the tutor, that I was a disgrace both to myself and the subject matter. But it wasn't that at all. Inside was a typewritten message, just two lines long. I had been given homework.

Task No.1
Build an Anti-Boredom Machine

I walked the high street, I took a seat on the green, I looked in shop windows. In the cemetery of St Matilda's I stood before my little brother Frankie's grave. He died of pneumonia just before his first birthday. I never met him, as I arrived two years later. I left a square of Cadbury's Dairy Milk on the stone for him. Then I walked on, all the time thinking of the task I had been set. I really didn't have a clue, neither about what Mr Holbrook was asking for, nor how to go about it. I went round to Denny's house to listen to records. His brother had a really great collection of long-players, including lots of bands with odd names: Moby Grape, Vanilla Fudge, Iron Butterfly, Canned Heat. Sometimes we experimented with those, but we always came back to our favourites: The Who, The Rolling Stones, Jimi Hendrix. Denny's mum and dad were famous for one thing: they loved each other. It was very strange to see mums and dads showing affection for each other in public, kissing and cuddling, and all that. Alan Portman was a weaver in a cotton mill, his wife Betty a sewing machinist. She worked from home, on a machine in the back room, and every so often she would come through and ask us if we wanted anything to eat or drink, and also to express wonder at the music we were listening to. We danced about the floor, playing invisible guitars and invisible drum kits. Then we settled down to writing a new comic book. We drew our made-up heroes and villains on sheets of paper, giving them a name and a costume, adding lots of arrows and captions pointing out the various gadgets and superpowers they possessed. Then battle would commence. *Blamm! Screech! You're doomed, Captain Mayhem! I, Spellcaster, banish you! Never again will you plague the town of Ormsley!* Lots of exclamation marks, of course. The Portman's front room had a white shag-pile carpet, which, in my memory, reached as high as my knees. Amid the long grass we both lay on the floor, listening to "Light My Fire" by The Doors. We had spent a good two hours working and laughing and telling each other silly jokes.

Then Denny said, "We should ask Eileen over, one time."

"Eileen Barlow?" (Playing it cool.) "Sure, why not?"

"I'll bet she'll have some good comic ideas."

"She doesn't read comics, does she? I'll bet she reads *Jackie*."

"She'll like some of the music. We could play her Simon and Garfunkel."

But the idea of being in the same room as the two of them suddenly seemed a bit awkward. I couldn't help thinking of the stories Mum loved to read in her weekly magazines: *They fought over the same woman. And they both lost everything!* Ridiculous, of course. My thoughts returned to my homework. I could ask Denny to help me, because he would have the imagination to work out what an Anti-Boredom Machine was. But after all, the task had been set for me, and me alone; I had to do this on my own. But I could still seek advice, without actually letting on.

"Denny, do you ever get bored?"

"No, of course not. There's always something to do."

"Right, and somewhere you can go."

"Sure, you can always run off somewhere, and see what's happening."

"And usually, right, something is happening?"

"Always." He gave me one of his looks. "Why, you're not bored now, are you?"

"Me? No way. I never get bored."

"No, me neither." He got up from the floor to choose another record. "What do you fancy?"

"I don't know. How about *Sgt. Pepper's*?"

"Nah, it's boring."

"Ah! You just said you never get bored."

"I'm not bored, it's the album that's boring."

"Oh come on, there's nothing boring about that album." I joined him at the record player. "I mean, there's always something new coming along in every song, and all the songs are different from each other. It's not boring!"

"Yeah, but when you've heard it too many times, even the exciting bits become boring."

"Right, right."

I flopped down in an armchair, draping my legs over the armrest. I set my mind to the task. According to Denny, people get bored when they know things too well, when they've experienced them too many times, so they always know what's going to happen next. So, an Anti-Boredom Machine would have to work against that feeling. It would have to make everything new, all the time. New, new, new! What would such a thing look like, how would it work? I had no idea. And even if I did, how would I build it? I had lots of assorted Meccano pieces, and a Preston Heyes conjuring set. I also possessed a Philips Junior Electronic Engineer Kit. I could use valves and wires and transistors, combined with some Meccano pieces, and maybe throw in a magic prop or two. But what exactly was I building? More than ever, right then, I missed my dad. He would bring out his toolkit, stick a pencil behind his ear, and have something planned, drawn up, and constructed in a couple of hours.

Denny chose a record. "Something we've never heard before. Then we can't be bored, right?" The music started. He handed me the sleeve. It was very interesting to look at, because the group (The Mothers of Invention) had taken the cover design of *Sgt. Pepper's Lonely Hearts Club Band*, and, basically, made it ugly. The seven members of the band were the weirdest of the weird: weird hair, weird outfits, weird expressions. As my mum might say, "They look like they need a good wash." One of the musicians (Frank Zappa, the leader of the group) had a speech bubble coming out of his mouth. It said, "Is this phase one of Lumpy Gravy?" What did that mean? (The gravy at school was never lumpy, just the opposite in fact: too runny. But Mum's sometimes had lumps in it.) And the album? Well it certainly wasn't boring, or lumpy, there was far too much going on for that. It was wild and unpredictable; it kept jumping from one style of music to another, often in the same song. Bits of it were recorded backwards. And there were lots of burping noises. Some of it sounded brilliant, some of it made us laugh, some of it we thought was rude, filled with references to bodily practices that we had no knowledge of. Even the title of the album was a puzzle: *We're Only In It For The Money*. Why would a group admit that? Like they didn't care about the music. I mean, The Beatles would never say such a thing.

SPEAKING BACKWARDS
A Rock Opera in the Style of The Mothers of Invention

DENNY: What's that weird noise they're making?
JOE: It sounds like it's going backwards.
DENNY: It is. They're speaking backwards.
JOE: But why?

A moment of contemplation.

DENNY: It's probably really, really rude.
JOE: You reckon? Really?
DENNY: It must be. They recorded it backwards to hide the rudeness.
JOE: Oh.
DENNY: Yeah.
JOE: I wish we could play it forwards.
DENNY: Yeah. We could…
JOE: What?
DENNY: We could make the record go the other way, maybe?
JOE: The other way?
DENNY: Yeah, so then we could hear it properly.
JOE: Yeah. I'll bet it's so rude!

The two boys examine the record player.

JOE: We'll have to do it by hand.
DENNY: Okay.
JOE: Put the needle on the record at the right bit.
DENNY: Mick will go mad, if we scratch it.
JOE: We'll be careful. That's it… Now, I'll spin the record
    the opposite way to normal.
DENNY: Like a clock going backwards.
JOE: I'll turn it by hand then, shall I?
DENNY: Aye, go on.

*Joe makes the record spin by hand, turning it anti-clockwise. A
    voice is heard, speaking in a low, drawn-out grumble. The
    two boys giggle.*

JOE: Can you hear it?
DENNY: It's too slow. Speed it up.
JOE: I can't! This is as fast as it will go.
DENNY: He sounds funny.
JOE: But what's he saying?
DENNY: Wait. Let's play it again. And this time…

Mrs Portman enters the room.

MRS PORTMAN: What are you boys up to in here?
    What's that horrible noise?
DENNY: Nothing, Mum.
JOE: Nothing, Mrs Portman.

Our little experiment came to an end with us none the wiser
about the rudeness or otherwise of the backwards voice. And
anyway, by the end of side one, we'd had enough. The different
types of music, the weird noises, and the spoken word sections
were very jarring, and that too seemed a quality of anti-boredom,
even if this particular long-player took it too far. So my machine,
when I built it, would have to have a jarring element to it.
Perhaps it was a broken machine, something that kept going
wrong, and that would keep people on their toes. They should
always be asking, *What is going to happen next?* But the whole
thing was just a pile of vague ideas in my head, and I felt like
pulling tufts of white grass from the shag-pile in my frustration.

I said my goodbyes to Denny and his mum and walked back to the high street. I had a plan in mind and that involved visiting the library. Surprisingly, there was only one G.K. Holbrook on the shelves. If he had ever been a popular writer, those days were over for now, otherwise there would be a lot of books to choose from. I didn't have my library card on me, so I took the book over to a table and started to read. The novel was called *Dreams of Brendle*. I learnt from one of the first pages that the book had been published in 1963, so not that long ago. Perhaps the library stocked this one because of the word Brendle in the title; it was seen to have "local interest". But I now had further knowledge of the author's mind, that he thought or believed that Brendle referred to a much more exciting area of land where all of history was happening at the same time, or something like that. Anyway, if the phrase "Anti-Boredom Machine" turned up in the pages, if such a device was featured, then I might well gain a clue and be able to make my own version. That was my plan, such as it was.

First of all, the cover. It featured a stone tower on a hilltop, so exactly like our Pike, I had to assume it was the same structure. Lightning sparked around the top of the tower. The evening sky was a lovely muted blue colour against which the lightning bolt really stood out. A lone figure stood on the hill next to the tower, a woman, with one arm raised up as though to summon even more of the lightning bolts. I spent a good few minutes examining every aspect of the image, gathering what information I could, just like Denny and I did with record sleeves.

Next, the dedication. *To Margery*. That made me happy, for some reason.

Now, the first paragraph of chapter one.

Petra was a night-talker. She spoke with owls and bats. She whispered to the black-petalled flowers that blossomed in darkness. Such was her role in the town, to bring news of the nighttime world back into the daylight hours. The moon was her guardian, her tutor. But Petra was old now, and she felt herself weakening, growing tired. Her steps were slow upon the ground as she walked up to the tower that evening to begin her work. Who would take on her role, once she had passed over into Fade and Fall, the land beyond both light and darkness? At the summit of the hill, she looked out over Brendleshire and wondered upon her fate. The moon was full and vast storms raged upon its surface, visible to eyes that were keen enough to see that far. And Petra had eyes worthy of any nocturnal creature. The sight of the moon's torment worried her, and she took it as a sign, a portent of forthcoming trials.

I reread the paragraph, trying my best to understand every word, every sentence. In truth, the book was too old for me, and parts of it I struggled with, like two wrestlers in the ring, me against the book. But I made sure to read every page carefully. Sometimes I had to get up to consult the library's dictionary for words I did not understand, such as *nocturnal, wherewithal* and *besmirch.* Oh, it was slow going! But thankfully, the biggest and strangest word of them all was explained in the book itself: *dustsceawung,* an Old English word meaning "contemplation of the dust". Well, I was always doing that myself, every day and night, staring and staring. Brendleshire, as portrayed in the novel, was similar to Lancashire, but with some fantastical elements added. The land was both real and unreal at the same time. Further to this, and connected to it, there was a mystery in Petra's life, a puzzle. At six minutes past three every morning she would visit an old well that stood near a gate. She would gaze into the well as though looking for something, but the water had long ago dried up and only a smell of putrefaction (another visit to the dictionary) came up to meet her. Of course, I noticed the time of these visits, the same as the public viewing in our world. Satisfied there was nothing of interest in the well, she went off on the rounds. At the end of her work, she would return to her cottage at the foot of Cropley Hill and write up a report of the night's findings: *The stories told to her by animals and plants and the tower itself, and the river and the underground streams, and the trees of Brendle Woods and the eggs of birds and the motionless wind.* Petra Tey (to use her full name) lived a lonely life. Some people did come to see her, not friends as such, but local villagers in need of a nighttime story or two, which she told for a shilling a go. This is how she made her living. But then, at the end of chapter two, this happens:

The moon was full. By its light she looked into the dried-up well and saw, within the darkness, a pair of eyes staring back at her. They were human in appearance, these eyes, yet oversized, and with a reddish glow to them. Petra Tey felt her heart stirring at the sight. She climbed down, using a rope ladder. She was old, but her hands and feet were secure on the rungs, and soon she reached the packed earth that filled the circle of the well. Weeds and lichen covered the walls. Insects crawled about. The only sound was that of her own breathing. She took an oil lantern from her bag and lit it, allowing the flame to catch.

I had to stop reading, to gather my wits. What in God's name was she going to see? Was there a monster down there with her, or a demon of some kind?

The eyes were wide open. Each was as big as a hand, corner to corner. They glistened. Their redness was that of the fiery plains of Mars, which Petra could see from the Earth's surface, such was her sight. The rest of the face and head were buried, but there was an indentation in the soil where the mouth must lie. Long strands of silvery hair lay tangled about, like the vines of a plant. The old king slept on for untold years, awaking every month or so, but then only for a few minutes. This event always took place at the same time of day. This was Petra's only clue, which gave her a fixed point in her nightly wanderings: the well at Widow's Gate, six minutes past three in the morning. She knelt down and laid out the tools of her trade. By the lantern's light she went to work. The eyes of the king looked at her. Was that fear she saw there? Petra had performed this task on many, many occasions, and each time the king showed her a different emotion. If only he could speak! Once, a few years before, she had removed some of the dirt from the mouth, only to reveal an empty toothless maw that seemed to sink down to the centre of the world. The breath that came from it was so rank it made her feel sick, and she had quickly pushed back the soil. Working quickly now, with a small silver spoon especially made for the task, she scooped out the granules of sand from each of the king's eyes, first the left, then the right. Most of the gathered stories she sold on or gave away as gifts, but this, the golden dust secreted from the dreams of the old king, was hers alone. It was a great treasure, and she used it for a special purpose.

Well, what a way to end a chapter! Yet, up to now, I had counted only one exclamation point. One! *If only he could speak!* I mean, what kind of writing was that? Yet it excited me. I started on chapter three, keen to know what Petra could possibly want with the sleep dust from a long-buried king's eyes. But right then, Miss Stockton, the assistant librarian, walked by reminding everyone that the library was closing in fifteen minutes. So I placed the book back onto the shelf, promising myself I would read the rest another day. Before leaving, however, I took a chance to ask about old maps of Ormsley Vale. Miss Stockton was happy to see my interest and she directed me to a large book, an atlas. "Be quick, though. I have a home to go to, you know." I flipped through the pages, finding the earliest map of the area. There was an extra letter *e* in the name of the town: *Ormesley*. I searched for Ormsley Woods, much larger in area than now, and yes, there it was, clearly named: *Brendle Woods*. Mr Holbrook had spoken the truth. I tried to find where our house would be. But the estate was just a patch of land back in 1742, the date of the map, with a few buildings dotted here and there, and a cross to show St Matilda's. There was a blue line marking the course of a brook through the fields, but instead of it being called *Stoneybrook*, it was called *Brendlebrook*. Oh, I liked the sound of that.

My head was spinning as I walked along towards the green. The little town of Ormsley Vale seemed different to me now, affected by the passages I had read. In a comic everything was drawn out for you; but now my imagination was set to work, conjuring in my mind's eye the fields and villages of the novel, as well as the face and voice of Petra Tey. I wished most of all that I could uncover the hidden stories of the town I lived in, in the same way she did with the flowers and animals of her county. "Brendlebrook, Brendlebrook, Brendlebrook!" It was astonishing. But sadly there had been no mentions of any Anti-Boredom Machines in the book, at least in the chapters I had read. So I was no nearer to completing my special task.

Customers were sitting outside the Weaver's Arms, happy to drink away the day's aches from factory and shop-floor. Mr Yardley was there, the town's oldest resident, feeding crumbs to his best friends, the pigeons. Only Tom Halfpenny was missing from the scene. I sat on a bench facing the war memorial, admiring the sculpture of the soldier on top, forever charging forwards, bayonet fixed to his rifle. Then I read the listed names for a while. There was a Sutter among them: *Osbert Sutter*. He was my granddad's brother, my great uncle. Also engraved were the names *Albert Sykes*, and *Clifford Sykes*, from my mum's side of the family. All three of them had died at Flanders Field. It was good to see the two surnames there. But what did I have to offer the town? Only the dust that flowed around me, painting the memorial with soft speckles of violet. It cascaded through the air in happy spirals, it chased the pigeons, it lighted up the trees with golden flickers. Koag had always been with me. I saw it collected on the pages of books, in the grooves of every record. According to Mrs Pierce it sought out lost pathways, the ways of the land, the secret tracks. Koag spoke in silence, or a whisper. But it did speak, I was sure of it. As the Grand Beholder liked to remind us whenever she came on the radio: *Greot talks in words of dust. Let us open our hearts.* I was aware of it from my earliest days, as a faintly coloured powder, or a sudden darting movement of darker air across the room. At the age of four I surprised everyone by running onto a school football pitch, chasing, as I called it, "the little red cloud, the little red cloud!". It was a shape made of scarlet dust which darted among the legs of the older boys who were playing the game. I nearly came a cropper that day, kicked by a pair of boots. Now, people knew me for what I was. "Eeh, have you heard, there's a new witness in town, a little scrap of a thing." Everything changed from that moment on.

I got up from the bench and walked home. We had a family supper, all four of us, dining on fish, chips and mushy peas from the local chippy. There was nothing good on the tele, so I went up to my room, searching under the bed to find my old toys. I looked again at the message I had received that morning. *Task No.1. Build an Anti-Boredom Machine.* The first part implied that if I got this one right, there would be further tasks set for me, *Task No.2, No.3,* and so on. It was important that I worked this out. So I messed about with the Meccano pieces and the valves and transistors from the Junior Engineer's kit for a while, trying to combine them together in interesting ways, sometimes adding a marked playing card or a special vanishing coin trick from my magic set. Who was I kidding? It was useless. In fact, it was *boring!* I did try to sketch some designs, only to end up writing the name *Eileen Barlow* ten times in a row, as though it were some kind of magical spell.

I gave up and decided instead to listen to some records. I had nothing to rival the collection of Denny's brother. In fact I only had one long-player, a *Top of the Pops* compilation given to me by Grandma because I had finished junior school without getting expelled. It was a collection of twelve recent hit records, including "Young Girl", "Can't Take My Eyes Off You", and "Jennifer Eccles". I played the album quite a lot, mainly so Grandma knew I was listening to it. But all my other records were singles, 45s, as we called them. Some I had bought with pocket money, others were presents, and a few I had inherited from Chloe as her tastes changed. They were a mixed bunch: pop songs, soul ballads, novelty numbers, and a few prized rock singles by groups like the Kinks and The Hollies and The Stones. Many of my records had scratches on them, and greasy fingerprints. But I loved them all, no matter their condition or their quality, as they were mine. I had twenty-seven singles altogether. I looked through them now, wondering which to play first. I usually blasted out "You Really Got Me", because that was great to jump around to, while playing power chords on my invisible guitar. But this time, probably because of the strange mood I was in, I played the B-side, "It's All Right". It was pretty good, a bluesy rocker. I had two pennies sticky-taped to the arm of the record player to make sure the records didn't skip. I got to thinking. I decided to play all the B-sides of every record I owned. I arranged them in any old order, stacking them eight high on the record-changing spindle, so that each one dropped down automatically once the previous one had finished. I lay on my bed. Melodies, beats, scratches and crackles. I think Koag liked the music, as the dust crept in at my open window and started to make psychedelic patterns on the ceiling. It was easy to imagine it was portraying the music in some way. Unless it was all a pattern created in my head, not in the world, in my head, not in the world, real, not real, real, not real…

I floated off into one of my daydreams. I was Anti-Boring Man. My special Anti-Boring suit protected me from harm. My raygun shot out Anti-Boring rays, which made all things interesting and bizarre. Everything was turned upside-down, inside-out, and back to front. Nothing was recognisable, not unless you thought about it from a sideways direction. The needle got stuck in one place on the final record of the stack, and that woke me up from my little fantasy, those same few notes repeating like a drum struck by a malfunctioning robot.

I'm not sure when the idea came to me; at that moment, or some time later in my deeper sleep. But waking up the next morning, I set to work immediately, putting together all the components I needed: a safety pin, a tub of glue, and even Mr Holbrook's silver lighter. After I had finished I went downstairs and joined in with breakfast. In a little while, when Grandma and I were alone in the house, I asked, "Grandma, have you ever heard of a man called G.K. Holbrook?"

"Who?" She was doing the washing up, I was drying.

"George Holbrook."

"Can't say I have, why?"

"He's a beholder."

Now I had her attention. "He's not from around here, is he? Only, I don't need any rival for my young men and women."

"Don't worry, he's not like you."

"He doesn't blow the dust in their eyes?"

"No, he doesn't do anything like that. At least, I think not."

She looked at me suspiciously. "It sounds like you know the man."

"I've heard of him, that's all." A little white lie. "Someone told me that he lives around here, somewhere."

"Well, if you ever see him, just tell him to stay off my patch."

"If I ever see him… I will."

"This isn't to do with the mysterious letters you've been receiving?"

"Sorry, Grandma, things to do."

I stole a handful of sugar from the bowl and then went up to my room to make the final adjustments to my Anti-Boredom Machine. The sugar was a cool idea, although I didn't bother testing it first. In the spirit of the task, I would surprise myself. Last of all, I drew a moustache, pointy beard and round glasses on a young woman's face. I also added a speech balloon. All was done. I needed something to carry the machine in, and I thought my new school briefcase would be best for the task. To match the case, I wore my Daniel Defoe tie. A first outing. Now I was smart, now I was ready. I crept downstairs, hoping to avoid Grandma, and her persistent questions. But the coast was clear, she had retreated into the parlour. I could hear her talking to Coco.

I snuck out of the front door and set off for Pike View.

12

It was the hottest day yet of the summer. At ten o'clock by my watch, I lifted the metal ram's head to knock on the door. A single yap from Nipper answered the sound. Then Margery welcomed me in with a smile, saying, "We're just working at the moment. Come and join us." I had a quick look through the open door of the living room, checking for any sight of the girl in the blue dress, but the room was empty. I followed Margery into the office, to the left of the hallway. Mr Holbrook was sitting in a well-worn armchair. He was wearing round wire-framed spectacles; I had not seen them before. His eyes were closed, his hands steepled against his chin, and the lines on his brow furrowed into a V-shape. He made no acknowledgement of my arrival. Nipper was curled in a basket near the window. A movement drew my eyes upwards. At last, I had found my Fancy. It was clumped around the light fitting. But my appearance in the room acted as a signal, and the dust quickly spread out until it covered the entire ceiling in a thin layer, all rosy and pink and silvery in its beauty.

Margery whistled. "Look at you, all dolled up with your neck-tie and your briefcase. Don't you look the gentleman? George, have you seen the boy? He's dressed up for us."

Mr Holbrook did not stir.

She went on, "I don't know what you did to his Lordship the other day."

"Me?" I was confused.

"Yes, you two jolly boys on a jaunt to the tower. He's been writing like nobody's business ever since." This pleased me, I must admit. "On top of which, I've been informed that from now on, I must refer to Old Greot as new, young, exciting Koag."

Which pleased me even more.

Mr Holbrook grunted and sat bolt upright in his chair. Seeing this, Margery took her place at the desk, where a typewriter awaited her attention. Mr Holbrook began to narrate a story while she typed away, capturing his words on paper.

"The trail of dust had brought him here, to this smoke-filled alleyway. A neon sign announced the stage doorway of the Alhambra club. Underhill narrowed his eyes. Three men were standing beneath the sign. Their faces were the faces of… the faces of…"

He got to his feet as he searched for the right words.

"Their faces were the faces of ghosts. He had met such men before, people haunted by their own evil doings, who would rather look into a pool of blood than a mirror."

"Oh, I love it," cried Margery, her fingers working at speed. "Pool of blood! I love it."

Encouraged by this, Mr Holbrook went on with his storytelling. From my careful listening, I learnt that this was the story of a private eye, Tod Underhill, a beholder so attuned to the floating dust trails that he could trace the lost people of the city, the helpless cases, the victims of neglect and betrayal. He had taken on a new job, tracking down a young woman who had disappeared from her flat in Camden Town, London.

Margery wound a new sheet of paper into the typewriter, saying, "I've never seen him this inspired, not for years."

The writing continued. The chapter ended as the private eye descended into the cellar of the Alhambra nightclub, only to find a series of cages, each containing a strange beast, creatures half-animal and half-dust in nature. *"Underhill felt the hairs on the back of his neck rise as he looked into those fathomless eyes. The beast's claws rattled at the bars of the cage. The red mouth opened to spit out a cloud of black dust, dark enough to blot out the cellar's only light. In the darkness a voice whispered of the lost lands."* It was stirring stuff. The words flowed on and on as he paced the floor. Margery's hands flashed over the typewriter, the keys clicking and clacking and the carriage return going back and forth, a little bell sounding at the end of each line. But a bout of coughing halted the story's progress.

"That's enough for now, I think, George."

He nodded, leaning against the desk for support. But he was smiling, obviously pleased with the morning's progress.

"What happens next, Mr Holbrook?" I asked. "I really want to know."

"It's all up in the air," he answered. "Just swirling around. But these weird animals, they have come through to our world, from Brendleshire."

"Yes! I knew it."

"But Underhill has never heard of Brendle. It's an unknown land. I want to end it when he travels north, still on the trail of the missing woman, right? I see him, in the final chapter, climbing up to the Pike tower and viewing this other land through a shimmering curtain. The moon shines down... No, wait, yes, *two* moons, one in each sky. He can see them both. The young woman leads him on, and he follows her, into... into..."

His words faltered and he looked puzzled, lost among the possibilities. But then he turned to face us, saying, "Margery, I want to change the title."

"Very well. To what?"

His eyes lit up. "*Moon Over Brendle.*"

"Good. I'll do it later on."

"You like it?"

"Yes, it's good, I said that."

He turned to me. "What about you, Joe, eh? How do you like it?"

Here I was, a young lad, witnessing this moment: the creation of a title. But I could hardly put my excitement into words. "It's amazing, Mr Holbrook." That was all I managed.

He tried to smile, but with an effort. I could tell he was doing his best to hold back yet another cough. This time Margery looked away; there was tiredness in her eyes.

I said, "It reminds me a bit of *Dreams of Brendle*. The title I mean. Is it a follow-up?"

The question roused him. "Not a follow-up, as such. But it's connected, the same universe." Then he looked at me with a suddenly suspicious eye. "But how do you know about *Dreams of Brendle*?"

"I started to read it yesterday, at the library."

"Keen, eh? I shall give the boy a copy. A gift. Come on."

We went into the living room. He pulled a copy of his novel off the shelf.

"Thank you, Mr Holbrook."

Margery encouraged him further. "Sign it for him, George, go on." He did so, with a flourish. "That makes it even more special, Joe," she said.

I had a grin bigger than that of Batman's arch-nemesis, the Joker.

Mr Holbrook sat in the armchair nearest the fireplace. Margery perched herself on the piano stool. They were both staring at me, and smiling, and nodding their heads.

Now it was my turn. "I have done what you asked," I told them. "I've built an Anti-Boredom Machine."

"Excellent, Joe. Very good."

Margery agreed. "I can't wait. I get bored so easily."

I was suddenly nervous, more than I'd ever been. They were going to laugh at me, or banish me from Pike View forever. My hands were trembling, my tie was too tight. I had trouble breathing. I walked over to the radiogram and lifted up the lid, revealing the record player. I clicked the *on* switch. The valves warmed up. I checked that the turntable speed was set to 33 rpm.

"Are you going to play us some music?" Mr Holbrook asked.

I didn't reply. I couldn't trust my voice not to stutter, or crack. I took the *Top of the Pops* long-player out of my briefcase and placed it on the platter, side one uppermost. I pressed *play*. The arm moved across and the needle dropped into the lead-in groove. The first track was "Young Girl" by Gary Puckett & The Union Gap. I turned to face my audience. Mr Holbrook looked perplexed, but Margery was tapping her foot and smiling.

"I like this one," she said.

I turned back to the radiogram. I let a few bars of the song play through. Then I switched the speed of the turntable to 45 rpm. Now the voice of the singer was a high-pitched whine, it made the song feel sinister; he really was telling the girl to get out of his life, in no uncertain terms, but his own voice sounded girlish. I heard Margery murmur something, I don't know what. Sweat dripped down from my brow.

I switched back to the correct speed, 33 rpm. Then I suddenly pushed the needle onto the next track, not worrying at all about it ruining the vinyl. It made a horrible noise, and Mr Holbrook cried out, "What's he doing? Is he damaging my radiogram?" The needle landed in the opening groove of "My Name Is Jack", as performed by Manfred Mann. But the song was ruined. I had deliberately scratched the track with the tip of a safety pin, many times. The music juddered from one beat to the next, one word to the next. But I didn't let it play all the way through, no, I had to keep my listeners on their toes; I pushed the needle on its journey, finding track number three, the lovely "Can't Take My Eyes Off You". Not so lovely now. My hand was on the volume knob, twisting and turning it left and right, raising and lowering the volume at sudden unexpected intervals. Soft, loud, soft, loud! Poor Andy Williams, he must have been cringing and cursing, wherever he was on the planet at that moment.

My audience was very quiet by now, behind my back. But I could hear Margery's fingernails on the piano lid, tapping, probably in irritation. I set the volume back to normal and pushed the needle on once more. Each track had been ruined in a different way, and I wanted to give each one a short time in which to be heard, a minute or so only: no boredom! Track four was "Blue Eyes", a forgotten record these days, but a hit back in 1968, sung by Don Partridge. I enjoyed this track because it featured a kazoo, and Don performed it on the television as a one-man band, with a giant bass drum strapped to his back. I had dribbled drops of glue on this track, letting them dry into little clumps to form obstructions. The needle found itself locked in place, so that one portion of the music kept repeating itself over and over, a little riff that might go on forever if I hadn't knocked the arm again, letting the needle find another drop of glue to come up against, another riff locked into place. I did this one more time, and then something quite remarkable happened.

I heard the piano playing.

It was Margery. She was improvising a tune over the repeating patterns of notes coming out of the radiogram's speakers, adding a layer of beauty to the chaos of my Anti-Boredom Machine. But I couldn't let it settle. I lifted the needle over its last obstacle and placed it on track number five, another unknown song of the period, The Paper Dolls singing "Something Here In My Heart (Keeps A-Tellin' Me No)". Here I had used Mr Holbrook's cigarette lighter, holding the flame at such a distance to only bend and warp the vinyl a little, rather than melt it completely. The effect was bizarre: the three girls of the group lost their voices to a kind of wibbly-wobbly effect. The words of the song stretched out this way and that. I increased the effect by pressing gently on the record to slow it down. I also made the record stop with my hand, and then go backwards, just like Denny and I had done yesterday at his house.

Finally, "Jennifer Eccles", a love song by The Hollies, complete with wolf whistles and lots of *la la las;* the addition of sugar crystals had sharpened the melody, making it spikier, crunchier, sweet to the point of sickliness. I had dipped the crystals in glue and sprinkled them on the track, like hundreds and thousands on an ice-cream cone. The needle bit into the crystals, jumping over some, cracking others, skipping about in a carefree manner that suited the song's mood perfectly. Margery's piano-playing followed this new direction, taking on strange chords and mismatched bunches of crotchets and quavers.

The record ended.

The piano played a final few notes.

Silence.

I felt weak, and very tired, as though I had run all the way from Ormsley to Ashton and back. I lifted the record off the spindle. It was a sight to see, each track looking very different from its neighbour, some of them nice and clean where I had employed outside effects like the volume and speed controls, and the rest damaged and decorated with marks, scratches, glue and so on. I held the record in one hand, with this side facing out, while in the other hand I held up the sleeve, showing the front cover. I turned around and walked towards my audience, hiding myself behind the two objects. When I lowered them after a few steps, I was amazed, utterly amazed, to see that Koag had accumulated itself in the living room, in all its colours, all shapes and variants, taking up most of the space. The dust clouds were mostly focussed around Mr Holbrook, but Margery too had her accompanying halo. Had my Anti-Boredom Machine caused this gathering?

I looked at my two listeners. Mr Holbrook clapped his hands together, not in applause, but to scatter Koag from the room. He reached for the record sleeve, examined it, and then asked me, "Did you deface this pretty young lady?" I nodded. Margery came over to have a look for herself. All the *Top of the Pops* sleeves featured young models dressed in the fashionable clothes of the day. This one sported a sailor's cap perched on her long blonde hair. I had drawn a moustache, a beard and a pair of spectacles on her face, in black ink. A speech balloon rising from her lips said, "YUK! This gravy's got lumps in it!" Margery laughed at this. Mr Holbrook ran his fingers over the different surfaces of the reworked tracks. He was smiling. I took that as a good sign, but I was too nervous to actually ask if he liked my performance or not.

But instead of any praise or criticism, he said, "Everything fades into blandness. Everything, lad. Everything! Unless you consciously fight it." He waited a moment. "This is my first rule of creation. Do you know what it means?"

"No."

"Do you know what *blandness* means?"

"Is it a bit like softness?"

He sighed. "Do you know what *consciously* means?"

Now it was getting embarrassing. "I don't have a lot of words." Seeing his quizzical look, I went on to explain, "Our dictionary at home isn't very big, Mr Holbrook."

He nodded. "Well, you followed the first rule precisely, Joe."

Was that it, was that a compliment? Well, I took it as such. Yes. That was it! It was enough, more than enough.

"Margery, how about a bit more music, eh?"

"All right. What would you like?"

He thought for a moment. "Bartók, I think would be suitable. In keeping." He smiled at me, as though at a shared joke. "*Allegro Barbaro*." And he added for my benefit, "*Allegro* means fast, and *barbaro* means 'like a barbarian'."

"What, you mean like Conan?"

"Yes, exactly! Ha ha. The boy knows his stuff."

Margery lifted up the seat of the piano stool and searched within. She was now facing away from us, so I took the opportunity to return the cigarettes and lighter to Mr Holbrook. He pocketed them swiftly, nodding his thanks. Margery had found the music she needed. She arranged this on the music stand and then sat down, ready to play. Seeing her there reminded me of the child of dust I had seen sitting in the same place.

I asked, "Is this house haunted, Mr Holbrook?"

"Here? No, I don't think so. Have you seen any ghosts, Margery?"

"Only when I've had too much to drink."

"She does like to drink."

Were they lying? Had they really never seen Henrietta Tudor walking the rooms?

Mr Holbrook stamped his foot. "Come, Margery. Play!"

She was sitting in complete stillness. The silence stretched out as her hands hovered over the keys. Then they slammed down, finding angry rhythmical clusters of notes, dancing like a pair of madly crazed spiders over the keys. Up and down the keyboard they ran, this scuttling pair, chasing each other, sometimes pounding away at the bass notes like a war drum, and then jumping up to the high notes to make a series of sounds like glass breaking into shards.

Slammm! Thuunk!
Ping, pang ping pang!
Pound POUND!
Jitter, skitter.
Berang!

I looked to Mr Holbrook. His eyes were closed in bliss. In his head he was perhaps listening to some lovely tune, a ballad, the wild feverish notes transformed. But to me, it was a nightmare made real, turned into noise. It lasted for two and a half minutes, this song, that's all, yet it blistered me, hypnotised me, set my teeth on edge and made the floor shake. I was flung about. A giant had me by the scruff of the neck. Margery was bent over the keys, angled at the wrists and elbows, lost, totally lost in the moments, each note, each chord. Where two days ago sweet Henrietta Tudor had sat, with her dainty fingers and her butterfly melodies, now Margery Adams, Barbarian, was in charge. Her hands were sledgehammers, her fingers were needles. And even in the quieter middle section, at the centre of the whirlwind and the sandstorm and the battlefield, still she burned to make each note count. I wanted to shout, to sing along even if this music had no tune to sing, but just to cry out, to chant and howl at the moon, at the broken moon of broken stories, to worship Koag, mighty Koag, to be taken up in the dust clouds, part and parcel, in particles, and float high above Brendleshire, seeing the unseen county from above, there I was, a kestrel over the patchwork of fields, mapping the hidden course of rivers, the nests and dens where the animals dart and dance, where the people of the unseen villages might look up to the skies, in wonder at the schoolboy in flight...

And then the music stopped.

The last notes rang out. Margery's fingers were raised above the keys.

Two and a half minutes. Everything was revealed.

Even in my slow falling back to earth, I was exhilarated.

Mr Holbrook nodded his approval. "Very good, Margery. I enjoyed that."

Then he stood up with an effort and left the room. I packed up my *Top of the Pops* record, and the copy of *Dreams of Brendle*, putting both of them into my briefcase.

Margery said to me, "He liked what you did, Joe."

"Really? I wasn't sure."

"I know his little ways, I understand him."

We heard him coughing, all the way from his office across the corridor. *Hack, hack, hack!* She frowned. Her voice lowered as she asked, "Why did you ask about the house being haunted?"

I had the feeling she didn't want him to hear this. It made me uncomfortable.

"Have you seen something, or someone? Joe, have you?" Little strands of scarlet Koag crept around her eyes, making them shine.

"I might have done. I came in alone, while he was up at the tower."

"Yes, and?"

I wanted to tell her all about Henrietta Tudor, really I did. I started to. But then Mr Holbrook came back into the room, carrying two pieces of paper. "These are for you," he said. "They may be of help." I took them, stuffing them into my case, not even looking at them. He had taken off his glasses. His face was drawn to the bone, and pale. Flecks of spittle and blood decorated his chin. He was holding back pain, physical pain, just so he could talk to me. I had a sudden desire to leave this house of secrets. I needed fresh air. But he grabbed me roughly by the arm and said, "When I was younger I used to think I was visiting a zoo, peering into the cages, making fun of the animals." His eyes burned into mine. "But now I'm trapped inside the cage, looking out, yearning for life."

The day was done.

PART THREE

BRENDLESHIRE

13

The fact that I'd become so much closer to the occupants of Pike View meant, in some odd way, that I could no longer just turn up on the doorstep and expect to be welcomed. Nor could I just go snooping about, like I did at first. No, I felt that I had to wait for an invitation, or better still, for my second task. I was hoping for a letter to be delivered. But none arrived, and the days passed. I met with Denny a few times, often with Eileen in tow; it was only a little bit awkward. Apparently, she was now a fully-fledged member of the Slew Hill gang. In the meantime more people came to see Grandma, sometimes three or four a day, but there was no repeat of the May Harper incident with the horrible voice and the message from the dust.

I wrote down everything I could remember of the "Anti-Boredom" day into my diary. The two pieces of paper Mr Holbrook had handed to me at the end of my visit were taken from a dictionary. He had torn them out, which struck me as a crazy thing to do. I could tell just from seeing how many words there were on each page, and how tiny the lettering was, that this dictionary was far, far larger than the one we kept on the bookshelf in the living room. Of course, they had been chosen for a purpose. One of the pages contained the word "blandness" (*noun; the condition of having little or no interest or excitement, nondescript*), and the second page the word "consciously" (*adverb; in a deliberate or careful or active manner*). These were the two words he had asked me about, when he had told me his first rule of creation. "Everything fades into blandness, unless you consciously fight it." Using the definitions I managed to work out the meaning of this. In fact,

I made up my own version of the rule, something a little easier to understand: *Everything becomes really, really boring, unless you work, work, work.* But that didn't sound nearly exciting enough, so I beefed it up with some capitals, an underline, and an exclamation mark:

> *Everything becomes really, <u>really</u> boring, unless you work, work, WORK!*

But still no word or message from Pike View. What were they doing up there, the two of them? Over the days of waiting, I finished reading the novel Mr Holbrook had given to me. One of the things I realised is that he would never explain everything all at once, but would wait a while, often a few chapters, before giving up further information. For instance, only in chapter three did the reader learn how Petra was gathering her stories: *She watched the petals of the flower open and the various names of the honey bee emerge, sticky with pollen. These she collected from the air, one by one. In this way, world becomes word becomes world becomes word, and so it goes on down the ages.* As you can imagine, this took some deciphering, but in the end this is what I came up with: Petra Tey had a superpower, a way of looking at a thing that revealed not just the object, the tree, animal or gatepost she was examining, but also every word associated with that object, over time. This was a bit like Superman's X-ray vision, but revealing hidden words and names rather than people's skeletons or a concealed gun. In this way, Mr Holbrook's idea of Brendleshire was brought to life. But only in the final pages of the book does the reader find out why Petra has stolen dust from the eyes of the dead king. After many a setback and misadventure, she sets off across the vales, reaching after a full day's walk a meadow called Lynden Lea, where once, centuries before, opposing forces had clashed and shed their blood in pursuit of the rightful crown. The king buried in the well had met his end during this conflict. But now, the old battlefield held very different spectres.

All across the land as far as the eye could see lay a vast curtain of dust, its grains lightly spread and swathed into bands of red, blue and green with yellow stripes in between, and dots of other colours here and there. The curtain of dust sparkled in the night air. Petra was soon embraced by it. She heard the song of the dust, which was made in equal parts of silence and the shimmer of a thousand tiny bells. Her ears tingled. Here was the veil of words, where the story of the land was told. She stood amid the cloud and smeared her face with the sleep dust until it masked her. Even her eyelids were covered, and her lips were painted a dark orange. Over the last years of her life she had collected this rare substance from the dreams of the old king. Under its spell, Petra was aware of the many stories told through time, each a part of this land, each merging with the next until they blurred into life. Through the powder of her eyes she saw the troops, the farmers, the maidens and the roustabouts and rogues, the lords and ladies, the May queens, the holy fools. All were portrayed, all equal under history, and all fashioned of dust. Among them danced a girl of seven years, a ragamuffin of the village, whose body was more delicate even than those around her, a ghostly child. Petra felt her own age dearly, but she looked on with love in her heart. Here was her daughter, long lost in time, but nonetheless a story still being told. The old dreams of Brendle were told again and again as the old woman stepped forwards, calling out the girl's name.

And so the novel ended, not with a fist fight or an explosion or a deadly shoot-out, but with a few steps forwards. The lost daughter was not named, but surely this must be Henrietta Tudor. Mr Holbrook was imagining a life for the girl within the dust fields, a ghost seeking companionship. I could not help but think of Grandma's words during the viewing session: "Little girl, poor little girl! Come to me." It was the same desire.

I turned to the title page and studied the author's signature, and the message he had written for me: *To Joe, my number one pupil. G.K. Holbrook.* This made me happy, of course it did. Even if, as I suspected, as I wished for, I was his *only* pupil. I wanted to see him again, to learn more, to learn everything that could be learnt. Why wouldn't they contact me?

A couple of days later I saw Margery's bicycle tied to a lamp post on the high street. I looked in one shop window after another, and found her as she was leaving the butcher's. I tried to talk to her, but it did little good.

"Just stay away, Joe," she said, "That's for the best."

"But why?"

"Never mind why, just listen to what's good for you."

But I couldn't leave it there. "Margery, what's wrong? Is it Mr Holbrook?"

She went quiet, and then she made three very quick little nods. "He's not very well, and the writing has stopped, and now... I just have to do what I can for him."

"But I can help."

"No, you can't." And she hurried away.

Could I carry on my writing work without Mr Holbrook's help? Perhaps if I did, it might impress him, it might even jolt him a little, bring him some life, some health. But what could I do? I needed a second task. I had to imagine I was him, and try to work out what he would ask me to do next. I thought back over our meetings, looking for clues. I went home and reread the notes I had made of our conversations. But I had no brilliant ideas to offer myself. So in the end I wrote out a very simple task, as a starting point.

Task No.2
Write a Short Story

Now then, where to begin? Mr Holbrook had told me of the four levels of invention, and that my made-up name, *Sutter's Fancy*, occupied the lowest level. I thought it rude at the time, but why not take him at his word: assume that he means well, that he's telling me the truth? My task, then, was easy. All I had to do was climb further up the levels of invention. I consulted my notes, but I had taken little notice of that part, probably due to my being upset at the time. *Genius* was the highest level, I remembered that. But what were the other three? Did he mention *unique*? Maybe, maybe. But it didn't matter what they were called, only that I had to think of a top-level idea, a genius idea, because that's what you were meant to do, right, get to the highest level? My mind drifted to the talks I'd had with Grandma ever since she'd moved in with us. Dotty Sykes was a mystery, it had to be admitted. She was a woman of many stories, but she kept most of them secret. Except for what happened that evening at the Ashen Society. Why had she told me that one story, and why now? There had to be a reason. So, then: I could possibly write about Henrietta Tudor. But not like Mr Holbrook had done, in *Dreams of Brendle*, no, but more from Grandma's version of events.

Well, that was interesting. But what was the girl's story? What would Henrietta actually do? I had no idea. I didn't have anything to write about, not of my own, that was the trouble. Everything was shared with Denny; games, jokes, magic tricks, comics, music.

Wait, wait... Everything was *shared* with Denny. That was it! *Shared* ideas. That was level one. Shared ideas, and then, and then, yes, *unique* ideas. Then something else, and then *genius* ideas. I looked up the word *unique* in the *Family Dictionary*. *One of a kind, having no like or equal.* Right, so that was the opposite of shared. *Shared ideas: belonging to everybody. Unique ideas: belonging to one person alone.* It was starting to make sense. I walked to Brendle Woods, as I now called it. This was a special place, because of what Mr Holbrook had told me. I felt within the trees a sort of ghostly presence. I don't know if it was a real presence, or just a feeling inside, something conjured up from the words of a wise, but probably quite mad, gentleman. But slowly, day by day, the idea of Brendleshire was taking me over, that land where different time zones intersected. It appeared in my dreams as a shimmering moonlit realm. In my waking hours it was just as magical; often I heard the clash of swords or the neigh of a warhorse, or the sparkle of spurs, only to have the trees alone for my company. I followed the old railway line until it vanished into a tangle of roots and giant weeds, and with every step I thought about my story. Various opening lines were spoken aloud: *Henrietta Tudor kept getting lost, no matter where she went.* Or: *One day Henrietta looked into the mirror, but the mirror was empty.* Or: *Henrietta really, really loved to play the piano, but the music kept disappearing from her fingertips.* Birds and beetles were my audience. I walked up to Brendle Pike and watched the kestrel hover and dart, and Mighty Koag floating free over the land all the way to Manchester and beyond, into the haze of the world. I looked down the slope towards Pike View, and felt my heart stinging with pain. So I wrote, and I wrote, and I threw away page after page, filled with one or two lines only, oh, such rubbish! The blank page expanded in my mind, filling my eyes with its emptiness. Nowhere Man was Everywhere Man.

From under the bed I pulled out the shoebox where I kept my most prized treasures, the eight things my father gave to

me on the day of his leaving. I examined each item carefully.
First up was the pair of binoculars (already mentioned). Next a
Parker fountain pen, the nib split. Thirdly, an instruction leaflet
explaining how to tie five different neck-tie knots (including
bow-tie). This had proven very useful with my Daniel Defoe
tie. Next, *The Book of Common Prayer*, a small leather-bound
edition. The fifth item no longer existed. It was a pound note,
long since spent on comic books and model aeroplane kits.
Item number six: a photograph of Jim and Lilian Sutter on
their wedding day. (Very handsome couple.) Coming next was
an autograph of Bobby Charlton. I wasn't sure about the truth
of this one, as it looked like the name was just printed on the
card, not handwritten. Still, Bobby had played in the England
football team in the World Cup final, so nothing else mattered.
And finally, in eighth place, a spirit level from my dad's toolkit.
He gave me a bubble, a bubble that lasts forever! Now all seven
items were laid out in a pattern on my bed, with a gap to
represent the invisible one pound note. Koag was very curious
about all this, I must say; the dust had come down from its
ceiling perch to hover over the gifts, each in turn.

My father's name was James Sutter. Mum always called
him Jim. He called her by her full name, Lilian, never Lily.
Lilian and Jim. He started work at Bradshaw's Mill at the age
of fourteen, straight out of school. He was taken on as an
apprentice maintenance engineer, learning how to mend the
giant machines that made nuts and bolts of every size and shape.
Lilian Sykes started her working life at the same factory, in the
wages office. They got to talking through the grilled window
where the wage packets were handed over every Friday, at the
end of the shift. My dad only had a few minutes' time to chat
with Lilian before the men behind him in the queue started
to moan and groan. But that was enough, over one Friday
after another, for them to get to know each other. They were
married when he was twenty-one, she twenty, their first child
being born a year later. That was Chloe. I followed five years
later. In between was Little Frankie. I often wonder now if
Frankie's passing was the beginning of my father's problems.
Jim and Lilian Sutter had a troubled marriage, I do know that.
He took to drink. It cost him his job in the end. He had worked
hard, becoming a skilled engineer, and then a foreman. But

darkness would not leave him alone, and so he retreated from the normal, expected life. I was eight years old when he left home.

I picked up *The Book of Common Prayer*. Our family was not particularly religious, we only went to church for weddings and baptisms and funerals, but my father kept this little book close by him for some reason, and he had passed it on to me. I turned to the passage circled in black ink: *I am the resurrection and the life, saith the Lord: he that believeth in me, though he were dead, yet shall he live: and whosoever liveth and believeth in me shall never die*. I could guess why this was picked out; he must have been thinking about Frankie at the time. I stared at the words. Koag danced. My eyes were troubling me. *Dad, Dad. Where are you? Won't you come home?* Something terrible happened then. I can't explain it. The dust started to vanish from my sight, every grain, every colour in the room, gone. I tried my very best to find it again, concentrating, looking this way and that. But it remained invisible. I closed my eyes and kept them closed.

I woke up the next morning to a dustless room, and a dustless house. I went outside and saw the dustless skies and streets. I started to panic. There was always a cloud or two hanging about, around the postboxes and the road signs. But there was nothing to be seen. Even the people on the street were empty of the dust, no shimmer, no shine, not a speck of air-force blue even, or chalk-white, the most common of the colours. I looked for Koag everywhere, seeking its special hiding places. All were empty. I felt sick. I blinked the sweat out of my eyes. I cried out.

Koag, show yourself.
Koag, talk to me. Koag, dance!
Koag, don't leave me.

People were looking my way, thinking me mad. I sat down on a wall. In one of my *Spider-Man* comics, Peter Parker loses his superpowers during a fight with Doctor Octopus. I felt as weak as he did, and as helpless. I ran home as fast as I could, straight into Grandma's room, not even bothering to knock or call out first. She looked up from her knitting. I saw the bowls of dust arranged on her shelf, ready for the next viewing session. But the bowls were empty. I picked one of them up and turned it over, in an attempt to find one single grain remaining.

"What on earth is wrong with you?" The bowl fell to the
carpet with a soft clunk. "Now look what you've done, there's
dust everywhere!"

"Grandma."

Just that word, her name, as though it might save me.
Grandma, Grandma. She stood up from her chair and came to
me. She was no longer worried about the scattered dust. Her
eyes were full of kindness and she patted me on the shoulder.
She knew. She didn't have to be told.

"There, there. It happens to all of us."

"It... It does?"

"Of course. Especially at your age. It's all part of growing up."

"How long does it last?"

"A few hours."

Okay, that wasn't too bad.

"Or a day or so. Or maybe longer, who can tell? A week,
sometimes."

"A week!"

I was no longer a witness. Perhaps my ability would never
return. I recalled the story she had told me at our early morning
discussion: "Just like Tom Halfpenny, the same thing."

"Oh, don't be daft. It's nothing like–"

"But you said, Grandma, that Tom never saw the dust again."

She nodded, admitting the truth without saying it.

I thought of going round to Denny's house; not to confess
my loss, but just to mess about for a bit, until the dust came
back. But I couldn't face seeing anyone. I stayed in my room
for the rest of the day, only emerging for supper, and even
then I didn't really speak or join in with the jokes and the
gossip about the neighbours. Grandma was good to me, never
mentioning my trouble. Mum wanted to know if I was coming
down with something, but I shrugged it off, and left the table
as soon as I could. I went to bed early, having set my alarm
for three o'clock in the morning. I was already awake before
it went off, already in place at the back window, watching as
the skies above the houses were lit up with streams of pink
and gold dust, starred with emerald. It was glorious! My eyes
opened wide to capture as much of it as I could, darting here
and there. I wanted it to last forever. But the time ticked
down on my Commando watch. Two minutes and thirty-nine

seconds. And the skies were dark once more. I don't think I'd ever felt as lonely. Lights clicked off at windows, a few final voices went quiet as doors were closed.

I lay on my bed, thinking of Eileen Barlow. At that moment she seemed to me an angel, of a kind. The way she talked, and smiled. Our own private moment, that day at Slew Hill when Denny hadn't turned up. Her sun-browned legs, swinging back and forth. That perfect sphere of golden yellow dust hovering above her head in the haze of the sunlight. I had boasted that I was going to be a writer, and we talked about Preston Heyes making a woman disappear in a cloud of dust, and Eileen had admitted her fantasy of becoming a magician's assistant, like Topaz, because then she would know what it feels like to... What it feels like to *vanish*.

I sat up. An idea was approaching.

Something about the magician's assistant, and Henrietta Tudor, and the thing that connected them both. But it would not stay in place. I had said something to Eileen that day, something to do with Helme's Threshold. I'd been trying to show off to her, and failing miserably. What had I said? Come on, Joe! Something about Helme's Threshold working backwards, because Grandma had told me the story of Henrietta a few nights before, of that special moment when Greot becomes visible to the eye of a witness, when the dust crosses over into sight...

Henrietta appeared out of the dust, Topaz disappeared into the dust.

The same journey, back and forth.

Preston Heyes. Hey Presto!

And here I was, a victim of the same process: the dust vanishing from my eyes.

I remembered the song that had been playing on the radio when I had followed Sutter's Fancy for the very first time, after Eileen and Denny had made fun of me. It was "King Midas in Reverse" by The Hollies. Mrs Pierce had told us about King Midas, about how everything he touched turned to gold. But the character in the song has the opposite effect: everything he touches turns into dirt. Not nearly as exciting! But I liked the song's title so much I treasured it now, saying it over and over to myself, and then changing it slightly as I fell asleep.

Helme's Threshold in Reverse.

In the morning, first thing, I started work on a new story. Perhaps I could tell the story of a magician's assistant. She knows how all the tricks are done, the gimmicks behind them, the trap doors, the hidden compartments, the fake blades, and so on. She's really good at squeezing into tiny spaces and contorting her body this way and that. But then, one evening, during a stage performance, she really does vanish. That moment, could you imagine? You're inside the magical cabinet, waiting for the trap door to open, when you actually start to disappear, but for real this time – your body fades away, *you* fade away.

Okay, so I needed a name for the assistant, something glamorous, like Topaz. I chose Amber. That sounded similar enough. But the trouble was, I still couldn't *write* anything, no matter how I tried. I had my story, but making it happen on the page, making people speak and move and cry and argue, all that kind of thing, no, it was hopeless. I looked over to the drawings for our latest comic. The six panels per page format was good, for Denny and me, because it enabled the story to be simply told, and to be honest, it was the exact same story every time. Panel One: Evil supervillain (Captain Mayhem, or the Needle) does something horrible. "Ha ha, my scheme to rob the Ormsley Bank will make me rich!" Panel Two: Our superhero turns up (Nowhere Man, Zigzag Woman, or Spellcaster) to find some clues. Panels Three, Four, Five: A mighty battle takes place. *Clang! Humfff! Arghhhh!* Panel Six: Evil supervillain defeated. The End. Now, this wasn't the kind of story that would impress Mr Holbrook, or Margery. Yet maybe I could use the same basic model, but instead of drawing six panels, I would write six very short chapters, each one just a few paragraphs long, nothing fancy.

I worked out what each little chapter would describe. *One.* Amber, in her sparkly costume, inside a cabinet, waiting for the trap door to open. It does, and she drops down out of sight. Now she runs along under the stage, to get into position for her magical reappearance at the back row of the auditorium. *Chapter Two.* Amber cursing the magician, because he gets all the applause, while she's been doing most of the work. *Three.* She finds an old book of magic spells, including a spell to make people disappear. She decides to use this on the magician. *Four*. First, she tries the spell on a neighbour's cat, and *Poof!* It's a success, the cat vanishes. *Five*. She tries it on the magician, but it doesn't work. And finally, *Chapter Six*. Amber in the magical cabinet once more, but this time the trap door doesn't open. She panics, thinking the trick is going wrong. The magician swings open the doors, but Amber is still there. He's surprised at this. But then, in front of the entire audience, she disappears, just fades completely away, with a terrified look on her face. The magician is shocked. The End.

I worked so hard on this outline that I forgot all about my current dustless life, until suddenly the thought would pop up again, and I would shiver and look around my room, hoping for a sign. Would I end up as the new Tom Halfpenny? Joe Farthing, they would call me. *You see that poor bugger? He used to see the dust, summat special, eeh, he did that.* And a penny would be thrown my way. Tomorrow, I said to myself, tomorrow I shall awaken to see the dust returned.

Keep working! I had to be honest: was this new story idea really any higher than level-one invention? The whole point was to make Mr Holbrook feel better. It had to be level-two, at the very least: a *unique* story. I was stuck. But writing, and thinking, about magicians had stirred an old interest of mine. I pulled my Preston Heyes Conjuring Set out from under my bed. Who could resist the slogan on the box: *Twenty-one Incredible Tricks to Amaze Your Friends!* Most of them involved guessing chosen playing cards correctly, or changing one object into another, or making things vanish. Coins, cards, handkerchiefs, all these things could be made to vanish, using the gadgets in the set. I kept asking myself the same questions: what happens to someone when they vanish, what does it feel like, where do they go to? This was the question Eileen Barlow had asked, and she was willing to vanish herself in order to know the answer. Well I, Joe Sutter, would answer the question for her. And at that point, I knew: this story wasn't just for Mr Holbrook, it was also for Eileen. Perhaps more for her than for him. Perhaps totally for her. And after this, it all became a lot easier.

A playing card vanishes from a conjurer's hand.

A coin disappears into thin air.

A silk handkerchief is folded over and over until it no longer exists.

A rabbit slips out of sight down a top hat.

A dove flies away into a puff of blue smoke.

A woman steps into a cabinet, and doesn't step out again.

And where do they go? They all go to the same place. Another world, a special world, where all the vanished objects end up. The story could begin where my first attempt left off; with Amber vanishing for real from the cabinet: that moment when the door closes, and the darkness creeps in, and she can still sense the audience out there beyond the door, and her heart is beating madly, expecting the trap door to open at any second, but instead the world slowly fades away around her, and now she's in this other place entirely, a very mysterious place. Along with all the missing coins, playing cards, hankies, doves and rabbits. So many doves have been made to vanish over the years, there's a whole room of them. And Amber is alone, she's the only human being to have vanished for real. Or even better, she finds a dead body, a skeleton in a spangly outfit. This is a warning to her: she too will die here unless she can find a way back. And how does the story end?

I was still stuck on that one. So I went back to something else Mr Holbrook had said to me at the tower, his second goal in life: "Solve the puzzle of yourself. The beautiful puzzle of yourself." He was very serious about the *beautiful* part. Maybe I could make a (beautiful) puzzle for Amber to solve. What if she wakes up in this place, surrounded by playing cards and coins and handkerchiefs galore, and with a good number of rabbits hopping about, and hundreds upon hundreds of doves flying everywhere, perched on every surface, cooing away? Poor Amber! She has no clue where she is. And so the story, maybe, is all about her finding out where she is. So there's no escape at the end, just the realisation, the solving of the puzzle. I liked that. A twist ending. The reader only finds out where she is when she does, in the final sentence.

I read over my notes so far. At some point I realised that my magician had made six different things vanish, the same number of panels in one of our comics. Maybe I was actually writing a comic? I set to work. In the first panel I drew a playing

card, the Seven of Diamonds. In the second I drew a coin, in
the third a handkerchief (with the initials *E.B.* embroidered in
tiny letters, a secret message for Eileen). In the fourth panel
I drew a rabbit, in the fifth a dove in flight. In the last panel I
drew a portrait of Amber. As mentioned, I wasn't very good at
faces, but I did my best, using a photograph of Lulu from one
of Chloe's pop magazines as a model.

This was a very different sort of comic to the ones Denny
and I usually created. The first five panels contained either a
single object or a single animal, and the last a human face. Now
for the words. I needed these to be in Amber's voice, because
the final panel would reveal the twist, from her own point of
view. So in the first panel she says, "I don't know where I am.
I'm lost. These playing cards keep appearing, but I have no one
to play poker with! I'm alone!" I didn't use speech bubbles; I
wrote the words in tiny capitals all around the playing card.
In the second panel Amber finds a room filled with sparkling
coins. "But I have nothing to spend them on!" And so on,
through each panel. "So many doves, lovely and white. But
they never stop cooing. It's driving me mad!" I included some
good sound effects here, filling the background space: *COO!*
COO! COO! Finally we get to see Amber herself, for the first
time. But I messed up her face, making her look lopsided. I had
to start again from scratch, drawing each panel more neatly this
time, in pencil first, and then going over all the lines in black
ink. I added the title of the story along the top of the sheet in
fancy lettering: "Helme's Threshold in Reverse". And this time
I made Amber look really mad in panel six, with crazy staring
eyes, gritted teeth, furrowed brow. I gave her these words:
"My name is Amber. I was a magician's assistant, but now I'm
trapped here, in the land where all the vanished things end
up. And I can't get out, I can't escape!!!" A rabbit peeps into
the bottom left corner, and a dove is pecking at Amber's face.
Her hands are pressing at the panel lines on each side, and in
a moment of inspiration I made the two lines bend a little, as
though she were trying to escape the comic itself. Her final cry:
LET ME OUT!

I was happier now. I felt like I'd moved on from the original
task I had set myself. So I turned the sheet over and wrote on
the back, with as careful a hand as I could manage:

Task No.2
Write A Story That Isn't A Story

Yes, that was a much better name for the task. And a wicked thought came to me: I'll bet Denny Portman would never go to such trouble to please Eileen. Against all the odds, I was going to win this battle. But that nasty Anti-Boredom Machine kept prodding at me. *Jab, jab, jab! Make it better, make it unique!* I needed a special effect, like in a horror movie or a haunted house mystery. These six different things are disappearing from our world and entering the Vanished Realm. I wanted to show that happening. So I went downstairs and rooted about in the sideboard cupboards until I found the tissue paper that Mum used to wrap presents. I watched *Vision On* and *Blue Peter* every week, and the presenters on those programmes were always teaching us how to make toys out of anything we could find around the house. I chose plain tissue paper, rather than coloured, as it was almost transparent but still a bit cloudy. Perfect. I cut out six little squares and used sticky tape along the top edge to fix them in place, over the playing card, the coin, the handkerchief, the rabbit, the dove, and lastly, over Amber. You could still see each image through the paper, but not clearly. Now the reader could lift up each square of tissue to reveal the drawing beneath. There, it was done. I had set myself a task. I had completed that task. What I had to do now, somehow or other, was get it into Mr Holbrook's hands. And then (if I dared!), to let Eileen read it.

14

I took up the same position as I did on my first ever spying expedition, flat on the grass near the gap in the drystone wall, peering through my binoculars at the farmhouse. The Land Rover was missing. Hopefully that meant Mr Holbrook was alone. I had a fear that Margery would stand in my way from seeing him, if he was too ill; she was very protective. I waited for fifteen minutes, just in case he came out for a bit of air. But there was no activity. I placed the binoculars in my briefcase and set off. The briefcase had five different compartments inside, with zipped pockets and little loops to hold pens and propelling pencils. But I was carrying only two items today: the binoculars and my "Helme's Threshold in Reverse" story. It was too important to trust to the Royal Mail. I wanted to keep the story flat, and safe from damage, so I had placed it between two pieces of cardboard cut out from a cornflakes box. The special-effect tissue squares were very delicate.

Nobody answered my knocks on the door, nor my shouts through the letterbox. Nipper made not a bark nor a whimper. I walked around the entire building, peeping in at each window as I went along. But every room looked empty. The back door was locked. I had a sudden upset: they had left home, moved away, found somewhere else to live. Their possessions would be sent on later, when the removal van turned up. It was too distressing to even think about. No, I refused to believe they would do such a thing. Mr Holbrook was ill, he needed to stay in one place, surrounded by the hills, the Pennines, and close to Brendleshire, real or otherwise. For a moment I considered breaking in, and leaving my story in his office, or on his bed, so he could find it later. But there were limits.

And then an even more terrible thought came to me, that Mr Holbrook had died. Walking up to the tower, I could not shake this fear. At the peak I looked down the length of the vale, seeing the various landmarks for the first time without their colourings of dust. The map was strangely drawn without those dots and speckles and whirlwinds and spirals and sudden becalming clouds. And yet this was real, I had to remind myself. This was the sight that greeted most people whenever they climbed to this viewpoint. I shared in that same sight now, the glory of the fields and towns under the sun. Brendle Woods looked especially enticing in the misty air, quite capable of its own beauty, unadorned. I sauntered down that way, briefcase in hand, entering the shade of the trees. The branches rustled thickly, though there was little or no wind, and the leaves were closely packed together, and overly green and filled with life, if such a thing makes sense. And the further I went, the darker it became, even though the canopy was not tightly wound at that point. I thought to find that clearing where I had first spotted Sutter's Fancy in the act of making itself anew, hanging in a clump from a branch. Surely, a place like that must hold some magical power, enough to renew my witnessing. Yet I could not find the railway track. Soon I was lost, and bewildered. I seemed to be walking in circles; every tree was the same tree. The heat of the day increased. My shirt was sticky. Would I ever escape this place? Mum would be panicking. They would have to send for the police, to search for me with hound dogs. The temptation to run blindly ahead was overwhelming. I came to a halt, drawing breaths heavy with the smells of weeds and sap and soil.

Save me, Koag, be my friend. Rescue me.

I shouted it out: "Help me, Koag, please. Help me!"

My words vanished into the tangle of branches, flittering away.

I closed my eyes.

The bark of the tree felt squishy under my palms. I think an ant or some other insect crossed my hand, I did not care to look. I had to keep my eyes closed. I liked the darkness, the soft dark. It felt safer there. Little fragments of story occupied my mind, breaking apart as soon as they were told. Flecks of orange and turquoise light disturbed me. I screwed my eyes tighter shut. They would not go away, these interior blotches of colour. Blood from the wound of the dustless world. A single blackbird was singing unseen, each note pinning the colours into place.

Once more I prayed.

Koag, come back to me.

I opened my eyes, expecting so much, seeing only the trees. I set off walking, and this time a pathway opened up, narrow, but enough for me to follow. And with great relief I found the tarmacked lane that ran through the woods. I followed it a little way and there, parked exactly as it had been last time, was the Land Rover. There was no sign of Nipper, nor of Mr Holbrook, or Margery. The rear door of the Land Rover was shut. I crept forwards. What on earth would I see through the glass? Nakedness? That strange act of which so much was whispered? But no, the vehicle was empty. I just didn't know what to think. Those little flecks of orange and turquoise that had marred my interior darkness came back to me, though my eyes were wide open. Could I hope for Koag? They drifted around the trees on the other side of the lane, these colours, yet disappeared as I approached. I had never been a Boy Scout, but I did own a copy of *Scouting For Boys* which Dad had bought for me at a jumble sale, so I knew the basics of tracking. I noted the broken twigs and the small pile of dog dirt where the woods took over the lane. I saw footprints in the soil, freshly made, and paw prints. I decided to follow, deeper into Brendle Wood. The mood changed again, darkening further, silent whenever I stopped for a breath. I could not see Koag, but I could sense its presence. I was moving towards a centre, perhaps a nesting ground. I felt I was approaching Helme's Threshold, with every step exploring a new world.

Then I saw the flicker.

Turquoise, orange.

This time I captured it with my eyes, closing them over the sight, keeping it there.

Opening, opening, slowly…

Yes, it remained, a firefly glow.

I wanted to sing out loud.

But I kept quiet, hardly daring to breathe.

I moved on.

The trees were laden with dust, in as many colours as you could picture: aquamarine, lemon, scarlet, tangerine, indigo, and bright gold. And out of them all, slowly forming, the rose-pink and silver of Sutter's Fancy. I was dizzy with it, this sudden return, and I had to lean against a tree as the colours dazzled me. My head was aflame. But I set off once more, for something was waiting for me here, in the woods, something good, or something bad. The colours led me through weed beds, through swarms of midges, through nettles and thorns, through reeks of rotten stench, and onwards, until I heard voices among the trees.

First of all I saw the dog, curled up in the undergrowth, sleeping, or more likely hypnotised, for the drowsiness was heavy in this place, and I felt it myself. My eyes were weary. I had to force them open, to stare ahead from my hiding place among the branches. What I saw wasn't a clearing as such, more a secret bower, enclosed by trees on all sides, and overhead. I heard the trickle of water, but could not see a pool or a stream. Yet despite its enclosure there was a soft eerie glow to the scene, made of many different shades and sparkles of light.

Next I saw Margery. She was dressed for a country walk in tweed and sturdy shoes. She was holding the handle of a small spade, the kind used to build sandcastles at the seaside, and was using this to dig in the earth. My first thought was that she was burying something. But no, it wasn't that. She was digging something up.

Then I saw Mr Holbrook. He was standing near the edge of the bower, his body upright, his face at rest, unmasked, the three lines on his brow finely etched. His face looked thinner, even more sunken at the cheeks. His eyes were narrowed to slits. I did not think he would venture so far from the house, but Margery had driven him as far as she could, to the bend in the lane, and then they had travelled here on foot. So this place was important to them. What they were doing could only take place here, I suspected, or was easiest to perform in this location.

Then I saw Koag, completely and utterly. The trees were filled with great sticky clumps of the dust, of all colours and mixtures intermingled, and it was these strange objects that gave the bower its multicoloured lighting. They hung down from the lower branches, dripping their viscous off-white secretions onto the ground below. Ugh! Lumpy gravy! The bluebottles were buzzing about in a joyful dance, as they supped at the droplets of liquid. It must have tasted very sweet to them. I could not count how many of the clumps there were, but I knew instinctively this was a favoured meeting place for Koag, rather like Ormsley green on a Friday night when you can glimpse courting couples kissing beneath the trees. I felt woozy and sick from the heat and the smell.

Margery had finished with the spade, and was now down on her hands and knees, working with a garden trowel. I dared to creep a little closer. I need not have feared exposure, for both Margery and Holbrook were each in their different ways totally focussed on the task in hand. She reached inside the hole, to pull something loose from the soil. It would not come easily, whatever it was, and I knew then it was alive, a creature of some kind. Something from a nightmare, it had to be. The creature was resistant to her demands, preferring to remain in the dark of its proper home. But Margery would not give up; she dragged the thing free with a heave and a grunt. It lay on the ground twitching, a mass of whitish flesh the size and shape of a half-deflated football, but it was never quite the same from one moment to the next; it quivered, it slurped, it bubbled and frothed, and most of all, it oozed.

I thought I knew what it was, at least to make a guess. When I had seen the solitary clump of Sutter's Fancy hanging from the branch, in another part of the woods to this, I had seen how the dripping liquid had seeped into the earth below. Perhaps over time this liquid solidified even further, and settled into the creature I saw before me now. Was this another stage of Koag's life, like the tadpole to the frog, the caterpillar to the butterfly? Would the living dust emerge from this mass at some future time? What was obvious, I think, is that the two intruders into the bower had pulled the creature too early from its nursery bed; the growth was not yet complete. Part of me wanted to step forwards, to put an end to this cruelty. Another part, the greater part, stood in fascination as the scene unfolded before me. And then, and only then, did the most surprising aspect of the affair come to me: Margery Adams could *see* the creature. She could *touch* the creature. How could this be? It didn't make sense. Yet I had seen her at work, unaided by Mr Holbrook's directions, pulling and struggling. There was only one explanation; that in this weird, jellylike state Koag was visible to all. Within the dark of the soil it coagulated into a semi-solid form, glueing itself together in such a way as to become visible, and tangible. Oh, Koag! Who will ever truly, truly understand your mysteries? To begin with it was invisible to all; then it crossed Helme's First Threshold, and became visible to the witnesses and beholders; then it crossed the Second Threshold, becoming visible to everyone; and then it travelled back again, this way and that, appearing and disappearing, according to the time of day, and the current nature of its body.

What on earth were these two doing with Baby Koag? The thing looked angrier than ever. I thought it might crawl up Margery's arm and attack her, like a monster from a flying-saucer movie. But she seemed to have some control over it. She picked it up in both of her hands. She was actually stroking it, like a pet animal, trying to calm it. Yet I could tell from her expression that she was not happy with this task. I had picked up a huge slug once, under Denny's instructions, and I imagined Margery felt a similar feeling as I had then: utter repulsion. But she was also determined; this was something that had to be done, no matter what. She stood up and walked over to Mr Holbrook, the creature held in her outstretched arms. She presented it to him.

I leaned forward a little further, pushing myself through the leaves.

Mr Holbrook's eyes were open. His mouth formed a smile. But then he grimaced, as though in fear of what might happen. His brow crinkled deeply. He need not have worried, for Baby Koag took to him gleefully, slipping quickly from Margery's hands onto his face. It clung there, perfectly still for a moment. Then it began to move over his skin until it covered his features from brow to chin. And once in place, it slowed, and settled. Now I understood. A new mask was being made, or more accurately, being grown, precisely formed and moulded. Not constructed of wax, as I had first thought, nor of plastic or rubber, as Eileen had surmised; no, the mask was made from the younger form of the living dust.

I was shocked. I was amazed.

Baby Koag!

I was shivering with excitement. I wanted to jump up and down.

Baby Koag is clinging!

I wanted to shout out in joy.

Baby Koag is clinging to his face!

Yet at the same time I felt sick to my stomach, and my legs were shaking. How absurd it was, that I had my school briefcase with me, still tightly clutched by the handle. I felt something rubbing against my legs, and it scared me. I looked down, expecting to see the little brothers and sisters of Baby Koag crawling over to the soil towards me. But it was only Nipper. He had come awake. His wet tongue slathered at my bare shins.

Margery attended to Mr Holbrook, making the final adjustments, pressing with nimble fingers to ensure the mask fitted perfectly. A sculptor at work. She poked out the little holes necessary for him to breathe, and to speak. The mask was now his face; his face now the mask. There was little difference between them. The woodland creaked about me. A fly buzzed. Nipper barked. Margery looked over, wondering what the disturbance might be. But she had not yet seen me. Just in time, I ducked back into the leaves. More than anything I wanted to run, tunnelling my way through the trees at such a speed that not even the Flash could catch me. But then, if I did that, wouldn't my Anti-Boredom Machine turn into a Boredom Machine? I could not face such a thing. So I stepped forwards into the bower.

Margery stood where she was, one hand on Mr Holbrook's arm, staring at me. Her mouth opened, and then closed. I did the same, copying her gestures automatically, like a robot boy. Neither of us spoke. Mr Holbrook was shaking, trying to escape Margery's grip. But her fingers held on tightly, squeezing. His mask was very dark, and cloudy, not at all translucent; it was still forming itself. And I realised that he was blind behind that covering. For the time being he was helpless, completely in the hold of his companion. The moment stretched out. Then Margery burst into action, first calling to Nipper, who came obediently. Then she strode towards me, dragging Mr Holbrook along with her. I stepped back from her approach, but she said to me in a stern voice, "Get the spade and the other things. Quickly!" I did so, gathering the tools she had been using and wrapping them in a canvas sack I found on the ground. Then I rushed to keep up with the pair of them, the dog at their heels, as they made their way through the woods. We soon came in sight of the Land Rover. Margery guided Mr Holbrook into the back, helping him to climb the metal steps. He was uncomplaining during all this. Nipper jumped in as well, yapping to show his happiness. I went to follow, but Margery had me by the arm. "No, in the front, where I can keep an eye on you." Again, I followed her orders, not wanting to anger her further. She looked livid.

We set off, taking the lane deeper into the woods, away from the town. I had never ventured this way before. The woods petered out and the lane joined with a more substantial road, which curled around the hill and led us back towards the Pike. The tower was stark against the sunlight. I had not seen it often from this angle. The Land Rover ground to a halt in the yard of the farmhouse, and we all got out. I tried my best to be helpful, taking Mr Holbrook by the hand to lead him from the van, carrying the tools, and so on. I needed to please Margery. But no matter what I did she just glowered at me. "In there!" She pointed to the front room. She led Mr Holbrook up the stairs, out of sight, and Nipper went off to find his bowl in the kitchen. I was alone. I went into the living room, first checking to see if Henrietta was sitting at the piano. Not a glimmer, not a shimmer. I put my briefcase on the table, and waited. Should I sit down? Best not, it might seem like I didn't have a care in the world. So I stood by the fireplace. I could hear movement upstairs. She was probably putting him to bed. I guessed he needed time to recuperate, when a new mask first took him over. Then came the sound of her feet on the stairs, slowly now, taking her time. She appeared at the doorway. I was shaking with fear. I knew I was in trouble, perhaps the biggest trouble I had ever been in. But what exactly was my crime? I had gone for a walk in the woods and stumbled across a private scene, that was all. But, of course, I was kidding myself. I had deliberately spied on them, wanting to know everything.

Her first words echoed this. "You're a nosy fuckin' bugger, aren't you?"

Nobody, I mean… *nobody*… had ever spoken to me like this. It only increased my fear. I had one eye on the door, wondering whether I should take off on that run now.

"I want to join in," I said, stuttering.

"To join in? This isn't some stupid kid's gang."

"I know, I know that. I don't want that."

"You should have friends of your own age."

"I do. I have Denny, I have–"

"Not some old bastard like his Lordship, upstairs…"

"I have Elaine."

"… snoring away behind that stinkin' mask, grunting and snuffling, dreaming of God knows what."

"But they're not like you and Mr Holbrook. Nothing like."

"Look! Look at my hands. They're filthy, all the muck on them."

But she didn't go off to wash them, or anything like that. Margery rubbed the palms together. She kept glancing towards the piano, and her fingers twitched madly, grimy or not, as though she really wanted to take out her frustrations on the instrument, to pound out some more of that violent music. Instead she veered over to the drinks cabinet. But then she stopped herself. Her whole body trembled, and now her hands were tightly clenched at her sides.

"Margery–"

"Shut up!"

She might as well have slapped me across the face, her words had such an effect. I darted for the door, but she jumped in my way and slammed it to, and then instantly regretted this. She looked up to the ceiling, worried that she might have disturbed Mr Holbrook. Then she turned to me. Her features were all screwed up, like something out of a horror comic.

"Sit down, please, Joe, will you?"

She was making an effort to get back under her own control. I nodded, then sat at the table, on the edge of the chair. Even the idea of comfort sickened me. Taking a seat opposite, she smiled at me. It was a ghastly affair, for I saw now that she had been crying, and the marks of her tears were white on her cheeks. I waited, expecting the worst.

She said, at last, "Oh, I don't know why I'm so upset. After all…" She stopped.

After all, what? I was mystified by adults: they were always contradicting themselves, and grimacing, or looking maudlin, or then a funny little grin might appear, or else they suddenly screamed in frustration. It was all so very, very complicated.

"After all, you've done nothing wrong." Her eyes were red-raw, and she wiped at them with her sleeve. "It wasn't always like this, not this bad. Once, I…"

The dust that floated around her was sickly looking, a dull vomity green, thinly textured. It acted as a guide to her mood. She took a breath and then spoke the truth. I was expecting some kind of explanation. Instead, she went back into the past.

"I was at a loss in my life, living in London. I wandered around Soho, working bars, playing in the jazz clubs when I could get a gig."

I was glad her mood had changed, and that I was no longer in danger of being hit. I was also, and more importantly, very interested in her story. I didn't know where this Soho place was, but a clear image formed in my mind. The younger Margery Adams in a sequinned gown, playing a grand piano while a handsome singer crooned into the microphone and the audience clapped politely.

"Filthy clubs, they were, stinking of sweat and cheap booze, filled with smoke, and the men swearing all the time, and making a play for whatever they could get their hands on."

A quick readjustment of the picture was needed. But it was still exciting.

Now she had a wistful look about her. "I fell in with the wrong crowd. Bohemians, we called ourselves. Miscreants, more like. God, what a lark! Painters, jazzmen, poets, harlots. Aye, it was a lively place back then, Soho was."

I wanted to ask about the harlots, but thought it best to let her carry on.

"You play and you play, every night of the week, often two or three sets a day, and you learn all the tunes. "I Get a Kick Out of You", "Someone to Watch Over Me", "Summertime". And you never stop, you never give up, and one night you suddenly realise you're better than you used to be, that now you're beginning, you're actually playing for real, you're improvising. It's electric! The music is just flowing out of you in a sparkle of notes that never seem to end... They never end, they just never end!" Her expression was glorious, but it quickly fell apart. "Until the melody palls, and sickens under your fingers." She paused, gathering herself. "And then you just have to carry on, even when your friends kick you out onto the street."

"I don't understand, Margery. What do you mean?"

"Oh, Joe, sweet Joe, you're just too young."

"I'm trying to be older. But... But I don't know how to manage it."

At least that made her smile. And she said, "In that scene, that Soho scene, there are various temptations on offer. It's to do with music and love, and getting lost in both, and losing both, and well... with *drugs*." This last word was said in a whisper. She bowed her head.

Oh, believe me, I had studied the headlines: *Sex-starved drug addicts caught in Vice Squad swoop*. I had consulted the *Family Dictionary* many times.

But when she next looked up, her eyes were blazing. She was defiant. "Christ Almighty, but I wish I were young again. I'd do everything the same but with double the intensity. I would wring life dry, and sup on the juices!"

Another pause. She shook her head.

"Who am I kidding, eh?"

She stared at the dirt on her hands.

"I didn't know what to do. I was in desperate straits. 1961, this was. There was so much hope in the air, and there I was at Euston Station, wondering whether to go back to Yorkshire or not, to run home to Mummy. I had nothing else to do, nowhere else to go."

Once again my mind was forming pictures. She hadn't mentioned the weather in her story, but in my image of her standing outside the train station, it was definitely raining. It was pelting down.

"I had just enough for a train ticket. But at the W.H. Smith & Son's stall, I glanced at the situations vacant in *The New Statesman*. The words jumped out at me. *Amanuensis required by renowned author. Good rate of pay (monthly), full board.* I took a gamble."

I tried to repeat the first word of the advertisement, but failed halfway through.

She repeated it for me. "*Amanuensis.* It means a clerk or scribe, a person who writes down the words or music of someone who is ill, or disabled in some way."

"So you came here, to Pike View?"

"I met his Lordship in London first, in the tea rooms of the Mayfair Hotel, no less. He treated me to scones with cream and jam. That did impress, I must say. He was polite back then, very well dressed, with a lovely smell of cologne about him. English leather, it was."

"Had you heard of him before, or read his books?"

"No. I was never a science fiction fan. But the job turned out to be a good one. He pays well enough, the house is nice, the views lovely, the walking. I have lots of free time. I learnt some of the classical repertoire for him, his favourite pieces. He bought me Nipper. I started to paint while I was here, and he provided me with all the equipment I needed." She smiled. "It's perfect. Really, it is." But something was off; it looked like her expression was lying about her feelings. "It was meant to be a stop-gap," she went on. "A pause between running away, and running onwards. And yet here I am, and here I remain, seven years later."

She hid her face in her hands.

I had so many questions to ask, so many that I could not think of a single one. I concentrated. I went back to my original list from the tea party, actually to the very first question on the list.

"Margery... Why does he wear the mask?"

She was still hiding herself away within the crook of her arms.

"Margery?"

Slowly she unfolded herself. But instead of answering me, she said, "Oh, look at my hands, they're filthy." She had mentioned this already. She would not leave them alone. Her eyes were glazed. "Excuse me, please." She left the room. I heard the taps running in the kitchen. She was washing away the stink and the muck. Now was my best ever chance to escape.

I stayed where I was.

She came back into the room, looking refreshed. But she would not sit down. She stood near the table. It made me feel awkward, as though I were back in the classroom and Mrs Pierce was standing over me, tutting at my work. But Margery did not tut.

"Come visit us in a few days."

"When? Which day?"

"Let the mask do its work first."

"Yes, but when?"

"It needs at least three days, to get started properly."

"Three days. Right." It was Monday. "I'll be here on Thursday."

"Okay, yes, fine. Around five o'clock, can you manage that?"

"Yes."

"And then, well... all will be revealed."

"About the mask?"

"Yes. Everything."

"I'll be here."

She nodded. "Although God knows, I wish I could make him stop."

I was reminded of my original intention, so I opened my briefcase to take out the short story. I removed it from its protective cardboard layers. "I wrote this for Mr Holbrook." I went off on a rambling explanation. "I set myself a task, *Task No.2*, to write a short story. But my first go wasn't good enough. So then I decided to write a story that wasn't a story. See, here, written on the back: *A Story That Isn't A Story*. I redid it, completely changed it, and then I stuck these little bits of tissue paper to it, do you see, Margery, look, the tissue paper. I did that because..."

She had a distant sort of expression. I placed my story on the table, saying, "Will you show it to him?"

She nodded. But her mind was still elsewhere.

"Margery, will you promise, please?"

"Of course, of course."

She moved over to the piano. She did not sit down. The fingers of one hand picked out a tune without a tune. I thought I recognised it, but the melody kept slipping away. And then it came to me: she was playing the same nursery rhyme I had heard the child play.

"Where did you learn that?" I asked.

"Oh, it just came to me, one day. I was trying to learn a sonata by Mozart, but my fingers kept moving to different notes, not on the score. It's just one of those things, you know."

"Is it?"

"Yeah, one of those silly tunes you can't stop singing, or playing."

"I've heard it before."

She turned to me. "Really? I thought I'd made it up."

"A little girl was playing it."

Now she stared at me. She looked worried. I remembered how she had asked me about having seen ghosts in the house. It was time to tell the truth.

"She was sitting right there, at the piano. A girl, seven or eight years old."

"No…"

"A child of dust. Really. I saw her."

It was too much for her to hear. She turned back to the piano, away from me. Her shoulders were tensed up and she was shaking. Now both hands moved to the keys, playing a single chord. She was mumbling to herself.

I stayed where I was at the table, feeling very awkward and uncomfortable.

She said, "George talks about her all the time. He writes about her. I thought he was losing his mind."

"No, she's real! Or almost real. Her name is Henrietta. Henrietta Tudor."

"You've spoken to her?"

"No, not exactly."

"George gets so angry that he can't hear her speak. Only the music she makes, and her little footsteps on the stairs in the night." A desperate smile came to her lips. "But if you've seen her as well, Joe, then he's not having visions. He's not mad."

I nodded eagerly. "Grandma and I gave her the name Henrietta. We tried out a lot of names, all based on the initials."

"Initials?"

"Yes, we have a handkerchief. My Grandma is a beholder, and she saw Henrietta years ago." I told her the story, as quickly as I could, all about Mr Dunham and the Ashen Society, and the fallen handkerchief with its embroidered letters.

Margery thought about it all, then said, "I never truly believed him, I mean, how could I? But now... But now..." Her eyes had a fierce intensity to them. "George first saw her a while ago, some years ago, after he started using the mask. He has let his imagination run wild. He's obsessed. The child infects his dreams." Her voice faltered. Then she explained, "When madness takes over a person, it's sometimes best to go along with it, to encourage their delusions." Her face tightened. "And I did that with George, for so long a time. I thought that his stories had taken him over. And lately, with his illness, it's all gotten worse." She stopped herself, to take a breath. "Much worse, so much worse. But what else could I do, in his final days upon the world, what else could I do?"

Was I supposed to answer this question? Luckily, Margery carried straight on.

"But now, if you've seen the girl as well... Joe, you have seen her?"

"Yes. I'm not lying. Cross my heart."

"Describe her to me."

"Okay, let me see. Henrietta is seven or eight–"

Now she looked irritated. "You said that already. Anything else?"

"She wears a blue dress. With white ruffles, here at the sleeves, and the neck. And her hair is yellow. Not a proper yellow, not blonde, I mean, not like Marilyn Monroe, but brighter than that, because the dust made it, you see, her hair is made of dust, bright yellow dust. Everything about her is made of dust, everything! Koag made her."

Margery whispered, "It's real, then. She is real." Her eyes darted about the room, and then up to the ceiling, as though she could peer through the floor above to the bedroom where Mr Holbrook was sleeping. Koag was as agitated as she was. It flitted about like a trapped butterfly from window ledge to mantelpiece. Finally it alighted on Margery's face, clouding her with flecks of glitter. Her eyelashes sparkled. Perhaps inspired by this touch, she took her seat at the piano and started to play. Her fingers danced softly across the keys, finding the notes of that same nursery rhyme tune as they went on their wandering way, up and down, up and down. She spoke to herself, or to another, not yet present: "Often I feel someone is sitting here with me, at the piano. They play along with me."

"So, that's how you know the tune?" I asked,

"Yes, I suppose it must be. But... But I thought it was my imagination at play."

"No, Margery. It's Henrietta, I know it is."

"Yes, probably. Who else could it be?" She gasped. "I feel her now, here with me! Can you see her?"

"I'm not sure. I don't think so."

"Joe, tell me."

I concentrated. There was a shiver in the air. Strands of Koag were arriving through the open doorway of the room. They gathered around the piano, lending themselves to Margery as she played. That same tune, over and over, but with each repetition more and more notes were woven around it. She was improvising. Koag danced, Koag trembled. Then Margery started to sing, putting words to the melody, turning it away from a nursery rhyme into something more elaborate, deeper, darker, greener, brighter, ever-changing, as Koag changed its colours to match the mood, painting the music in the air, in dots of light. Margery had a lovely voice.

A late lark twitters from the quiet skies...

The melody never quite settled, but was shifting all the time as the verse progressed.

A late lark twitters from the quiet skies;
And from the west,
Where the sun, his day's work ended,
Lingers as in content,
There falls on the old, gray city
An influence luminous and serene,
A shining peace.

I believe that was the first time I had ever been at the exact centre of beauty. Certain notes, the highest ones, caused explosions of silvery light in my head. It was extraordinarily pleasurable, and I have sought that out in my later years, listening to sopranos, for only they can trigger that specific reaction in me.

The dust ascends
In a rosy-and-golden haze.
The spires shine, and are changed.
In the valley shadows rise.
The lark sings on.

I stood up. Koag drifted about in waves of blue and copper and little specks of whitish grey. My senses were adrift, stripped from my body. I was, quite literally, light-headed. Headed with light. I swayed from side to side in a dance. If Denny or Eileen or Chloe could have seen me then, they would have laughed and made jokes, but they weren't there, only Margery was, and she was lost in the music. She didn't care. She just wanted to play. Koag danced with me and I felt for the first time, the *very* first time, a slight waver in the dust as I moved my hands. I could hardly breathe. Was I now entering that magical world where my Grandma lived, along with Mr Holbrook? At last I would no longer be a witness, but a beholder, and so the dust would be my friend, and we would play together in the fields and streets.

Sadly, no, or at least, not yet. The effect lasted a few seconds only.

But Margery kept the song going, even if the notes, by now, were far away from the original tune, floating free. The dust trembled about her, collecting itself into a new shape. Some other presence was taking over Margery's body; no, not taking over, but occupying the exact same spot as her. The visitor. The child. Henrietta. Margery might not be able to see her, but she could certainly feel her spirit; after all, she had heard or imagined the child's music before now. One note at a time the tune returned to its simple beginnings, once more a nursery rhyme. Two people were playing the same instrument, a duet, but the shared melodies were slightly out of time with each other, so that the music was blurred, and fragile at the edges. I moved until I could see Henrietta's face in profile. Turned-up nose, lips in a smile, enjoying the music. But the features were not quite complete; tiny scatters of dust drifted away from her. I was fearful of moving any closer, even one step, in case the girl started to fade away. She had done so previously, when I had first heard her play. So this time I waited until the very last notes had turned into silence before I made my way from the room, the spell of the house, into the sunlight.

15

I ran to all my favourite hideouts and secret dens and places of mystery, trying to exhaust myself, to make the days go by at a quicker rate, but in fact, time slowed down in the heat of summer. I wound my Commando watch as tightly as possible, and moved the hands on, gaining five, ten, fifteen minutes, anything to bring Thursday afternoon a little closer. I borrowed science fiction novels and short story collections from the library, and read them in single sittings, lying on my bed, or atop Slew Hill. I made up my own tales of interplanetary conflict and robots going crazy, copying ideas from Isaac Asimov and Arthur C. Clarke, but failing, always failing, after the first or second paragraph. I spent some time with Denny and Eileen, but they kept making jokes about each other, so much so that I couldn't join in. So I went off on my own merry adventures in the woods, revelling in my rejuvenated powers, Kid Koag once more, leaping and bounding, getting scratched and dirty at knee and elbow, contemplating the dust non-stop. Until at last the appointed day and hour arose, and there I was on the dot of five at the door of Pike View. Margery was dressed in a smock covered in daubs of different coloured paints. Leading me into the dining room, she said, "Give me a minute to get ready." I recalled my first visit to this room, the cakes and crustless sandwiches on the table. But this time the table was bare but for a small pile of torn paper squares. With a shock, I realised what they were: the remains of my story, the second task. I looked at each square in turn; they had been torn without care, the tissue paper crumpled, each marked with a word or a phrase: *Clever-*

clever. Shallow. Devoid of meaning. Gimmicky. Schoolboyish. For some reason, that one last hurt the most: I was a schoolboy, and this was an example of what I did, so why was that so bad? A further disappointment came over me: that now I would not be able to show the story to Eileen. That plan was ruined.

"Ah, you found them, did you?"

Margery came back in, dressed now in smarter clothes. I don't think I had ever been as angry before; even Mum and Dad arguing never made me feel this way.

"What did you say to him?"

She looked surprised. "Me?"

"Did you tell him I set myself a task? *Task No.2*? Did he read the back of the sheet?"

"I don't know, I suppose he did."

"Margery!"

"I have a lot on my plate, as it happens. What with this, and what with that."

"I told you to tell him."

This time she didn't answer me. But I was seething.

"I want to be a writer, like Mr Holbrook. I really do. I want to astonish people! And he said he was going to help me."

"He is, Joe, believe me." She spoke softly. "He was under the mask most of that day, into the evening, late. It's always that way, when he begins anew; he likes a good long sleep with the mask in place, to get it settled. It was gone midnight by the time he came downstairs for something to eat. I made him eggs and bacon, but that wasn't enough, so I opened a tin of peach slices and he ate the whole lot."

I tried to imagine this scene: Mr Holbrook wolfing down his food, the mask on the table next to his plate, an exact copy of a human face moulded by a living substance.

"And then, Joe, he looked at your work."

"Did he say anything?" I was arranging the torn-up pieces of paper on the table, putting them back into their original shape, a jigsaw puzzle.

"He read it through very carefully, twice over."

"Did he lift up the tissue-paper squares?"

"He did."

Now I looked at her, filled with hope. "Perhaps he didn't understand them properly, what I was trying to do. You see…"

"Joe?"

"Yes?"

"He understood."

I went quiet again. My story was laid out properly, the eight different pieces correctly aligned, but the ripped edges were on show. But it was too painful a sight. I scrunched them all together and shoved them into my pocket. Margery shook her head.

She said, "George's first ten stories were rejected by magazines. And then the first novels he wrote, they were also turned down, and by a lot of different publishers, one after another. He just couldn't get it right. So, you see."

I suddenly felt stupid, really stupid. Schoolboyish, in fact.

"He was thirty-one before *Lost Between the Stars* was published. That was his debut novel."

Thirty-one? Could I wait that long, and with so many rejections along the way? I mean, what would I do in the meantime, for a job? I really didn't fancy mending the lathes at Bradshaw's, like my dad had done for so many years.

Margery must have seen the look in my eyes, because she smiled. "Don't fret, young man. Here. Look." She opened a drawer in the table and pulled out an envelope. "He made this for you last night. A proper one, this time."

"A task?" My fingers were already working at the glued-down flap.

"Don't open it now, Joe. Put it away."

I nodded, and did as I was told.

"We have work to do."

I followed her into the hallway. But instead of walking on towards the office, as I expected, she stopped at a door close to the kitchen. She opened this, revealing a set of stone steps leading down into a cellar. The smell of damp came up to meet me. I was suddenly nervous. Margery went down first. I stayed where I was, watching as she turned away at the bottom of the steps. I waited. Nothing could be seen down there. Then Margery reappeared. "Come on then, don't dither." Still, I hesitated, one foot on the step. In all the Saturday afternoon films I had watched, going down into a cellar was always a bad idea. Evil dwelled in such places.

Eleven steps altogether.

I counted them as I walked down.

I could sense the earth around me, as though the walls and floor were paper-thin, but they were stone, heavy stone. There was a single light bulb hanging down on a flex. A rusty tap dripped water into a washbasin fixed to the wall. A table and two wooden chairs were the only pieces of furniture. A white teacup, turned upside-down, rested at the table's centre. Next to it was a large hardback book and a fountain pen. What did all this mean? Was there something hidden beneath the cup? But I had no time to ask any of my questions, for a sudden noise made me turn towards the archway of another room further into the cellar, further, darker, eerier. And there the Mask of Koag floated, disembodied, alone. I gasped. It glowed with a spectral light, as though lit from within. I had never witnessed this effect before. Mr Holbrook's features were seen through the waxy material as a series of blurred smudges. The rest of his body came into view as he walked forwards. I was suddenly aware of the cold. The tap at the basin released one of its droplets. *Plink*. Then two more. *Plink, plink*. A sparse cloud of dust accompanied the old man as he took a seat at the table. Margery sat down opposite him. Her expression was stern, her backbone straight, head held high. I was reminded of a priestess in a Tarzan movie, someone about to take charge of a cruel ritual. My fear would not go away. Mr Holbrook made a gruff noise from under the mask, and his chest quivered. The dust particles danced, each no bigger than the point of a pin: blue, violet, lilac, orange, white, rose-pink and silver, each colour fizzing into life.

Margery opened the hardback book at a blank page, towards the end of the volume. She asked gently, "George, are we ready?"

He nodded. She lifted up the teacup, revealing the hidden object. I expected a deadly spider or a worm to crawl out, but no: it was a bird's egg patterned with brown splotches on a reddish-fawn background. A quantity of whitish liquid had dried on a large crack in the surface. It was a kestrel's egg. I knew that because, after first seeing the bird of prey hovering in the sky, I had read up on its habits and lifecycle in my *Observer's Book of British Birds*. To use Mr Holbrook's own way of speaking, this naming word (egg) would never turn into a doing word (flying).

"Nipper and I found it this morning," Margery explained. "It was lying beneath a tree along Pike Ridge. I thought George here would like to have a good look at it." She was right. He was staring at this object through the mask, nothing more than that, staring, staring, staring!

"What is he looking for?" I asked in a whisper.

"The egg's story. Or rather, not the *one* story, but all of the stories."

Now, this set off many a question in my head, but she shushed me into silence.

"Let him work, Joe." She picked up the fountain pen and held it at the ready.

Occasionally Mr Holbrook's upper body would shiver a little but otherwise he was perfectly still, his entire focus on the broken egg. Then the mask began to speak, in a voice I could at first barely hear.

Sun bright dreaming bright, wings of brightness brightly winging, to trees darkly set where nesting darkly, little ones are chirruping.

Margery must have become accustomed to his voice, for she wrote each word down as it was spoken, until Mr Holbrook paused. He made an adjustment of the mask and then began again, this time a little louder. The pen nib scratched on the paper.

From the tower high around the fields perching, then falling shadow darkly falling, sudden falling, diving low with claws and beak, blooding vole and mouse and mole, following high above sunlit figures walking slow on fields of greening silvery flowers, and high smoking plume reaching high from stone tower misting air, following on till lost in fog and shadows winging high amid the song to charm the sky.

I listened. I dare say I have never listened to anything before or since with the same intention, even though I could hardly work out what I was hearing. His voice had a quality to it, not so that he was speaking, but more writing a poem one word at a time, or praying to the Bird God, murmuring in a dream this message from the interior of the egg, the broken egg whose story or potential story he was somehow able to retrieve. It was magical! But it didn't last long; already I could see he was tired. His body slumped forwards and the mask dipped down.

"That's enough, George. That will do us." Margery lowered the teacup over the egg.

Mr Holbrook shifted about in the chair to face me directly. His lips moved behind the mouth-hole, as though there were stories yet to be told, but he remained silent. His eyes were as blank as the mask's eyes, almost invisible, but I wondered: if he saw so much inside a broken bird's egg, then what on earth must he see when he looked at me, at my greasy hair, my tatty clothes, my grass-stained knees? The very idea of it made me fearful, and yet excited at the same time. What secrets he must know! It made me want to run upstairs, making my escape, but instead I waited and watched as he raised his hands, placing one on each side of his head. Using his fingernails he started to peel the mask away from his skin. There was a horrible slurping sound. Little bits of it were clinging on, making long strands of goo, like pulling a piece of chewing gum out of your mouth for as long as it could go. One after another the strands snapped. Now his face was on view, his eyes, his nose, then his lips, as the mask surrendered its grip. Margery took charge, taking the mask and cleaning it at the wash basin with cold running water. Mr Holbrook breathed heavily, with a sound like a broken accordion. His face was white and powdery, as though he had just removed the make-up of a clown. Yet the three lines on his brow were as deep as they had ever been. His eyes blinked rapidly. Grains of dried dust fell from his shirt and collar. He coughed a little. Not much. Not too bad. No blood. Then he said, "All that matters is the dust, and what it produces, what it gives to us."

I nodded, not daring to speak, to break the mood.

He went on, "The dust tells the story of the world in each second passing: what now, and now, what next? The story never ends." He took the mask from Margery's hands and looked into its blank eyes. "The mask is made from the dust. Therefore it sees the story from within, as it tells itself, and untells itself, over and over." He sighed heavily. "Show him, Margery, please."

She turned the book so that I could see it clearly. The title page read: *The Book of Brendle*. Again, the fictional and the real world merged. Margery opened it at various pages, each of which held a paragraph only, always made up of a single sentence, whether long or short.

I read:

From grazing shadow climbs the tree where jackdaws squabble, stark on branches making their chitter chatter in words of tumble beak worm-hunger clacking.

I read:

Muted shallows of pond beetle shadows skittering surface, light flickering greening brown floating flicker spawn clusters.

I read:

Torn open lamb belly tooth marks red where flies lay eggs, worming.

I read:

Petals opening sunlight glisten bee buzz traces left from pollen dance across ages, Roman soldiers marching in mud of the long field, breaking ghosts of mist, where the dead lie slowly rotten flesh sinking, fading.

I read:

Old shiver skin woman witch tearing roots from dry dirt, seeking poison.

That was enough. I felt dizzy from seeing too much in the words, so few words but seeming to contain whole stories hidden or half-hidden. Mr Holbrook and Petra Tey were living a kind of shared life, approaching the same task from different directions. I looked up from the book. It was Margery who explained the process to me.

"Every object in the world," she said, "living or otherwise, has a story, a collection of stories in fact, from which they arise, and which they possess. Even the simplest of objects, this cup for instance, will have a collection of stories that surround it. And the mask allows the viewer to see these stories as they arise." And then, after a pause, she repeated Mr Holbrook's phrase: "The dust tells the story of the world."

How amazing that sounded! *Koag is the storyteller of the world.* I looked to Mr Holbrook for confirmation. I thought of my very first sight of him lying on his bed, covered head to foot in the dust as it took on Tom Halfpenny's appearance. Now I understood, or believed I understood, that all the stories of Tom's life were being recovered by Mr Holbrook. Why, his brain must be close to overflowing! No wonder he couldn't stop writing.

His voice broke into my thoughts. "I know only what the mask has shown me..." He stopped, as a tremor disturbed his features. The dusts of Koag danced away from the wall to attend to his shivering form.

Margery went to him. "George? George, are you all right?"

He coughed violently. "Help me." His body folded up, losing all of its strength. He would have slipped off the chair to the floor if his companion had not taken charge, holding him in place. I went to help, but then felt useless. What could I do?

He was back upright, the coughing fit having passed. Margery frowned and tutted.

"You have something to say to me?" he asked.

"Oh, I do, believe me."

"Spit it out then."

Her face was set firm. "This will be your last time, I swear it will."

"Enough now!" He spluttered, and his face grew red.

But she went on, regardless. "George, I beg you, put the mask away. You are seeing too much, far too much. You must know that!"

"I have to, I have to see! The girl needs my help." He turned his attention back to me. His eyes were wet with tears, although whether from the pain of coughing or from sadness I could not tell. "I have heard," he began, "that you have witnessed her?"

"The young girl?"

"Yes, yes."

I nodded. "I have, Mr Holbrook. She is called Henrietta Tudor."

"You have a name for her?"

"My grandma and I made it up between us."

"I could never tell her name, her true name. It was blurred."

The statement was a mystery to me. "How can a name be blurred?"

He dismissed this question with a pained smile. "It begins with her, with the girl, and those who came before her, the earlier ones seen by other witnesses, figures who appear to us in a cloud of dust." His voice grew steadier. "History speaks of the Ecklam Man of 1472. And Our Lady of Hilderburg from the eighteenth century. And then, closer to home we have the Children in the Ruins, spotted in London in 1942." He glared at me. "But *Henrietta*, as you call her, she is the strongest yet. In her we see the dust forming itself into a bodily shape. And when I saw her for the first time, truly for the first time, through the mask..." Phlegm rattled in his throat. "Show him, Margery, please."

She turned the pages of the book until she reached a certain passage, close to the beginning. As I looked at the words written there, Mr Holbrook read them aloud. He knew it by heart.

In the music of her notes, softly singing, she, a girl in blue, white at neck and wrist, playing piano playing softly upon the keys, fingers dancing.

"There she is, you see, the first ever mention. And over time, over the years... This girl, she is almost with us. She approaches. If I could only... only..." He struggled as his chest heaved with pain. Margery frowned. "Oh, leave me alone." He pushed her hands away. "Koag wants to exist as a living being, to arrive out of the stories. And so, to be alive, fully alive!"

I was excited, and I couldn't help asking, "Can I use the mask? Please. Can I look through it? Please, Mr Holbrook. I'm ready, really I am."

They both stared at me. Until, with a trembling movement, he handed the mask to me.

Margery cried, "No, George! I forbid it. He's too young."

Whatever might have happened next, what wonders I might have seen, I cannot imagine. But a loud rapping at the front door put an end to my venture. It was so violent and insistent we could hear it from down here in the cellar. The frown lines on Mr Holbrook's brow stood out against his powdery skin.

"Who's that, now? Not one of your fancy men, I hope, Margery?"

"No, of course not. I don't know who it is."

"Find out, then."

She climbed the steps. I felt embarrassed, now that we were alone, the old man and myself. I didn't know what to say. Nor did he, it seemed. He had taken back the mask. Then we heard Margery at the top of the steps, calling, "Joe, you'd better come up." I was glad to leave the cellar, and I ran up to the hallway. The ram's head was still being pounded against the front door. I heard a voice shouting through the opened letterbox.

"Joe? Joe, are you in there? Joe!!! Open up."

It was my mother's voice.

16

Margery opened the door. There was my mother, red of face, her hair awry from the climb up the hill. My sister Chloe was with her, which only made it worse. There was a number 12 bus that stopped at Weeping Cross Lane, at the foot of the hill; they had probably taken that from the stop opposite our house and then walked the rest of the way.

"I told you, Mum," Chloe said with glee. "I saw him going into this house, more than once."

Had she been following me?

My Mum looked angry. "Joe, get out here, this minute."

I tried to, but Margery blocked the way. "He's not doing any harm, Mrs Sutter–"

"It's not *you* I'm worried about. I'm worried about my son coming to harm, from a bunch of maniacs."

"There's only me and Mr Holbrook here, no one else. Hardly a bunch–"

"Oh, don't you clever-clogs me!"

Well, here we were, finally, it had to happen:

WHEN TWO WORLDS COLLIDE
An Intergalactic Space Opera by Joseph Sutter

Margery tried to calm my mother. "Joe has been helping out around the house, what with my Mr Holbrook being so ill. Joe here, he's a godsend."

My mother was a little consoled by this, it must be said. "Well, of course, he's always been a good boy. Well brought up, he is."

"I knew that, from the moment I first spied him." Then she turned to me. "Joe, I thought I'd told you to let your family know about your visits?"

I nodded eagerly and said, "I meant to, Mum, honest, I did. But it slipped my mind, and then everything... everything else got in the way."

My mother stared at me. Chloe sneered and mocked me with her smile: she loved it when I got in trouble. And she pushed the nail in a little further: "Don't let him fool you, Mum, he's been coming here every day since the holidays began."

"No, I haven't. Only a few times."

"He's lying."

I felt that marvels were about to be taken away, leaving me a boy bereft. I could see the doubt in my mother's eyes.

She asked, "How do I know he's not being... interfered with?"

I had no idea what this meant, none at all.

"You may come inside, if you like." Margery stepped aside and welcomed them both.

"Aye, I think I should. But hang on a minute, whilst my mother catches up." Then she shouted off to the side. "Dotty, come on. Hurry up! Chloe, you go and help her."

I went outside and looked down the slope to see Grandma struggling with the pathway. Oh, this was a real family outing! Chloe went to her and helped her the rest of the way. Dotty was wearing a chequered headscarf and had put on her rouge and lipstick. She was huffing and puffing. "I'm here now, I'm here. Stop fussing!" We all traipsed into the hall. Coming towards us was Mr Holbrook. He had taken up his walking stick and was leaning on it, bent forwards as though he had a bad back. I had to admit, he looked a fair old codger in his brown shirt and his dark green demob-style trousers. Nipper danced about his feet.

"There you are, George," Margery said. "Come and meet Joe's family, the Sutters."

He shook hands with each in turn, leaning on the stick the whole time. "He's a grand lad, Mrs Sutter, a grand lad. The best of lads!" Then he winked at Grandma. "I see I am in the presence of a fellow beholder."

"That you are."

"And a fine one, at that."

"Don't start all that with me."

"I would not dare."

"I've been in the business since I was nine years old, and there's none better at beholding, not in Ormsley, nor the surrounding towns."

Mr Holbrook held up a hand in surrender. The dust swirled about them both, Sutter's Fancy included. It was a fine display. We went into the living room. I showed off the books on the shelves, saying, "Mr Holbrook is an author, Mum. He's teaching me how to write."

"Is that so?"

"I really think this will help me at the big school. I'll get much better marks, just watch me!" I was laying it on a bit thick, but what else could I do?

"And what kind of books does he write?"

"Science fiction. You know, flying saucers and men from Mars."

"I like romances, myself."

Mr Holbrook took a book from a shelf. "Here you are then, a present for you. *The Glare of the Sun*. I wrote a series of love stories under the name Eleanor Dale. Years ago it was, and no doubt they're a bit tame compared to nowadays, still, you might like it."

Mum looked at the lurid cover of the book with its handsome brooding lord of the manor and the trembling maid in his arms. She slipped it into her handbag.

"Mr Holbrook has written lots and lots of books," I told her. "All under different names."

"Why, is he ashamed of his own, or something?"

"Not at all, madam," he answered. "I do it purely for commercial reasons. Otherwise I would be competing with myself in the marketplace."

Mum nodded at this, sagely.

Margery came in carrying a tray of tea and biscuits. Mr Holbrook took charge. He paid special attention to Grandma, serving her himself. Koag floated between them like the long flowing veil of a wedding gown, its whiteness speckled with turquoise, gold and scarlet. What a sight! The specks of colour were flowing back and forth along the strands from one end to the other, from Grandma to the old man. I imagined they were speaking to each other in a language I could not yet understand, the Beholden Tongue. The adults sipped their tea and dunked their biscuits. Chloe walked around the room with curiosity in her eyes, taking it all in, gathering ammunition, probably, for further jokes at my expense. I stood in front of the bookshelves, wondering where this merging of my two lives would lead. I clung to the shelves, one on each side, tightening my fingers. I was worried that I might float away at any moment.

"This is all very strange, I must say." Everyone looked at my mother as she said this. "Yes, very strange. I'm not quite sure what to make of it."

Margery did her best, urging, "See it as an act of kindness on your son's part."

"Oh, I don't know... Chloe, what do you think?"

"Me?"

"Yes, you. You got us here."

She shrugged. But then said, "It looks all right, I guess. I mean, they're a bit weird, the both of them. But maybe they're harmless. I don't know. But if... if Joe's enjoying himself here..."

Sometimes my sister really did surprise me.

My mother nodded. "Yes, I suppose so." But doubt remained on her face.

I let go of the bookshelves and crossed the fingers of both hands behind my back as I waited for her to give the word that I could continue to visit Pike View. But the moment of acceptance was ruined by a sudden cry from Grandma. Her teacup fell to the floor, spilling its contents. For a moment there was silence. No one moved. Even Grandma was frozen to her seat. She was staring with wild eyes at some object in the room. What was it? I could not see. The dust fluttered madly, breaking the bond between her and Mr Holbrook. Then she pointed over to the piano and said in a voice that seemed far too deep for her, "There she is."

But there was nobody there. Not to my eyes, anyway.

My mother stood up and went over to her. "Dotty, are you quite all right?"

"There's a ghost."

I looked, expecting to see Henrietta Tudor. After all, Grandma had seen the young visitor once before, years ago. So, why not now? It made sense. But the room was empty of all spirits, beyond maybe a shimmer at the edge of my vision. But, of course, Dotty Sykes had far more witnessing power than I did. I saw that both Margery and Mr Holbrook were worried. He could probably see the ghost of dust as well. But he made no sign of having done so. In fact, he laughed at Grandma's suggestion. This only made the situation worse. She stood up and repeated her claim, this time with a tremor in her voice. "A ghost in the room. A little girl. It's her. Oh, she's moving now… She's walking over towards… towards Joe. She's reaching out–"

"Right, that's it!" my mother cried. "We're not staying in a haunted house. Chloe, Joe! Come on, this minute." She grabbed us both by the hands. "You too, Dotty. Now!"

Grandma obeyed. But she kept looking back over her shoulder as we left the living room. I could hear Margery saying, "Please, Mrs Sutter, wait!", but that was that. There was no stopping my mother once evil spirits were involved. She managed to get us all outside, bundling us through the doorway. Grandma was still muttering about the ghost.

"It was her. The girl with the handkerchief."

Mum had no way of knowing what this meant, but she didn't like it. She pulled me about by the shoulders, as though she could shake some sense into me. "You're not to go there ever again, do you hear me, Joseph Sutter? Do you?!"

I nodded, hoping this was sufficient. It wasn't.

"I want you to promise me. You won't go back there. Promise me."

"I promise, I promise!"

And with that, I broke away and ran further up the hill. I had to get free of her, of all of them, as quickly as I could. I needed to be alone, so they couldn't see the state I was in. But they already knew it. They knew it, everybody knew it. I ran and ran. I would have taken the ridge as far along as Oldham, as fast as Superman, or Quicksilver, from The Avengers team. But the stone tower drew me, as it always did. I sat down on the further bench, out of sight, and put my head down in my arms, pressing my sleeve hard against my eyes to bring on the darkness, the lovely darkness. I could smell the damp cotton of my shirt. I could hear Dad repeating over and over in my head, "You're the man of the house now, Joe, the man of the house, you have to be strong." I don't know for how long I stayed like that. I could feel a breeze through my hair, I could hear birdsong. Far away, the sound of a tractor's engine. Then I heard a voice, a real voice this time, calling my name. I looked up. It was Chloe. She sat down next to me.

IN THE SHADOW OF THE TOWER
A Radio Drama for Two Characters

The sound of a breeze blowing, and birdsong. A boy (11) and a girl (16) are talking.

JOE: Where's Mum, and Grandma?
CHLOE: They're waiting at the bus stop. Come on, shove over.

A peewit calls.

JOE: Why did you tell Mum, sis? Why?
CHLOE: Because I'm worried about you, silly.
JOE: There's nothing to be worried about.
CHLOE: That's not what Denny Portman says.
JOE: Denny? What's he got to do with it?
CHLOE: He told me about Pike View, didn't he, and how you were always hanging around the farmhouse.
JOE: He should have kept his mouth shut!
CHLOE: He said you weren't the same anymore.
JOE: Of course I'm the same, what else can I be but myself?
CHLOE: Snap! I wish I could be somebody else.
JOE: Yeah, me too.

A dog barks in the distance.

JOE: Denny's got a new friend now, anyway.
CHLOE: That girl, you mean?
JOE: Yeah.
CHLOE: Eileen Barlow. She's a toffee-nosed cow.

JOE: She's all right. She's not too bad.

CHLOE: You've got a soft spot for her, have you? I'll bet.

JOE: No! Of course not!

CHLOE: Joey's gone soft, Joey's gone soft–

JOE: Shut up! Girls are boring!

CHLOE: Just wait until next year, then you'll be feeling it.

JOE: Feeling what?

Chloe laughs, but will say no more.

CHLOE: So, that old codger, he's all right, is he? He's cool?

JOE: He's cool. I wish I could tell you why. But it's a secret.

CHLOE: You can tell me.

JOE: No I can't, and you know it. You'll blab to Mum, first thing.

CHLOE: Of course I won't–

JOE: Oh, look, there's a kestrel!

CHLOE: Where?

JOE: There, look! Can you hear his call? (Imitating) Quirrr-rr, quirrr-rr, kee kee kee.

CHLOE: (Laughing) Now you just sound daft.

JOE: Look at him dive. He's going in for the kill!

CHLOE: What's he caught?

JOE: A vole, probably, or a field mouse. Or a small puppy dog.

CHLOE: Oh, do shut up, a puppy, as if!

Joe whistles the tune of "King Midas in Reverse", a song by The Hollies. A flute picks up the melody, extending it.

CHLOE: I've got a secret of my own.

JOE: Really?

CHLOE: Sure. It's a good one, too, a special one.

JOE: What is it?

CHLOE: You first.

JOE: Okay. This tower here, Brendle Pike?

CHLOE: Aye. It gives me the shivers, actually.

JOE: That's because of what it really is, a doorway, like, to another world.

CHLOE. Get out!

JOE: Mr Holbrook explained it to me. It leads to a place called Brendleshire, where all the old kings and queens live, and the knights on horseback, and everybody else. And the dust blows here from Brendleshire, carrying all the old stories with it. It's true, sis!

CHLOE: Oh, you and your dust, you make me sick.

JOE: And if that doorway opens fully, well then... Two Worlds Collide!

CHLOE: You know what, I used to be dead jealous of you, I did. Because I wanted to see the dust, so much. I mean, we're brother and sister, I should be special, as well as you. But now, I don't care any more, because I have enough to see already, just with my everyday eyes, more than enough, hundreds of things!

JOE: I've told you my secret, now yours.

CHLOE: Brendleshire! You're off your head, you are.

JOE: Now yours, come on.

CHLOE: Okay, okay. Are you ready?

JOE: This had better be good.

CHLOE: Oh, it's good, It's juicy.

JOE: Well, come on then.

CHLOE: I've been to see Dad.

JOE: No you have not!

CHLOE: Yes I have, and a few times now, actually.

JOE: Where is he?

CHLOE: A really grotty place, in Clayton.

JOE: A house?

CHLOE: Nah, a bedsitter. Really smelly, as well.

JOE: What's he like?

CHLOE: Down in the dumps, scruffy, and his eyes were red.

JOE: Oh.

CHLOE: But he has a new job, on a building site.

JOE? And? What else? What did he say?

CHLOE: He wants to come home.

The ghostly flute melody slows down, is almost lost in the breeze and the birdsong.

CHLOE: He misses us, Joe, summat rotten. And Mum.

JOE: If you're making this up…
CHLOE: I'm not.
JOE: I'll knock your block off.
CHLOE: Oh aye? You and whose army?
JOE: My own army, that's who.
CHLOE: An army of dust. Ah, I'm scared. Oh, I'm shaking!
JOE: He wants to come home… he wants to come home…
CHLOE: But Mum won't let him, will she?
JOE: She will, she will!
CHLOE: Joe, I saw more than you did. I know what happened between them.
JOE: I'll make the house really special for him. I'll paint it with great billowing clouds of the most colourful dust I can find, red and blue and shining gold, just you watch me! I will, Chloe, I swear. I'll use my powers.
CHLOE: What powers? You haven't got any–
JOE: My super powers. Just like Mr Holbrook, he can move the dust, he can, I've seen him, just by using his hands, like this… I'll learn how to do it, too. (Shouting) Dust! Mighty Greot! You are under my control, do as I say. Turn our house into a palace!
CHLOE: Oh, Joe, please…
JOE: Paint it gold and green and blue and…

Joe's voice quietens, loses its power. He chokes back tears.

CHLOE: I'm sorry. For telling Mum on you.
JOE: Quirrr-rr, quirrr-rr, kee kee kee. Quirrr-rr, quirrr-rr, kee kee kee.
CHLOE: Come on, Joe. Let's go home. It's getting late.

We hear them walking away, talking together. The sounds of the birds and the breeze take over, as the ghostly flute describes the landscape through its melody.

We walked home through the first shades of dusk. All the way, I thought of Pike View and my time there, and how much I'd learned, and how much more I wanted to learn. But I would never break a promise made to Mum, not ever. At least, not a serious one. It was a rule.

The dust clouds followed us down the hill and along the lane, only leaving for other ventures when we turned into our street.

That night as I got ready for bed, I pulled the envelope out of my pocket. I hadn't forgotten about it, really, I knew it was there the whole time, I just didn't want to look at it. It worried me. Because whatever new task Mr Holbrook had set me, well, it was useless now, wasn't it? Because I would never be able to talk to him about it, not directly. Whatever I did from now on, I would have to do it off my own bat, without any help from Mr Holbrook, or from Margery. There was no other way. It made me think for some reason of my father, and what Chloe had said about him, how he wasn't coming home, even though he wanted to. Hidden things, secret things.

I sat down on the edge of my bed and opened the envelope. There were two pieces of paper this time. The first of them was a handwritten diagram of the *Scale of Invention*, as Mr Holbrook labelled it. It wasn't very neat, so I think he did this himself, rather than Margery, who would have naturally taken more time and effort with it. The diagram listed the four levels of invention, with the borderlines shown between them as solid lines, except for one, which was a dotted line. The second piece of paper detailed the task. Straight away I noticed Mr Holbrook had called this the *third* task. That was a good sign. He had acknowledged my own made-up second task, even if he did think it was rubbish. The numbering went on.

Task No.3
Cast a Magic Spell

My hands longed to pull Koag down from the ceiling and mould it into new fantastic shapes, but the dust remained where it was, clinging.

17

THE SCALE OF INVENTION

---

4. Genius

---

3. Crazy

---

2. Unique

....

1. Shared

18

A couple of days later, I met up with Denny and Eileen at the goods wagon and we walked on into the woods. I told them what had happened at Pike View. Denny was apologetic for telling Chloe all about the farmhouse visits: "Your sister forced it out of me."

"I know, I know."

"And I only said you were spying on a house up near the Pike, nothing else."

"I don't care any more." I was taking them to the part of the woods where I'd seen Sutter's Fancy hanging from the branches. "This is where it all started," I told them.

"What did?" Eileen asked.

"My adventures. I saw Koag hanging from a tree, right here, this branch. Two different strands all squirming together."

"You know what that means, don't you?" Denny said with a grin. "They're having it off!"

Eileen slapped him on the arm. It was a good hard slap, too. "Shut up. You don't know what you're talking about."

"I know. I know lots, me."

"No, you don't."

I interrupted their game. "One of the strands was my favourite ever. I called it Sutter's Fancy."

Denny laughed. "Is that the best name you could come up with?"

"Sure, it's stupid. But the thing is, I followed this one strand, silver and pink, it was, I followed it all the way to Pike View. And I went inside."

Eileen was sitting on a stump. Denny was using his penknife to carve his initials into the bark of a tree. I wondered if one day he'd add an *E.B.* under his *D.P.*?

But I went on: "That's how I found the man in the mask. He's called Mr Holbrook. He's a writer, a famous one. He's written hundreds of books, and he wants to make me into a writer as well. He's taught me loads of things, amazing things."

"Like what?"

I listed some of the lessons I had learned over the summer. I'm not sure how much either of them followed me, but I needed to tell them everything, as much as I could, anyway. I jumped to the most recent homework task.

"I have to cast a magic spell."

"What kind of spell?" asked Denny. "Oh, I know! You could turn your sister into a newt, that's a good one."

Eileen suggested, "How about a love potion?"

They had this habit, the two of them, of playing tag with each other's phrases.

"Nah, that's soppy," Denny answered. "How about putting the Evil Eye on someone?"

"Oh, yes. On your brother, Michael."

"On Micky, why?"

"He's a letch."

"No, he is not."

"Is! All the big girls talk about him."

"Who, for instance?"

"Sally Wayne's sister, for instance."

"Sally Wayne's sister? She'll snog anyone, she will."

"Aye, true enough. Once she snogged Corporal Boot."

Corporal Boot was the made-up name people gave to the bronze statue of the soldier on top of the war memorial. Eileen told us the story. One evening Sally Wayne's sister had climbed up the memorial with the help of her friends. She was drunk, of course, and she kept her mouth pressed against the metal lips for at least a minute and a half, before a policeman ordered her down. Then she tried to snog the policeman. Eileen mimed all this action for us, climbing onto the tree stump, squirming about and pouting her lips. We all fell about laughing, knocking into each other. I slipped and fell on my arse which set them off laughing some more. When we had finally quietened down, I remained as I was, lying on the ground with the weeds and moss at my back, the overarching branches above me, and then the sky, and Koag floating about in swathes of dandelion yellow and a scarlet as bright as the red of Grandma's hair just after she'd dyed it. Little birds were drowsily singing, lulling me, and so my eyes closed. The woods murmured with a hundred different sounds, but all of them quiet, or soft; soft and quiet went the clock of the woods, tick, tock, tick, tock.

My two friends were nearby, both also lying down.

In a voice as drowsy as the day, I said, "These woods are really called Brendle Woods." Neither of them responded, but I knew they were listening. "Mr Holbrook told me that. On certain days you can hear the Roundheads and Cavaliers fighting each other."

I heard Eileen sigh. It made me continue.

"Brendleshire is where all the stories of these fields and woods and villages are gathered, the old stories. They flow along the trails of dust."

My voice was a hush. I felt a daze taking me over. No one spoke for a while. Perhaps we were all thinking of magic spells and distant times, distant times just a few feet away, beyond the trees. One single letter away.

World becomes word becomes world becomes word becomes...

If I could only find a pathway.

Beneath me, not too far down, little Sutter's Fancy was slithering and squirming in the earth, a baby of the dust. One day soon perhaps, it would be strong enough to break free and take to the air, spreading its new colours wherever it liked.

Denny broke the silence. "I don't know why you want to be a writer, anyway, Joe. Just sitting in a chair all day. Boring."

"What are you going to do, then?" Eileen asked him, "When you leave school?"

He answered immediately. "Formula One racing driver."

"Oh yeah, that sounds brilliant."

"What about you?" he asked. "International fashion model?"

"Aye, I thought I might. Or else a pop singer."

She didn't mention *magician's assistant*, so perhaps it was for the best that I wasn't able to let her read *Helme's Threshold in Reverse*. I got to my feet, saying, "I don't even know how to cast a spell, never mind choose a spell to cast." I looked to them both. "It's like a puzzle, a jigsaw puzzle as big as the world."

Eileen cried out her joy: "Sutter blows up his own brain with dynamite!"

I added a suitable sound effect.

KARUMMPPPPPH!

We walked back through the trees until we reached the dirt track. We climbed the first gate, and then the second. Denny told jokes, Eileen sang songs. I fell back a little. They walked on ahead, and I saw her hand brush at his. He didn't flinch away, as I thought he might, no, he took hold of it. Even a few weeks ago he would never have done such a thing.

I was jealous.

Then I was glad for them both.

Then I was jealous again.

Then the child still clinging on inside told me it was, "Soppy!"

If I had the mask with me, I would have put it to my face, and the truth would be spelt out: the story of that moment in a series of words, one after another, joining us together.

"Koag," I whispered. "Koag, speak to me. Tell me what to do."

Silence, and silence. A bird twittering in the branches.

And so the days passed. We thought the holidays would last forever, until, suddenly, they were almost over. Such is the way. In little over a week's time I would arrive at the gates of Fairfields Secondary Modern, donned in uniform and cap, carrying my briefcase. I needed to finish the third task before then. I made notes about possible magical spells of my own invention. I didn't get very far before the conjuring came to an end. It wasn't easy, creating an entirely new magical effect. Ormsley Vale was as down-to-earth as any place could be. I went back over my diary and exercise books, summing up everything Mr Holbrook had told me.

Goal number one: Astonish other people.

Goal number two: Solve the (beautiful) puzzle of yourself.

Rule of Creation number one: Everything becomes really, really *boring, unless you work, work, WORK!*

Most of all, I studied the Scale of Invention. All the lines on the diagram were solid except for the one between *Shared Ideas* and *Unique Ideas*. Mr Holbrook had done that on purpose, but why? It was not a solid border. It was more like the borderline between Ashton-Under-Lyne and Ormsley Vale (just a sign at the side of the road), rather than that between East and West Germany, the Iron Curtain and Checkpoint Charlie. If only I could go up to Pike View and ask for further advice. But such an action was cut off from me. I stuck the diagram to my bedroom wall with a drawing pin. I stared and stared at it until the lines and the words started to blur in my sight.

Dotted line, dotted line, what on earth can you mean?

I made a little song of it, a tune of my own.

Dotted line, dotted line, will you ever be complete?

Will you ever be a solid line, or will you always be a…

But I couldn't even think of a rhyme.

I thought of sending a letter through the post: *Dear Mr Holbrook, would you kindly explain the dotted line, thank you. Yours sincerely, Joseph Sutter.* But then I would just be waiting for a reply that might never arrive. One thing I knew for certain, I had to finish *Task No.3.* It wasn't just about the summer holidays coming to end; there was also Mr Holbrook's illness to consider. It would be so good if I could just deliver my homework to him, before anything terrible happened. Lying in bed I tried to picture in my mind the ingredients of a spell: tongue of dog, a rose thorn tipped with blood, the silvery stuff coated on the back of mirrors. They all faded away as I fell asleep.

In the morning I was lying on my side, so the first thing I saw was the Scale of Invention. My mind was set racing. That very special word, *invention*, caught my eye. I thought back to Denny and me listening to The Mothers of Invention's album, *We're Only In It For the Money*. The Mothers of *Invention*. And that album had directly led to the invention of the Anti-Boredom Machine. There had to be a connection. If only I had my own copy of the album, I would play it now, and listen out for new inspiration. Instead, I tried my best to remember the music. The way the songs were tuneful one moment, and then suddenly really weird and noisy, and then tuneful again, then weird, then tuneful, and this was happening all the time, from one moment to the next. But so what? Think, Joe! The tuneful bits were an example of shared ideas, because we all love a good sing-along. And the weird noisy bits, they were unique ideas, belonging to The Mothers of Invention only: nobody else but that particular group could make those noises. So maybe that was the purpose of the dotted line, that constant give and take between *shared* and *unique*. That's what you had to do: to constantly cross over that borderline, back and forth. I thought of Jimi Hendrix, who could play wild shrieking feedback one second (unique), and then dip down into a blues lick (shared). The Beatles had that same superpower: their music moved back and forth across that dotted borderline, surprising us one moment, making us dance and sing the next. Or, to take another example: Spider-Man. In real life he's mild-mannered Peter Parker, high school pupil, not a popular kid, he gets bullied, he's a bit of a swot. All of these were shared ideas; I'd seen them acted out in loads of films and television shows. But then one day Peter is bitten by a radioactive spider, and then *TINGLE!* suddenly he's got these really cool super spider-powers. Unique! And so the game goes on. Shared ideas, unique ideas. And before I knew it, I was thinking back to a special moment from a few months ago.

NOWHERE BOYS
A Superhero Comic, Issue No.1

PANEL 1: *Seen from above, a record player, with an album spinning on the turntable. We are close enough to be able to read the label: Rubber Soul by The Beatles. Little notes of music float around the record player. Within these crotchets and quavers, we see the first two lines of the lyrics to the song "Nowhere Man".*

PANEL 2: *From higher up. The record player and a patch of white shag-pile carpet. Speech bubbles emerge from the grass, from two different positions.*

JOE: What is a Nowhere Man, do you think?
DENNY: A man who isn't there.
JOE: He's invisible?
DENNY: No. You can see him, but he's never there when you look.

PANEL 3: A little closer on the carpet. The speech bubbles continue.

DENNY: He sounds like a superhero, don't you think?
JOE: Who does?
DENNY: Like Spider-Man, Superman, Batman.
JOE: Nowhere Man?

PANEL 4: A boy sits up, appearing out of the long white carpet grass. This is DENNY.

DENNY: He's never there. Joe, Joe, listen to me!
JOE: What?
DENNY: Nowhere Man! He's never there!

PANEL 5: JOE sits up, parting the strands of grass. He stares in wonder at his friend.

DENNY: He can't be seen. Only... only... only heard!
JOE: You mean, like, with sound effects?
DENNY: Yes!

PANEL 6: The two boys have disappeared beneath a cloud of sound effect bubbles: KERPOW! KAZAM! OOF! PING, PING! THWIK! SIZZLE! BLAM!

That was the moment, when something unique arises out of a set of shared ideas. But what good was it, when I didn't even have a shared idea, never mind a unique one? It was a Friday morning. After breakfast I set off for the goods yard. The wagon was empty, no sign of my friends, but I really didn't mind. Everything sparkled in the sunlight. Streaks and strands of dust decorated the trees and fences, it floated in the air. Even the crow that flew past me was dustified, its black wings glinting with so many colours. I scrambled up Slew Hill, reaching the summit in less than a minute, easy! Here I sat down and surveyed my kingdom, the railway tracks, the rising chimneys of the factories, the canal, the line of the woods. And visible over the treetops, Brendle Pike, the border of my realm, a marker post. I lay on my back and closed my eyes. I chewed on a blade of grass. Dapples of dust tickled my face. I was happy to have worked out the Secret of the Dotted Line, at least as far as I could, but the third task remained. I drifted off halfway into a doze. For some reason the opening lines of *Dreams of Brendle* popped into my head.

Petra was a night-talker. She spoke with owls and bats. She whispered to the black-petalled flowers that blossomed in darkness. Such was her role in the town, to bring news of the nighttime world back into the daylight hours.

The dotted line between shared ideas and unique ideas started to move in my mind, to shape itself into the pattern of a woman. It became the dotted outline of Invisible Girl from The Fantastic Four. Nowhere Boy meets Invisible Girl. What a superhero team-up that would be! I dwelled on the idea for a moment or two. *I must tell Denny, I must tell Denny.* But the dotted line was on the move again, this time taking on the shape of Henrietta Tudor.

Sunlight crept over my skin. I felt the grass between my fingers.

Invisible Girl equals Henrietta Tudor.

That seemed important for my spell. Yes, because…

Something made me sit up.

Not a noise, not a shadow crossing me. But a shiver in my body, head to toes. I looked down over the goods yard, expecting to see Denny or Eileen, but the place was deserted. Standing up, I focussed my gaze, shielding my eyes from the sun with my hand. Yes, there was something else, a disturbance in the dust patterns. It was very subtle, a slight fluttering that moved from the goods wagon across towards the fence, before turning back and coming towards the hill. At a certain precise distance from me, this shape crossed Helme's Threshold, and there she was.

Henrietta.

She was only half-visible, but her blue gown with the white ruffles was very distinctive. Some other figures may have been present, further from my sight, some of her friends perhaps, but they had no more substance than a heat haze in a dream and they quickly disappeared, leaving Henrietta alone. She came to a halt at the foot of Slew Hill and looked up at me. Was she going to walk up the slope, to join me? No. She turned and moved away, towards the entrance of the yard. All my thoughts of magical spells flew away as I clambered down the hill and followed her, keeping a fair distance between us. She more glided than walked. I tried to copy her style, but my feet were too heavy and my sandals kicked at the gravel. She took the canal path, only stopping when she reached the wasteground alongside Bradshaw's Mill. Here was Monty's caravan, shimmering in the sunlight like some fantastical carriage from a fairy tale. But it was real, as real as Henrietta was real, in exactly the same way. I knew this for sure, as I watched her approach the doorway. She didn't need to step up onto the wooden boxes, like flesh and blood people did; she simply raised herself up in the air, hovering at exactly the right height so that her dust-made body merged with that of the dust-made vehicle. She was now an occupant of the caravan. Her form merged with that of the shelving units, the fold-down bed, the pots and pans in the sink. It was incredible! I had the feeling that she had led me here, but for what purpose?

I made my approach, slowly, one step at a time. And this time she remained fully formed, alive to my eyes. Reaching the edge of the caravan, I no longer hesitated, but stepped quickly up onto the first of the boxes and entered through the door that was not a door. I stood some two feet away from her. I wished Grandma could have been here to see this. But I was alone, alone with the ghost. Henrietta's face formed and reformed as Koag did its best to keep her in place. The caravan gleamed and glistened around us, this palace of particles.

She smiled at me. Her eyes and mouth were very dark, compared to her skin, but I don't know how much this contrast was an outcome of the dust's processes, or whether they represented her real colourings. The ruffles of her dress were made of delicate lace. Her lips parted, as though to speak. But she could not speak. We stood in silence. Dust trembled around her, as it passed from her body into the objects of the caravan; she was giving them solidity, each thing she touched in turn. Using this method she managed to open one of the cupboards, at head-height. The door kept its fragile nebulous shape as it swung outwards. Such an act hardly seemed possible. I moved forwards, stepping onto another of the boxes, to see what was revealed. There were objects inside the cupboard, arranged on three shelves, personal items that had once belonged to

Alfred Montgomery. I saw a folded razor, a tin cup, a slim
softback book, a salt and pepper set. Each item was delicately
modelled. She took out the book and showed it to me. The
cover shimmered, but I saw enough to know it was a diary for
1964, the year Monty had walked away from Ormsley Vale.
Henrietta opened the diary. She actually opened the book, a
book made of dust and dust alone, and the pages stayed intact
as her fingers flipped through them, searching. She found the
page she was looking for, the final written entry, which she
tore out. I could hardly believe it. She tore out a page of dust
from a book of dust and the page was whole in her hand of
dust, even as it shivered in its delicate state.

I looked at her. She stared back, her eyes the most solid part
of her entire body. She had made them so, using her willpower
to mould them into the exact shape, colour and texture. If only
she could mould her whole body to that same degree, then she
would be real, as real as the handkerchief she had made for my
grandmother. But as yet she lacked that final strength.

Henrietta reached out for me.

I brought my hand up to meet hers.

But we could not touch, not properly.

Her fingers broke apart and then reformed.

She drew back. I was now holding the page from the diary.
It was still intact. It did not drift apart or crumble, although I
felt it might at any moment. There was an entry written there,
perhaps Monty's final message before he left, but I could barely
make out the words, they shifted about too much. It was real,
not real, real, not real. Dust from the girl's fingers joined with
that of the page, making it slightly firmer. After one more
look at me from those darkling eyes, she started to fade away,
merging with the furniture and fittings of the caravan. Here
was a place for her to rest, a temporary home on the borderline
of Lancashire and Brendleshire. Perhaps Monty had left his
caravan here for that very purpose? He had to leave, so this
new occupant might take up residence. Yet this time when she
vanished a few strands of her remained behind, in the diary
page she had given me. But would it survive, away from the
caravan? There was only one way to find out.

I stepped down carefully from the wooden box, to solid ground.

The page trembled, almost drifted apart.

I stopped, hesitated.

The page came back together, re-forming itself.

I walked on, further along the path.

The page stayed with me.

I ran.

The page remained in one piece in my hand, no matter what I did. And I had so much to do, so much to see. I whooped in celebration. Let the Many Eyes of Koag see me now! Watch me! Clouds of dust streamed alongside, air-force blue, mint green, dappled gold, cloaking the pathways ahead and behind, departing from me only as I entered Stoneybrook Estate. Nothing could stop me, nothing and no one, not until I reached home and I fell at last onto my bed with a great sigh of delight. Only then did I open my fingers, releasing the diary page. It floated above my head, just hovering there, still intact. It was mine to treasure. And not just the page, no, not at all; for mixed in with it were tiny particles of Henrietta Tudor herself, ghostly girl. I sat up cross-legged to examine my gift in detail. In colour the page was pink and lilac and orange, all mixed together, with specks of emerald sprinkled in. A very nice pattern. The lettering, originally handwritten by Monty himself, was a deep purple. It wasn't easy to read, because of the constant shimmer of the thing. But I managed it.

> I hear her at the window. She whispers. I see her against the factory wall, a shadow moving, a shadow of dust. She draws near in the night, as I sleep. I know she is out there in the dark, in the dust, waiting, waiting. How can I help her?

That last sentence, that offer of help, chimed with my idea that Monty had left on purpose, that a ghost might use his caravan as a home.

The next entry was much shorter, a single sentence.

> To see a world in a grain of dust.

That was all. These were the last words he had written down, before leaving Ormsley. I reread the two entries, looking for clues. Maybe the very act of reading made it more fragile, I don't know, but the dusty paper became even dustier, and then dustier still, until it was only dust, and nothing but. The words disappeared. The dust remained, but not in the shape of a page, just as a tiny cloud floating above my bed. Working quickly, I wrote down the words I had seen into my exercise book. Once I had copied everything as best I could, I read the lines a few times over. *I know she is out there in the dark, in the dust, waiting, waiting.* Grandma had said something similar at the Living Eyes session I had witnessed. There was definitely something weird going on. The witnesses and beholders of the area were sensing the girl's presence, and had been doing so for years and years. Oh, she must have such a need to be alive, to walk among us fully formed. I lay on the bed. The Bradley sisters from number 14 were playing a game of hopscotch in the back alley. Through my open window, I could hear their jumping feet and the chanting of the rhyme, their laughter.

To see a world in a grain of dust...

These days, I know this as the opening line of one of William Blake's most famous poems; to my younger self it was simply a call to adventure, an instruction manual for a game or a wizard's device of some kind. The little patch of dust floated above my chest. Pink, lilac, daubs of orange, glints of green. I called them Henrietta's colours. It was the only dust in the room. I felt sure it was waiting for me, that it wanted me to act. Slowly I raised my hand, moving it towards the right. The dust moved with me, following the movement of my fingers. I waved my hand in the opposite direction. The dust followed, wherever my finger pointed. Left to right, right to left, zigzagging. Around and around in a circle. I was holding my breath. Only my hand moved, this way and that, and the dust copied me, every single time. *Oh, sweet Koag!* I sprang up and ran downstairs, full pelt, two steps at a time, jumping the last three in a single bound, shouting out, "Grandma, come see. Grandma, look!" I could hear Dotty in the parlour; she was singing one of the songs of her youth. There was a startled look on her face as I burst into the room.

"What is it, Joe? For goodness sake."

"Look, Grandma, look. See!"

The magical dust had followed me down the stairs, flying alongside. I showed off my new skill, making it dance and jiggle about, and Grandma clapped her hands and laughed with delight. I did the same, dancing with her. Coco the budgie chirped along.

"Grandma? Will you let me see into the dust now? You promised I could share the Living Eyes with you, when I was ready. I think I'm ready now, I really do. I am ready!"

"Well, well, I think you are."

She told me to close the curtains. Then we sat at the table opposite to each other. The handful of dust floated between us. I thought it best to tell the truth. So I said, "This is the dust of Henrietta Tudor, just like you saw at Mr Holbrook's house. She shared this with me."

"It was a gift?"

"Yes."

"Good, very good. Yes, I've been expecting her." She caught a little of the dust on a fingertip and watched it sparkle.

"What will I see, Grandma?"

"Well that depends. It's a bit like a dream."

"A dream of what?"

"It's different for every person. And because you're a witness, it might well be special."

"Special. That's good, isn't it?"

"Yes, let's hope so. But the thing is…"

"What?"

"Greot will tell you all you need to know, but you might not recognise it as such." She sighed to herself, and then added, "Remember this: Greot speaks the truth."

I had so many questions to ask, but she shushed me into silence. She grabbed the dust in one hand. I watched with great interest as her closed fist moved back and forth across the tabletop, each sweep releasing a few more of the grains. I was nervous now. What would be shown to me? Coco fell silent: small mercies. Grandma moaned. Her hands and upper body trembled. I had seen her do this at other viewings, and had always thought it a nice show for the customers. But now I believed utterly in what she was doing, and I watched with fascination as her face took on its most strained aspect, her neck stretching, her wrinkles deep at brow and cheek. This was the moment of passion. The dust rose up and fell again, and rose once more, guided not by my grandmother, I was sure, but by some other, further, darker power she had conjured into being.

Then her face calmed itself.

The dust floated in place, now glowing brightly.

"To see not the world, but something beyond the world, that is our purpose."

I found myself mouthing the words with her: I knew them so well.

"Something beyond this petty world. Something that cannot be seen otherwise, only with the help of Greot." She took a breath. "To see into the darkness that surrounds our pitiful ring of senses, the darkness encircling."

She slammed both her hands down onto the tabletop. *BANG!* It made me jump in my chair.

"Open your eyes, my child, wider, wider!"

I watched as she pursed her lips and blew at the dust with as much puff as she could manage. I felt her warm breath on my face, and a little of her spittle. But I didn't mind. My eyes were wide open, as wide as could be, to receive the gift.

"BEHOLD!" Her voice called out to me. "Do you see?"

My eyes closed, to keep the dust inside. And I found myself copying May Harper's response, exactly: "I see, I *do* see."

19

Ormsley high street came into view. It was night. The moon was low and hugely round and yellow and spattered at the edges where the storms raged across the surface. I walked alone, in the deathly silence. Only the faint shuffling and rustling of the dust grains could be heard as they formed this townscape around me, one building at a time – butcher, baker, post office, bank, clothing store – each edifice crumbling behind me as the next one appeared. Koag breathed this place into life. I walked on until I saw the library. My destination, apparently. Everything about it looked identical to the real building except for the sign above the door: *BRENDLE PUBLIC LIBRARY*. Inside were the usual shelving units and tables and the central checkout counter, all in their allotted places. I felt at home, and yet displaced, slightly adrift. The place was deserted, no customers, no one picking books off the shelves, no Miss Stockton or the other librarians. Only myself.

Mindful of the rule of silence I whispered, "Grandma? Can you hear me, can you see me?" There was no reply. I tried again, louder this time. "Grandma, where are you?" In a panic I went back to the door, only to see that now a dust storm raged violently on the high street, speeding by at so many miles per hour. It battered against the glass like hailstones. If I went outside I would be torn to shreds. I was trapped here and would have to sleep in a den under one of the tables, building a wall of books around me for protection in the night. I would read and read and read, seeking a map of escape: a new Robinson Crusoe, alone on his island. I explored my world, walking the aisles, choosing books at random. The words were clear and easy to read, yet I could never read the same sentence twice. Always, some other words took over, often written in an old-fashioned manner with long sentences and flowery speech, and at other times written in a more up-to-date fashion, but the next second after that, written in a futuristic language of tiny half-words and no punctuation. However, as far as I could tell, the stories were always the same, no matter the words used. Every single book I looked at had this same effect. History had seeped into the stories, ever-changing, backwards and forwards, and the pages and the ink rushed to keep up. In the science fiction section I found a copy of *Dreams of Brendle*. What would I find within? Would the story be ruined for me? Yet the opening lines were fixed in place, without any disturbance from other time periods. Perhaps this was the only book in the library that stayed as it was, no matter the date on Koag's clock. I turned to the last page and read again those final words. *Here was her daughter, long lost in time, but nonetheless a story still being told. The moon of Brendle looked down as the old woman stepped forwards, calling out the girl's name.* I carried on the story past the book's limit, this time saying the girl's name out loud.

"Henrietta, Henrietta."

I was suddenly alert. An answering sound had broken the silence, a single hard tapping noise. I listened at full attention. It came again, a few more times, the working of a mechanism, one tap after another at irregular intervals. *Tap, tap. Tap. Tap, tap, tap.* What could it be? I crept along the aisle like an army commando on a dangerous night raid. I peeked around the corner. On a table to one side of the main seating area were a pair of typewriters for the public to use. A man was sitting hunched over one of these machines. This was the source of the tapping noise, as the keys were pressed at a slow, almost painful, rate. I moved out from the aisle and crossed the open space, all the time keeping myself on high alert. The man's shoulders moved slightly as each key sounded. It only took a moment for me to work out who he was, thanks to his costume, with its purple cape and the ruby-red mask that covered his head and the top half of his face. My heart leapt for joy. It was Spellcaster. In everyday life Brian Chadwick was a quiet, unassuming junior-school teacher, but, when he donned his Spellcaster costume he became the Warlock of Ormsley Vale, Master Magician, the World's Greatest Sorcerer. His chin was peppered with stubble, which was unusual; I had always drawn him cleanly shaved. Also, his costume was dirty and torn, and his cape had a ragged edge to it and was splattered across the emblem of a golden sun with what looked very like pigeon poo. Poor Spellcaster, he was not looking his best. It was peculiar to see him there in his colourful costume, sitting at a library table, typing away, rather than standing atop Ormsley Town Hall conducting a ritual to send the Martian invaders back to their home planet. His magical amulet laid on the tabletop, alongside his wand and his bag of tricks. Perhaps he had been fighting an evil supervillain and was now writing up his exploits for the sake of history. That made sense, given the purpose of this library. But he was not satisfied with this work and he pulled the sheet of paper from the typewriter, screwed it up into a ball and threw it to the floor, where it joined countless other such cast-offs, hundreds of them. How long had he been sitting here, working away? I had not heard him until a few minutes ago, but that was easy to explain: I had in some way passed through his Forcefield of Deathly Silence, one of the spells Denny and I had made up for him. I watched as he rolled another sheet into the machine. He had not yet looked at me. His fingers went back to work, seeking out each letter in turn, each taking a while. *Tap, tap, tap.* The keys were depressed, black letters were printed. But I could not see what he was writing, not from this angle. I let him work on for a moment or so, then I spoke up.

"Spellcaster, sir? Is it really you?"

His shoulders trembled, ruffling his cape slightly. Beyond that he made no recognition of my presence. I tried again this time using his real name.

"Mr Chadwick? Brian Chadwick?"

Still no response. His fingers worked the keys.

"My name is Joe Sutter. You don't know me, but I... That is, my friend Denny Portman and myself... We invented you."

Nothing. *Tap, tap, tap.* But then he stopped, his hands frozen above the keyboard. Something had troubled him. I was suddenly cold, and I shivered from it. The idea of being trapped in a library in the middle of a desert of dust, a whole planet of dust, was frightening. I hadn't thought about this, not until now. Spellcaster's hands were poised for further action, should the urge come to him. I dared to sneak a look at the page he was working on, a few lines only. It came to me that Spellcaster might be casting a spell, that is, writing down an incantation of some kind and that my third task was now within my grasp, here, in the library of Brendle. After all, he had turned up, and not Zigzag Woman, nor Nowhere Man, nor Kid Koag, or any of the other Denny-and-Joe heroes.

Spellcaster reached up to loosen his mask. He pulled it over his head.

I had never drawn him without a mask.

He had my father's face.

Which meant that Spellcaster's secret identity was not Brian Chadwick, but James Sutter. This revelation did not disturb me. I simply accepted it. But my need to see the words typed on the sheet was now very real, and very intense.

But my reading was interrupted by a *shushing* sound, and when I looked round I saw that the shelving units and the tables and chairs were all crumbling away, the walls also, and the ceiling, and the books, every single last one of them, crumbling, crumbling into dust. *Shush, shush, shush*. That was the noise the dust made as it drifted apart, as though the invisible Miss Stockton was telling us to be quiet. The whole building was being drawn back into the dust clouds of this world. Soon only myself and Spellcaster remained in our little circle of solid things. Oh, this was bad. This was very bad! He made a few more stabs at the keys. I cried out, but could do nothing to help; the mighty superhero was disappearing, grain by grain. The table was crumbling away. The process took me over as well; my body started to disintegrate until I was a torso, a head, and a pair of arms only. In my last moments I pulled the sheet free from a typewriter that was no longer there. I had just enough time to read the few typed lines, and to do my best to memorise them, before the paper and my hands and my eyes and the words crumbled away into nothing, nothing at all, and all that remained then was the dust, the endless dreamless dust.

20

I came to with a bump, landing at the parlour table as though dropped from a height. In truth, I had not moved at all. I rubbed at my eyes to get the grit out of them. The mantle clock ticked on. Coco tapped at his bell. Grandma was staring at me intently from across the table. "What did you see, Joe?" she asked. "Where did Henrietta take you?" Her voice was distant.

"Henrietta?" I was confused for a moment, and then I remembered the gift of dust. "How long was I away for?"

"I don't know, half a minute, perhaps."

"Half a..." I shook my head to clear it. "But it was night. The moon was out."

Grandma was insistent: "Where did she take you?"

In fear of the vision slipping away, I made it real by speaking of it. "Brendle Library."

"Where?"

"Oh, it's just like Ormsley Library, but a bit weirder. Every book is a history book, even when it's telling a made-up story. And it all crumbled away. And Spellcaster was there!"

"Who?"

"A superhero. He was typing a letter. No, not a letter, but a... a... a spell!" I sprang up from my chair, almost tipping it over. "That was it. A magic spell."

"Joe, where are you going? Slow down."

"Sorry, Grandma, things to do."

In my room I pulled out my exercise book and wrote down the words I had read in that last moment. I saw them perfectly, each one etched in my memory.

In the dust, in the dark, words are waiting. In the dark of the dust, words are waiting, waiting. In the dusty darkness, dark dusty words are waiting.

Twenty-eight words, five commas, three full stops, no exclamation marks. I had heard them in a slightly different form, spoken by Dotty Sykes during the Living Eyes session, when she had cried out, "In the dark of the dust, she is waiting", *she* being Henrietta Tudor. Grandma had also said, "In the dust, in the dark". On top of which, Monty had jotted down something similar in his caravan diary. I consulted my notes to find the exact phrase he had used. *I know she is out there in the dark, in the dust, waiting, waiting.* Most probably, I had merely remembered these words, and then given them to Spellcaster to type. Dreams are like that, filled with bits and bats of everyday life mixed in with strange happenings. But these words were originally part of Koag, part of the world of the dust, and they had to be spoken, and spoken again and again, whether through my grandmother, or through Alfred Montgomery, or through Spellcaster, a made-up character. They formed a spell, but for what purpose? They were a set of instructions only Mr Holbrook would understand. *In the dark of the dust, words are waiting.* He would know how to draw the words out of the dark, surely, if anybody could. I would post them in a letter to him; I don't think that was breaking my promise to my mother, about not seeing him anymore. And so my third task would be completed. Was it enough? No, no, and no! I needed to make the message unique in some way. But no matter how much thought I put into it, I could not think of a way of crossing that dotted line between *shared* and *unique*. But one thing I could do was type the sentences out properly, as I had witnessed them. I set out for the library. I would use the actual typewriter I had seen in the vision. My fingers would copy exactly the movements of Spellcaster. Miss Stockton would be able to teach me how to type, at least enough for me to complete the task. After all, it was only twenty-eight words, not an entire novel. But along the way I started to think about the First Goal: I had to astonish Mr Holbrook. And that got me thinking about the First Rule: I had to fight against blandness and boredom. Oh, it was impossible. So many rules and laws and goals!

I stopped on the high street to look along its length into the distance where Brendle Pike was seen at the end of the vale, where the land rose towards the Pennines. The town was designed and laid out, Grandma once told me, to give precisely this view. Smoke from Bradshaw's Mill smeared the sky, fighting with strands of Koag for supremacy. A very odd feeling came over me. I could not walk any further. The library was wrong, the wrong place to go, but I could not think why. Shoppers came and went around me. A sudden cloud of dust took off at speed across the sky. That's right, Koag, you fly away on your holidays, leaving me here without a clue. I went to my favourite seat near the memorial, across from the Weaver's Arms. The pub had opened for its afternoon trade and a group of drinkers were sitting outside. Their laughter drifted by. I took out the piece of paper I had brought with me, containing the words of the spell.

In the dust, in the dark.
Words are waiting.

A nice little fantasy took me over, that by performing this spell I would cure Mr Holbrook of his illness. But no matter how I stared at them, or thought about them, or rearranged them in my mind, the words remained as they were. Even picturing myself in the costume of Spellcaster did no good, except to make me laugh at myself, with my cape draped over the back of a park bench, and the mask much too big for my young face. A bird flew from one branch to another, a dazzling array of colours, so weird-looking I would never find it in my *Observer's Book of British Birds*. As it landed I saw it for its true self, a shape made by Koag. A couple of hedge sparrows, male and female, were disturbed by the multicoloured bird of dust. And a strange thought came to me then: the magic spell needs to be more like the Koag bird than a common sparrow. But what did that mean? Any attempts at working out this riddle were cast aside by a shout from the public house, and a cry of alarm, a glass smashing on the tarmac. I looked over. A fight had broken out, two drunks at their play. But one of them had it worse than the other. He almost fell over, knocking into a table, hanging on like a man adrift in a storm. I stood up. That was all I managed.

It was my father.

The fight was quickly over, more of a scuffle really. The pub's customers were laughing at the drunkard as he clung onto some invisible rope, pulling himself along from one table to the next. He was causing trouble, arguing in public with strangers, and I don't know what else. My father rallied and went back for more punishment, shouting. His words were slurred. I ran to him and tried to pull him away. He struggled with me, a grown man with a boy.

"Dad! Dad, stop it. Please!"

He looked at me as though I too were a stranger, not his son. His eyes had a glazed look, and he was sweating badly. I steered him away from the tables, over to the bench, but he was too heavy, like a bag of semi-set concrete. He collapsed to the grass in a sprawl of limbs. I looked over to the pub and then to the other benches, where people were staring at us, passing comments, laughing. It was so embarrassing, but what else could I do? He looked up at me.

"Son? Is that you, Joe?"

"Yes, Dad, it's me."

"Playing hooky, eh? You should be in school."

"It's the holidays." How could he not know that? "Get up, Dad, please."

He made an effort to do so, and I did my best to help him. I levered him over to the bench, where we both sat down. He gazed at the war memorial, his eyes seeking focus. He raised a hand to wipe at the sweat on his brow and cheeks. His face was shiny and red, and his hair needed a good trim. He was unshaven. What a mess he was, nothing at all like the man I used to watch leaving for work in the mornings, so proud in his smart and freshly-ironed overalls, *Daily Mirror* tucked under his arm. This man had taught me how to take a penalty kick, how to play gin rummy, how to use a claw-hammer, how to pick up a worm without squirming. Even as I thought of all this, a clump of Koag rose from the nearest tree and came towards us. The dust hovered about my father's head. I watched in awful fascination. Koag clung to his face, taking on his features, his eyes, nose and cheeks. Koag masked him, in colours of dark blue and streaks of gold and little dots of white. He looked like a strange otherworldly animal sitting there on the bench next to me, an animal wearing a crumpled shirt and a half-knotted tie. He turned to look at me, but this time I could not see him, only the mask of dust. "Look at you, all big and strong," he said in his raspy voice. "You've grown up." He moaned quietly. "I didn't see it happen, and now, and now…"

Koag left his face. Revealed once more as a simple man he looked drained, startled by the everyday world. And then, and only then, I remembered from my dream of Brendle Library of the face behind the Spellcaster's mask. This same face before me now.

"Dad, what are you doing? Why have you come here?"

"I want to see your mother."

"She's at work."

"Yes, of course, right."

I had visions of him blundering into Bradshaw's Mill, making a commotion on the shop floor and in the wages office, and some big tough blokes chucking him out on his arse, or even worse, calling the police on him. I had to make sure that did not happen. I choked a little, as I spoke. "I don't think… I don't think she wants to see you." It was daft to say so. Of course she wanted to see him, she wanted him back. I saw it all plainly, Mum welcoming him back into the house, cooking a big slap-up meal for us, the whole family around the table, me, Chloe, Mum, Dad, Grandma, all of us laughing and joking and filling our faces with grub. What a picture!

He grunted. "Of course. At work." Then he stood up. With bleary eyes he looked around the green, at the pub, then the memorial, the high street, and finally to me. But he did not speak.

"You're not going, are you, Dad?"

He seemed to shake his head, and nod, at the same time.

"Do you want to come home? You could wait there for Mum. We've got chocolate teacakes in, and everything. You like those, don't you? They're your favourite."

"Aye, that will do nicely, that's it."

"Really?"

"Yes."

But even as he said the word, I knew he was in doubt. He thought for a long moment. Then he said, "The bus stop. Where is it? Point me in the right direction, son."

I was both relieved, and incredibly sad. I don't think either of us knew what we really wanted. How could we? I took him along the street to the stop, where the number 216 would take him back to Clayton and the grotty bedsitter, as described to me by Chloe. A little cloud of Koag came with us, floating nearby. I tried to think of things to say. Luckily, unluckily, it didn't take long for the bus to arrive.

"Do you have enough for the fare? I have some pocket money."

He shook his head. "No, lad, you're all right. I'll be off now."

And so he climbed aboard the bus and it took him away. I watched for as long as I could until it turned onto Lindhurst Street and vanished from sight. The shelter was now empty. Empty, that is, but for the cloud, which stayed with me. I could not stop thinking about my father. My head buzzed with his face, his movements, his voice, the things he had said. Koag mirrored my thoughts by recreating Jim Sutter's face for me, a very good copy that floated in the air, blue, gold and white as before, but more realistic, less of a weird mask, more like a human. I stared at it. Other people were coming into the shelter, waiting for the next bus. I moved on. The mask of my father's face followed behind. How long would it torment me? Would I be lying in my bed tonight, with the thing clinging to the ceiling? Oh God! I started to run, faster and faster, that I might outpace it. Faster, Joe! I took my usual shortcut through the churchyard, leaping the wall in one bound, heading for the mill, the canal, hoping to reach Slew Hill, my hideout. Surely Koag would not follow me all the way there? I did not dare to look back, nor to lose a single step, nor to slow down. Until, finally, out of breath and with a stitch in my side, I had to come to a stop. I was bent over, hands on my knees, panting, sweat dripping down from my brow, stinging my eyes. And when I looked up, through a haze I saw Monty's caravan before me. I would always be drawn to this place, it seemed. My unreal palace.

I looked around the wasteground. No sign of the floating mask.

Only the caravan.

The shimmer it made.

The sun had gone in behind a cloud, but the vehicle still gleamed with light, with flecks of every colour you could name. I hesitated, missing my father's dust-drawn face now that I'd escaped it. The image took over my mind. I could almost picture it, almost touch it.

I took the Brendle Library spell out of my pocket. For some reason Grandma's words came to mind: *At first it wasn't real. But then it was. At first it wasn't real...*

Of course. Now I knew what I had to do. And it would be so much easier if Henrietta were here to help me. I walked closer to the caravan and called out her name, but there was no answer. I stepped up onto the first of the boxes. It felt different than any time before, producing in me that feeling you get just before a really brilliant bit of a song is about to be heard, and you're waiting for it, skin already tingling. For a moment I stood still, letting the caravan settle around me. Then I called for Henrietta again, this time in a hush.

Henrietta? Henrietta Tudor, are you at home?

Even my softest whisper disturbed the delicate world Koag had made here. The caravan was breathing as I breathed, but there was no sign or presence of the ghost girl. I moved to the box nearest the fold-out table, so I could work easily. The typewriter sat there, its machineries of dust packed in enough to give it shape, but not enough to touch. Inserted in the roller was the letter to "Harry" that Alfred Montgomery had started, but not finished, back in 1964. There was a pad of paper next on the table, all this recreated and composed by Koag. I remembered how Henrietta had opened the cupboard, without breaking the illusion of a door, how she had revealed the pages of Monty's diary for me. But every time I had tried in the past to read the copy of *Mayfair* magazine, it had disintegrated in my hands. I needed to be as good as she was at working with Koag. But I was flesh and blood, jittery and awkward and butterfingered.

No more dithering, lad, let's get to work.

As gently as I could, I placed my finger and thumb around the sheet of paper in the roller.

Finger met thumb, with nothing in between.

The dust-made paper shivered and trembled and settled back into its proper shape.

My first attempt was a failure.

This was either going to be very, very difficult, or more likely, impossible. I tried again, this time making a quick, vigorous, and quite aggressive grabbing motion, like I was trying to catch a butterfly. All this did was disturb the paper even more, as well as part of the typewriter. I watched as the tiny strands of dust floated back into position. Perhaps this was a mistake.

"Koag, won't you help me a little?"

The caravan wavered in a breeze. I looked around for inspiration. A single strand of Sutter's Fancy floated in the corner, a thing of no more substance than a length of Grandma's cotton thread. But surely that was a good sign. I gritted my teeth, readied thumb and finger either side of the dusty paper, pinched them together… and pulled. Slowly, gently, yes, the paper was actually moving, I could feel it. There was no sound being made, but the roller was turning as the paper was dragged free. My hand started to shake. The paper broke apart, re-formed itself, allowing my fingers to retain their grip. Just a couple more inches, a little more. I brought my other hand into play, gripping the leading edge of the paper at both corners. This was easier and it was soon free of the roller's grip.

My hands were outstretched, holding the paper aloft. What should I do now? Screw it up and throw it in the waste-bin under the caravan's sink? No, of course not. Carefully I placed the paper down on the tabletop. It stayed there, dust on dust. The first part of the operation was over. Next I took up a clean sheet of dusty paper from the dusty pad and placed this in the dusty roller. I did this without really thinking about it, and the paper came away from the pad clean and complete. I had never used a typewriter before, real or unreal, but I had seen them used enough times in television shows and films, and I had seen Margery at work. I knew the basic principles. There was a knob on the side which I turned, drawing the new sheet of paper into the machine. By now, I had a feel for the dust and how it worked, how it stuck together, how it drifted apart. If I had tried this a few weeks ago it would have been a hopeless task, but my time at Pike View, and meeting Henrietta, and undergoing the Living Eyes session with Grandma, all this had given me some small ability. I wasn't yet Kid Koag, superhero saviour of the human race, but I was learning, bit by bit, and day by day. I had one, two, three, four brilliant teachers.

Now to begin typing. I had no idea how to make capital letters, so I just ignored them, using small-case throughout. Nor did I bother with full stops or commas. I searched for the letter *i*. It took me a moment to find it, because the letters were not arranged in alphabetical order, which seemed utterly crazy to me.

My finger was poised over the key.

I hesitated. It was one thing for Koag to copy a letter already typed out by a person, but for a person, a boy, to actually type a letter into the dust, surely that was a different matter.

I held my breath.

The caravan was perfectly still, for once.

I pressed down.

My finger went through the soft dust of the key and just carried on, right through the tabletop. I almost toppled over with the forward motion, and had to do a quick balancing act on the wooden box. *Oh, blast!* It was all an illusion. I was a useless kid, with too many stupid dreams stuffed inside his head. And of course the typewriter and the table re-formed themselves, exactly as they were before, mocking me. I tried again, concentrating as much as I could. My finger went through the grains of the key, to no purpose. I tried a third time, and a fourth. After my fifth useless attempt I screamed out loud and jumped off the box, swinging my arms wildly about me, smashing the caravan into pieces, scattering every last particle of dust. I broke a teacup. I splintered the table in two, I smashed the shaving mirror, I tore up the shirt hanging on a hook, I pounded the door and the seats into oblivion until all that was left was a great cloud of dust swirling about, nothing, nothing of worth, myself at the centre of it, useless, head bowed, the scream wasted. I fell to my hands and knees. There was something clogging my throat, and no matter how I sobbed and choked it would not come loose, the tears ran from my eyes, my body trembled uncontrollably. I retched and threw up the clog of dust that had near-suffocated me. It streamed out of my mouth. How it had got there, I don't know. It had been in place for a long time, I think, a constant troubling presence. It spattered on the ground, powder and spittle, all the colours of it dark, miserable.

Slowly I got to my feet.

The caravan was re-forming around me, taking its time, rebuilding all the broken objects, the walls, the door, the fold-out table, the typewriter, the empty sheet of paper still waiting for me. I climbed back onto the box and stood as before, breathing heavily.

Father, father? Are you there?

I thought of him, remembering how he had stood over me, guiding me, helping me, as I made my first ever Airfix kit, a model of Admiral Nelson's flagship, HMS *Victory*.

My hand moved to the keyboard, to the letter *i*.

My entire arm felt weightless, hardly a part of my body.

I watched in fascination as the fingertip reached the key, resting against it. I sensed that every last particle of dust in the caravan had concentrated itself into that exact point, the typewriter key, making it solid, or at least partly solid. I felt the plastic against the pad of my fingertip, hard against the softer flesh. It felt real. Now I pressed down, that was it. A little more.

A thin metal arm rose up from inside the typewriter, hitting the paper, and then fell back down into place. Every component was made of dust, and yet they all held together, working as one. The machine did this in complete silence.

I leaned over and examined the sheet of paper.

There was a letter *i* imprinted there in black ink, quivering slightly.

"Yes!"

Monty's caravan shook with the waves of my joy.

"Yes, yes, yes!"

Good. Very good. I was the world's finest dust-typist, no contest!

I saw that the paper had moved along of its own accord, ready for the second letter to be typed. It was working. I was a proper writer now. Fearful of breaking the spell, I carried on with my work, seeking out the letter *n* on the keyboard. And press!

It worked. I had now successfully typed out the first word of the spell.

in

I was exhausted, like after running four laps on Sports Day, or after that fight I got into with Kevin Mulvaney. But I had to keep on with my task. Okay then, the next word. But then I worried myself; hang on, I have to make a gap between the words. How do I do that? I looked at each key in turn, some of which had really strange symbols on them. At the lower left and right corners were two keys, both of them blank. That had to mean a blank space, right? I tried it. Nothing happened. Then I took notice of the long bar across the bottom of the keyboard. I worked it out, Sherlock Holmes style: typists would need to put a lot of blank spaces in a letter, so it made sense that the biggest key of them all would be for that purpose. But I was nervous, despite my reckoning. I pressed the bar. Yes, the paper moved one space, without typing a letter. I stood upright, steadying my nerves. I let a few moments pass. And then, one painfully slow letter at a time, I went back to work, managing to type out the entire first line. Now I wondered how to move the typewriter mechanism down to the next line. I thought back to watching Margery at work in the Pike View office, as Mr Holbrook told his story of the caged dust-beast. I recalled seeing her move the carriage along with her hand, using a special lever. A little bell had rung every time she did this, either just before she pressed the lever, or just after; I couldn't remember which. But I tried this now, moving the lever, slowly, gently. With a slight resistance, the carriage moved. There was no bell sound, so I made my own sound effect, saying it out loud.

Ting!

A man walked by on the canal path, with a dog on a lead. He looked my way. What would he be seeing now, assuming he was not a witness? Well, a boy standing on a wooden crate, nothing more, just standing there like an idiot. I waved at him, and waited until he and the dog had moved on. I wanted no disturbances. Then I took out my copy of the spell, just to remind myself of the next few words, committing them to memory. I started to type. One letter, the next letter. One word, two words, three.

Ting!

I was careful in this, extremely careful, making an effort to find the correct key each time and not pressing down until I was absolutely sure. It had to be right. If I made a mistake, I would have to start again from the beginning and I really didn't want to do that.

Ting!

For each of the three sentences I reread the original, and then typed it out. My father guided my hand: no longer drunk, not now, but clean-shaven, working hard, smartly dressed, hair trimmed, still at home, sawing wood, hammering nails, checking the pools, kicking a football, joking with Mum, laughing and loving. I was lost to the outside world, living on that dotted borderline where Brendleshire met with Lancashire. Nothing else mattered.

Ting!

Koag was kind. The caravan worked with me, gathering as much dust as it could into each key as my finger hovered over them. I don't know how long I was at work, no idea, but it felt like ages had passed since I had first entered the caravan. But finally the task was complete.

Twenty-eight words.

Ting!

21

in the dust
in the dark
words are waiting

in the dark of the dust
words are waiting
waiting

in the dusty darkness
dark dusty words
are waiting

22

The factory workers came home an hour early on Friday afternoons. It was a family ritual that we all had a sit-down tea together, always eating the same meal: boiled ham and quarters of pork pies, with cucumber and lettuce and tomatoes on the side, and slices of white bread and butter, all helped down with Heinz salad cream. I drank dandelion and burdock. I was keeping up the chat about the new school and how much harder I was going to work, once I was there. But all the time I was thinking about my day, first meeting with Henrietta at Slew Hill, then visiting Brendle Library (with Grandma's help), and then seeing Dad in his terrible state, then typing out the magic spell at the caravan. I didn't know which to think about the most! Anyway, there was nothing I could do about the spell tonight; tomorrow morning I would post it to Mr Holbrook, that was my plan, trusting it would remain intact on its journey. Even then, it would not arrive at Pike View until Monday morning, because of the weekend. It couldn't be helped. I would trust to Koag. As it was, I had no time to do any of that.

After tea my mother sat in her chair in the living room and read. She was in the middle of *The Glare of the Sun*, the romance novel Mr Holbrook had given her. Her eyes moved quickly along each line and she turned the page eagerly. It gave me hope, to see this.

"Mum?"

"Yes, Joe?"

"You know, about Dad..."

"What's that?"

"Dad."

She looked at me, taking her eyes from the page. "What about him?"

"Would you ever see him again?"

"Perhaps I will, at birthdays, and such like. Why?"

"No reason. I was just wondering."

"You know what they say about *wondering*, don't you?"

"Yes, Mum."

"What do they say?"

"Wondering never got a thing done well."

"That's right."

Her attention went back to the book, smiling as she read. I thought of Mr Holbrook writing those words, and how they had travelled through time and space to reach my mother's eyes. It seemed a miracle. And then the doorbell rang. Chloe trundled down the stairs, shouting, "I'll get it." I could hear her talking with someone on the step. With a sigh, Mum got up and went to see who it was. Her voice was quickly raised, an argument was underway. I looked out into the hallway to see Margery Adams standing in the doorway. I knew straight away from her face that something was wrong, and I feared the worst. She more or less forced her way into the house.

"Joe," she said. "It's Georgie, Mr Holbrook, he's awful bad."

"What... what do you mean?" I gulped.

"He's nearing the end, Joe, very near, and he wants to see you."

My mum intervened: "Now look here, lady, my boy's to have nothing to do with you, or that wretched house. Nothing!"

"Mum, please!"

"Go to your room, Joe, go on."

I stood my ground, something I hardly ever did with my mother. She glared at me. My sister looked on, her arms folded across her chest. But then she relaxed, and the sneer left her face.

"Mum, I think he should go," she said.

"And what's it to do with you?"

"If the old man is very ill, if he's..." She couldn't finish the sentence, it was too much to even say out loud.

Mum looked from Chloe to Margery, and then to me. She didn't say anything, she just stared at my face for ages. I know she could see what I was feeling; she was always good at that. Then she went outside and we all followed her. The Land Rover was parked in the street, drawing a fair bit of attention from the neighbours. Mum took one look at the huge green mud-splattered monstrosity and shook her head.

She said to Margery, "This had better be the truth you're telling."

"It is. It really is. I don't know how long he's got."

"And he's asking for Joe, is he?"

"He keeps calling out your son's name."

It was terrible to think of this, of the old man calling for me like that, just terrible. But Mum was still hesitant.

Margery tried again. "You can come with us, if you like, Mrs Sutter. Would that suit?"

"Me, in that thing? Not on your nelly."

"I'll go, Mum," Chloe said. "Let me."

Mum looked to Grandma for assurance and received in reply, "Let them go, Lily. They'll be all right."

"Are you sure, mother?"

"Very sure. I can feel it. The dust is good. The dust demands it."

There was a moment's further hesitation. Then Mum said, "I swear, if there's any trouble, any at all... I'll set that house afire."

Chloe and I made to get in the back of the vehicle, but then I leapt down and ran back into the house, up the stairs, three at a time. I pulled the magic spell from its hiding place in my room, then I ran back downstairs and jumped into the Land Rover. We set off. What a journey that was. Chloe was perched on a wheel housing, while I sat on a rug on the floor, getting buffeted about. There were dog hairs everywhere, and Chloe started sneezing from them. The Land Rover was not built for comfort, it was like being transported in an army vehicle. On any other occasion, this would have excited me greatly. But now, not knowing what lay ahead, I was worried sick. Margery drove in silence. I looked down at the piece of paper in my hand, dusty words on dusty paper, each grain safely gathered back together into its proper form and shape. Of course, I was the only person in the van who could actually see the spell. It had taken on even more magical power now, in my mind. It might even save Mr Holbrook's life. *Anything is possible, anything is possible.* The Land Rover was speeding along, clipping the branches on the side of the road as we made our way up the hill. We swung into the yard of Pike View. As I climbed out, I saw that the front door of the house was wide open. Margery shouted into the hallway, receiving no answer. Perhaps he was down in the cellar? We could hear Nipper yapping from within, but he did not scamper out to greet us. I imagined he was tied up by his lead to a chair leg.

Then Chloe touched my arm. "I think he's up there, Joe, at the tower. Is that him?"

It was, it must be, a lone figure standing next to Brendle Pike, just like on the cover of *Dreams of Brendle*. But there were no lightning bolts in sight, only a flat sky streaked with various shades of Koag, purple and lilac and slate-grey, and the sun nearing the horizon.

Margery cried, "He should be in bed. I told him!"

I set off running up the ridge, not caring if I left Margery and Chloe behind. I came to a halt a short distance from the tower. Mr Holbrook was bent over, his hands on his thighs, each laboured breath visible in a movement of his hunched back. His walking stick lay on the ground, cast aside. He rocked back and forth, enough for me to see that the Koag mask was on his face. He started to cough, really quite badly, and he had to pull the mask quickly away in order that the fluids could get free of his mouth and throat. Hovering over him was a thick clod of black and brown dust, like smog from a factory chimney, a pall of darkness.

"Mr Holbrook, sir?"

He made no answer. I thought he might have some trouble speaking.

Chloe came to join me, and then Margery. She went to her friend and companion and gently pulled him towards the bench, telling him off the whole while: "I told you, George, I forbade you from using that dreadful thing any more. I told you!"

"Margery, please stop fussing."

"Now, just you listen—"

"I'm all right, I tell you. I'm all right." But he wasn't, that was obvious. He had returned to his bent-over position. The mask was clutched in one hand.

Margery kept with him, speaking more gently now. "I have brought the boy to see you. Joe Sutter. Like you asked."

"Joe?"

"Yes, he's here. Look."

His head raised up enough to let one eye take me in. His free hand flailed about wildly, trying to brush the clouds of Koag away. But they always came back for him, either to protect or to hinder, I didn't know which. "Come here, lad." His voice was very gravelly. I went to him, hoping to guide him to the bench, but he would have none of it. "I'm not done yet." Instead we moved away from Margery and Chloe to the other side of the tower. They looked on from a few yards away. Margery's expression told its own story, and it wasn't a happy one. Chloe looked like a person lost in a strange land, not knowing how to speak the language. But I was glad to see her there, very glad.

Mr Holbrook grabbed me by the wrist, showing surprising strength for one so ill. His face was terribly sunken at the cheekbones, and his eyes were wet with tears that he would not let spill, these, his last ever emotions. Every so often the fits of coughing would take him over, and then I had to grimace in my own pain as he used me for his support; I felt the bones of my wrist might splinter under the pressure. I saw the flecks of blood on his hand as he held it to his mouth. He wiped this on his trousers, no longer caring for decorum. But I think the sight of this stain was bad enough that he surrendered a little. He took a seat and I sat down next to him. A few harried breaths followed. Then he made an effort.

"One last lesson, eh, lad? How would you like that?"

"I would like that very much, sir."

"Good, good chap. That's the spirit."

He held the mask in both hands now; he stared down at it, and his modelled face stared back at him with its sightless eyes. What a mirror they made between them, each for the other.

Then he said, "We are warrior poets, all of us, no matter the fight, and no matter the poem."

I tried my best to think about this lesson, to work it out, I really did.

"Are you following me?"

I nodded. "Yes, Mr Holbrook." Because to say otherwise, when he was in this state, well, it would have been cruel.

"Warrior poets. Indeed. This is how I think of *character*, you see, when I write my stories. Character! The heart of it."

I kept nodding.

"We fight, and then... and then we... we write a poem about the fight. God damn it!"

His throat seemed to close up on the words. Hearing his curse, Margery came to us. She stood behind the seat.

"How are you feeling, George?"

"I've been better, my dear."

"Oh yes." Her voice cracked a little. "Won't you let me fetch the doctor?"

He whispered darkly, "It's too late."

I felt cold inside. What was I supposed to do? I had no knowledge of such emotions. Over the hills and towns of North West England, Koag gathered in its streaks and patterns, its wisps and columns, its swirls and whirlpools. I saw the sandy pitch that floated above Fossett Moss cricket ground, I saw the rusty length of the canal mirrored by a line of green dust. I watched as flowery gold and red spirals rose up from Ashton-under-Lyne. In the distance, the city of Manchester held a tender cloud of lilac instead of its usual grey sootiness. Koag was in splendour, this day of all days. The dark smoky pall that had covered Mr Holbrook had now dissipated, and in its place a soft cloud of turquoise surrounded us, these four people, and the tower also, which seemed to glow with a new power. The treetops of Brendle Wood were coated with pink and silver, lemony yellow and speckles of aquamarine.

I reached into my pocket and pulled free the sheet of dusty paper. It was folded in quarters. I undid it carefully, revealing its contents, which, I was glad to see, were still intact.

"This is the third task you set for me. *Cast a Magic Spell.*"

Mr Holbrook took the paper into his hands, where it trembled. I looked at his face. His eyes were full of wonder, and he gasped.

Margery asked, "What is it, George? I can't see anything." Then she gasped as well. "No, wait, I can see it, a little. Oh, my God."

Mr Holbrook explained, "The words are crossing Helme's Threshold, for all of us, or at least trying to."

"No, it's gone again. Oh, George, I almost saw it. I really did."

He nodded. "The boy has written… he's written on the *dust* itself. On the dust!"

Chloe came up close, trying to see. I described the process for them. "Mr Holbrook asked me to cast a spell. I did so, with my grandmother's help. And Henrietta's."

"Grandma helped you?"

I nodded to my sister. "She blew dust in my eyes."

"Well, that's Dotty Sykes for you."

"I was in Brendle Library, Mr Holbrook. All I could see through the window was a great sea of dust, higher than a house, all speeding about it was, like mad. I swear, it's all true. You do believe me, don't you?"

He nodded to me. That was enough for me to carry on.

"Spellcaster was there. The superhero. Remember, how I'd told you that Denny and I made him up? Anyway, Spellcaster wrote the spell out for me, and now I've brought it to you."

"But how did you write the words on dust?" Margery asked.

"I did it in Monty's caravan. He left a typewriter on his table. I used that."

"Well, bugger me."

Chloe laughed at this. "What does it say?" she asked. "Read it to us."

I started to, but Mr Holbrook stopped me, saying, "More slowly, Joe, please." I began again, at a slower pace. He joined in, but only on certain words, so that on every *dust* and *dark* and *waiting* my not-yet-broken voice was underpinned by his gravelly rasp. It was a magic spell in which certain elements held more power than others, and his voice sent these chosen words out into the air.

Dust
Dark
Waiting
Dark
Dust
Waiting
Waiting

Dusty
Darkness
Dark
Dusty
Waiting

And then silence. I imagined Koag had taken our words and carried them far and away. Oh, it was lovely to think of that.

"Do you like it, Mr Holbrook?"

"I do, lad. Very much."

I wanted to cheer, but I kept it all inside, except for where it spilled out into a great big smile on my face.

Chloe broke the mood: "I don't know what it means."

"Well, I think it's beautiful," said Margery.

"It might be, I suppose. But what does it mean?"

Mr Holbrook had the answer. "Koag has sent us a message, I believe. A key to the door." He tried to get up but struggled with it, and then he doubled up in agony, coughing. I felt sure he might burst open at the chest, so bad it was. But when it was over he managed to stand up. We all did our best to help him, and to hold him steady on his feet. He clutched onto me.

"It might take years, Joe, my boy. But if there's a spark in what I've said, in the lessons, you will catch it, won't you? Set it alight?"

I nodded eagerly. "I will try my very best, Mr Holbrook, I swear."

"Now, I believe, it is time to close the book of life."

"No, no, no!"

He handed the mask to me, pushing it into my hands. That done, he took a few unsteady steps forwards. I made to follow, but Margery grabbed onto me.

She said in a hushed voice, "Let him go. He'll walk on alone now."

He set off down the hill, towards Brendle Woods. Without the aid of his stick, his steps were a bit doddery, but he kept going. He had the dusty spell with him, I saw it at his side as he shuffled along. The tower darkened me with its shade as the sun lowered further. I could hear Margery at my side trying to speak, failing to speak. Chloe's hand was on my shoulder. I felt a great desire to run after Mr Holbrook, to help him along the way. But my sister kept me in place. All I could do for now was watch his descent. As he reached the entrance to the woods, Koag cloaked him for the journey in gold and silver, rose-pink, saffron, with sparkles of crimson and orange. At the same time the skies above were unlike any other I had ever seen. There was so much dust in the air, scattered evenly across the fields and towns, reaching all the way to Manchester and beyond in a sheet of many different colours, more than I thought possible. A gathering. And it was constantly moving, shimmering, dancing, playing games of tag and leapfrog with itself, swapping about the colours and patterns of the various towns, so that my eyes would never be able to take it all in. I knew that a special time was upon us. At one moment Ormsley Vale sparkled, with tall red spikes topped with cascading yellow fountains, and the next it was cloaked in a purple mantle through which waves of motion passed like the billows of the sea at Blackpool. Just as suddenly, it was draped in a fog so golden and motionless it might have blown here from the Sahara, or from the ancient past, it might be the breath of a god, it might have fallen from the cape of Jason as he stole the Golden Fleece. And then it changed, the whole thing. All that was dark in the sky congregated over Brendle Woods, every particle of midnight blue, of black and sooty grey and autumn brown, of deep purple and deeper green and deepest red, all streamed at once to the woods, hovering in a thick layer over the trees. A shadow fell over the map.

I felt Chloe's grip loosen on my arm, and I started to move down the hill, slowly at first, and then gathering speed as I went. I soon reached the edge of the woods. It was like stepping into a fairy tale, but one read at night by candlelight. The lowering fog was thick among the trees. I could barely see more than a few feet ahead of me. Mr Holbrook had done this, I know he had, following the instructions I had given him. This was the dark dust, the dusty dark, of the spell. Henrietta's story was now trying its very best to become true. Birds twittered from the knotted twigs, their songs unlike any I had heard before. My skin tingled. I walked on with arms outstretched, hands touching at bark and twig. I almost tripped over a fallen log, but pushed on through a web of branches, and then I found him. Mr Holbrook was standing amid the trees, speaking to whomever might be listening, the mice and voles, the birds, the insects. The spell was in his hands and he offered this up.

In the dusty darkness, dark dusty words are waiting.

The words came out of his mouth not only as sound, but as dust also. He did not look at me. I did not call to him. He looked very weak, empty, without weight. I watched him at his work, this magician of strange books and pathways, here on his final utterance. He repeated the spell, slowly, slowly, and this time the paper drifted away from his hands, becoming once more a part of the mother dust. He stood in silence a moment longer before he fell quite softly to the ground. I went to him.

"Mr Holbrook, sir? Wake up. Mr Holbrook!"

But there was no waking him, not now, not ever. I stood alone, shivering. The woods stirred about me. The gloom gathered itself in the clearing, lit only by sparkles of Koag in gold and scarlet that darted about like fireflies. Without them, the darkness would be complete. The leaves were rustling on the nearest tree, revealing the shape of some as-yet unseen object. I kept my eyes on that one spot, concentrating all my efforts in order to see what could not be seen, that was barely seen, then almost seen, then finally seen as the shadowy figure of a girl. The clearing brightened a little, with her presence. She stepped forwards.

I still had the mask in my hand. I raised it to my face.

It was not made for me, so the fit was wrong, my boy's face too small and too smooth. But I pressed it more firmly against my features, feeling the material soften a little, to accommodate this new wearer. It reshaped itself, it clung to me. I did not have to hold it in place. It was cold against the skin. There were openings for the nose and the mouth, but none for the eyes.

And as clear as day, I saw Henrietta Tudor.

I saw her truly, because of the mask. Her many names coalesced, each different from the next, blurring her body. I saw the dust for what it really was. Now I knew. I saw what Mr Holbrook had been seeing, all these years. I knew the secret of the book in the cellar, why he had written down so many words. I was too young for such knowledge. It frightened me. But I kept looking. I saw the trees as well, and the little animals in the undergrowth, and the insects that flittered about, all in their true nature. Each leaf was seen, each twig throughout history, each leaf and twig that had ever grown on this tree. Even the twittering of the birds was seen clearly, in the air, in their true and oldest nature, as words, so many words that had once been said, and were now waiting to be said, and they were said, they were spoken, here, in the wild woods of Brendle.

I pulled the mask away from my face. It clung on a little, but came away easily. Henrietta was still there, still visible, more so than before; the dust that created her was packed so tightly together that she was almost solid, almost flesh, almost real. The spell had worked.

I heard a noise behind me. It was Margery.

"Can you see her?" I asked. "The girl?"

"Yes. Oh, yes, I see her." Her voice was a whisper. "I see her." Then she saw Mr Holbrook's body lying in the undergrowth, and her hands went to her mouth, covering her distress.

I reached out into the swirls of dust. Henrietta came to me and our hands touched, and I felt her skin against mine. It was warm, a living touch. I remember her face so well, even now, filled as it was with the need to live. But she moved on from me, towards Margery.

The two of them merged as one being, dust into flesh.

Henrietta vanished from my sight, entering Margery's body like a ghost at play. Did Margery even know what had happened? I do not know, I could not answer that question. But she trembled from head to foot. And then Chloe arrived, stumbling through the undergrowth, cursing loudly. The mood was broken. The darkness crept away through the trees. A blackbird sang. Margery went to Mr Holbrook, falling to her knees at his side.

I joined her there, and we both sobbed over what had been lost.

PART FOUR

SPECKLESOFT

23

The holidays ended, Eileen went off to Ashton-Under-Lyne Grammar, Denny and I to the secondary modern, Fairfields. Unlike the grimy grammar school, Fairfields was a new building, all concrete pillars and huge plate-glass windows. Once there, we quickly grew apart. Perhaps we had the first two terms together, then he fell in with a new bunch of pals, the toughs, the cool kids. By year two we hardly spoke at all, and there were no more hours hanging out at Slew Hill, no more listening to records at his house, no more making up superheroes. I didn't mind. I had friends of my own, the types who spent their breaks and dinner times skulking in corners, swapping obscure facts about rock bands and re-enacting Monty Python sketches. And more than occasionally getting beaten up. Sometimes Denny would step in to protect me. I'm not saying he dropped down from above like Spider-Man, but if he was around, he would put a halt to it. And then move quickly away, back to his own gang. But we hardly ever spoke. I kept my witnessing to myself, as far as I could. A girl called Mary McClean helped in this. She was the only other witness in my year and a terrible show-off, boasting continually of her powers, and using Greot to peep around corners or to sneak answers off other kid's exam papers. And yes, at some point in the first year I started to think of Koag as Greot once more. Denny's invented name faded away. Over time I became Invisible Boy, or at least Semi-Visible Boy, keeping myself to myself. Stories came to me. I had discovered progressive rock, and saw in the records' painted covers and their side-long, multi-part epics a great unfolding of fantastical tales. It fed my imagination. In the final year of schooling I was encouraged by the English teacher, Mr Castle, to "write, write, write!" He saw something in me, something first stirred into life by Mr Holbrook and Margery. But the urge was soon replaced by other, more teenage interests, and I put all the Pike View material into a cardboard box and shoved it into my wardrobe, and that was that.

I left Fairfields with no qualifications of any useful kind. But I avoided Bradshaw's Mill, and somehow or other (with Mr Castle's help, actually) managed to land myself a job as a shelf-stacker at Ormsley Vale Public Library. Eileen came in to borrow books on occasion, but we only nodded to each other, nothing more. One time she had a boy on her arm, one of those glammed-up orange-haired Bowie types. Later, I heard she had moved to a flat in Ashton, and that she was studying to be a nurse. Meanwhile, Denny joined the Royal Navy. I received this news from his mother, Betty, when we bumped into each other on the high street. She was proud of her son's endeavours. At the age of twenty-one I moved to the south-west side of Manchester, renting a bedsit in Chorlton. I signed on for a while and then took up a job in a bookshop in Manchester. I did write a few very bad science fiction stories, which I sent off to various magazines; but receiving rejection slips for all of them, I quickly gave up. It felt like some other person's dream.

In 1981 dear old, lovely old Dotty Sykes passed away. She had reached her seventieth year. Her funeral at St Matilda's was a striking affair, not just for the attendees (it was a good turn-out), but also for the clouds of Greot that settled over the cemetery as her coffin was lowered into the ground. I was not the only witness present. A number of people looked up at the dust clouds as they floated above the heads of the mourners. My father was there, and we nodded to each other, nothing more. But later, after the ceremony, I spied him on his own standing near another grave, that of Frankie Sutter, his first boy, and my older brother. The engraving on the stone read, "*Francis James Sutter. Forever in our hearts.*" Below that, the dates of his birth and death: 1954–1955.

We stood together side by side, father and son. I was taller than him now.

"All right, lad?"

"Yes, Dad. Sorry to see Dotty go."

"Aye, she was a grand lass."

Did he really think that? Probably not, but this was not the time for pettiness. What was it a time for? A good few seconds passed. I thought to move away. But then:

"You're in Chorlton now, I hear."

"That's right."

"How's that then? Posh, is it?" His voice was suddenly gruff.

"Nah, not really."

I was aware of how much I must have changed, in his eyes; my voice, my way of life, my post-punk haircut, even the cut of my best black suit.

"It's not that different to here."

He looked at me for the first time. His eyes were rheumy, and his hair grey and a lot thinner than it used to be. But I saw myself in his face. And I think he must have seen the equivalent, in mine: his younger reflection. Various thoughts went through my head, each with their accompanying set of words; but all felt trite, or hollow. Or a lie. We had not spoken together properly, I realised, since my sixteenth birthday.

At last I said, "I used to put half-chewed toffees on here, on Frankie's stone. When I was a kid, like. Something to share."

My father managed a little smile at this. But it left his face immediately, and he said in a low voice, "I have lost so much." His eyes never left mine.

For some reason a line spoken by George Holbrook came back to me, something about being in a cage in a zoo and getting old, I don't know. God, I hadn't thought about him for so long a time. What else did he say? So many rules. *Solve the puzzle of yourself.* But that wasn't it, or not quite that. There was another component. I really had to dig deep.

Solve the *beautiful* puzzle of yourself, that was it.

And here we were, two pieces of the same puzzle, my father and me. But what possible beauty could this moment contain?

Then he put his hand on Little Frankie's gravestone and he said, "I'm sorry, son."

Was he speaking to me, or to his first boy?

Both. The both of us.

He put his arm around my shoulder and we walked back towards the line of black cars, and the waiting family – my mother, my sister and her husband and their two kids – and the clouds of Greot that drifted away across the trees carrying my grandmother's spirit.

I stayed at the house on Stoneybrook Estate for a couple of days, helping out. My mother lived alone, now that Grandma had gone. I slept in my old room, the rock star posters and model Spitfires and Hurricanes taken down, but the place was more or less the same. Greot crawled across the ceiling, as it used to do, the old patterns. The next day, over lunch, I asked my mother if she had kept any of my writings and drawings, from when I was a kid. She had, which needn't have surprised me, as she treasured every little thing her children had ever produced. "There's a box in the attic, but be careful up there." *I will, Mum. Don't worry.* It was dusty and smelly, lit by a single bulb, filled with the usual detritus of family life. And hidden behind an old standard lamp and a roll of carpet, there was the cardboard box, as promised. Written on the front in black ink was *FICTION SCIENCE*. For the life of me I could not remember coming up with that, but I was always writing things backwards, and upside-down, making up anagrams, and the like. Mr Holbrook's influence. It was incredible to think of those days, my venturing into that strange house like I did. What was I thinking? My head swam with memories.

I levered the box down the attic steps and took it into my old bedroom. And there I sat for an hour or more, reading, and exploring. The box was filled with papers, far more than I remembered. There were drawings of superheroes, lots of single-page comics, half-completed stories, countless scribbled notes in exercise books that tried desperately to capture Holbrook's various sayings. I had misspelt the word pseudonym as *sudoname*. The drawings of Spellcaster and Zigzag Woman and Kid Koag made me smile, but the one of Nowhere Man actually made me laugh out loud. It was just a blank space in the middle of the paper with lots of arrows pointing to invisible gadgets on his invisible costume: *noise blaster*, *echo locator*, *sonic lasso*. Just a blank space! The innocence of childhood. But it got better. I unfolded a sheet of paper to find the *Scale of Invention*: the four kinds of ideas, the separating lines, that one dotted line that had troubled my young mind so. *Shared, Unique, Crazy, Genius*. It was too much, too much to even look at. I had forgotten… Damn. The years, the years.

I went on with my search, uncovering several attempts at "Helme's Threshold in Reverse", the story that wasn't a story, including the torn fragments of the final version, the sorry remnants of Mr Holbrook's anger at my failure. It was crazy, some of the things he was asking of me; I mean, you can't just go around astonishing people all the time! But he was forcing me to think ahead of my own thoughts and feelings, and my eleven-year-old self had run along at full pelt to keep up. And there it was in my hands: a broken tale about a magician's assistant who vanishes into another dimension, along with various rabbits, doves, handkerchieves, playing cards. I thought of my father bowed and trembling at the graveside of his first son. We all lose things to that impossible realm. Helme's Threshold gives, and Helme's Threshold takes, and that is that.

I found the quote I had tried to remember at Frankie's grave: *When I was younger I used to think I was visiting a zoo, peering into the cages, making fun of the animals. But now I'm trapped inside the cage, looking out, yearning for life.* At the time I had not understood this, except that it struck me as being a very exciting thing to say; but now, at the age of twenty-four and thinking of my father, I felt the true meaning of the words had been revealed. "I have lost so much."

The *Fiction Science* box held one last surprise, an object wrapped in a linen cloth. I knew what it was immediately, and was fearful of what it might look like, given the years that had passed. But the Mask of Koag was well preserved. The waxen face of George Kenneth Holbrook stared back at me, every line, every wrinkle, the blank eyes through which I once looked, on the day of his death, and the things I had witnessed, the wonder of it all.

I took the box back to my Chorlton flat and straightaway started work on a story; an old story, actually, a story that *was* a story, this time including a father and a little brother in the lost items accompanying the magician's assistant. That was the key. My God, I worked hard! So many drafts, all in longhand and then typed up at the local library. I used all the techniques

Mr Holbrook had taught me. I understood them more fully now. It can be reduced to one central concept: everything fades into blandness unless you consciously fight it, and that conscious effort is focussed on one act only, to place every single word, theme, character and plot point into that special area where shared ideas merge into unique ideas. That was the rule I followed, then as now, and always. Word after word, book after book. Finally the story was ready, good enough to be sent off. This time I used a pseudonym, reversing the initials of my first and second names, then taking the second syllable of Holbrook's surname, and adding an *s* to it. A.J. Brooks was born. Two magazines rejected "Helme's Threshold in Reverse". The third, a new British mag called *Interzone*, accepted it, and published it in their first edition. I can't remember how much I earned from the sale, a few pounds I suppose; but a fortune, in the truest sense of the word.

A few months later I met up with Dennis Portman for a drink, when he was home on leave. We fell into the old greeting without even thinking about it.

"Alright, Denny?"

"Yeah, not bad, not bad."

He was engaged to a girl called Katie Greenlaw, a Wren. He had a picture of her in his wallet. He told me of life aboard ship, and the places he had visited around the world. We talked a bit about the old days, about listening to music and running through the woods and the giant leeches that lived in the clay pool. I even showed him the drawing of Nowhere Man, and his eyes popped at the sight. He laughed and laughed, nearly spilling his drink. Our lives had separated and moved apart, far apart, but it was good to see that we could still chat, and make fun of each other. Then his ship sailed. And like I said, Helme's Threshold is always waiting.

In April of 1982 war broke out between Great Britain and Argentina over the ownership of the Falkland Islands. During the conflict HMS *Sheffield* was hit by an Exocet missile and went down, losing twenty-one lives. Petty Officer Dennis Alan Portman was among them. His body was never recovered; the sea took him for its own. His family held a memorial service. In place of a coffin there were lots of flowers, and a Union Jack draped over the table and a large photograph of Denny at his smiling best. Half a dozen of his shipmates were there, in dress uniform. Michael Portman spoke lovingly of his brother. One of the sailors recited Tennyson's "Crossing the Bar", a tradition in the Navy.

Twilight and evening bell,
And after that the dark!
And may there be no sadness of farewell,
When I embark;

For tho' from out our bourne of Time and Place
The flood may bear me far,
I hope to see my Pilot face to face
When I have crost the bar.

That evening we all met up in the function room above the Weaver's Arms. It was meant to be a celebration of Denny's life, but Betty Portman started crying almost straight away. Denny's father looked like a tightly-wound spring about to snap. But drinks were served, ham and pickle sandwiches and chicken legs were eaten, and soon enough the atmosphere eased a little. The disc jockey (Michael again) played some of his brother's favourite tunes, ballads to begin with, but then more upbeat numbers. I remembered some of them from our days together, while others were more contemporary songs. But the small dance floor remained empty. A young woman sat alone at a table, and I realised it was Denny's fiancée, Katie. But I really couldn't bring myself to speak with her, not yet, at least. Instead I spent time with Betty, telling her how much of a friend her son had been to me at school, admitting to some of the pranks and capers we got up to. She smiled at this and thanked me. But she was finding it difficult. "I wish someone would dance," she said. "Denny would have liked that." She went to join her husband at a side table. I stood alone for a moment. I didn't really know any of the people there.

And then across the room I saw Eileen Barlow.

She hadn't made the service itself, only arriving later with a friend.

I watched her for a while.

Would she even remember me? Perhaps it would be awkward between us? Ah, what the hell. I finished my beer and made my way over to her. Before I could get a word out, she said, "Joe! Joe Sutter, well I never!" Within half an hour we were both merry on Denny's behalf. She was a nurse at Tameside General. I told her about my job at the bookshop. We got on well, and, suitably encouraged, I admitted, "You won't know this, Eileen, but once upon a time I waited outside your house for, oh, forty-five minutes, easily, working up the courage to knock on the door."

"Really? When was this?"

"I was eleven. 1968."

"Eleven? What did you expect us to do?"

"I wanted to invite you to a tea party at Pike View."

"Pike View… sorry…"

"The farmhouse where the old man lived, the science fiction author, you remember?"

"Hm, a little."

"I was obsessed with him. It was crazy, thinking back, and more than a bit weird. I mean, I was up at that place a lot."

"What were you doing up there?"

"Learning. Learning how to be a writer."

"Oh, I remember now, you told me once, didn't you… It's coming back… That you wanted to be a writer." She spilled a little of her drink down her dress and dabbed at it with a paper napkin.

"I still do. I've had a few stories published, in magazines."

"Let me guess, you're writing a novel."

"I am, actually, but I'm stuck on chapter seven."

She shrugged. Then smiled. She looked lovely. The drink made the room warm and fuzzy. Her edges were blurred, as were her words. We laughed a lot. A new song came on: "Don't You Want Me" by The Human League. That was Eileen's cue: "Oh, I love this one!" She finished off her Malibu and Coke and walked onto the dance floor, the first to do so. She started to move. I could see that one of the sailors had his eye on her, and there was little chance my off-the-peg suit would compete against the uniform. But she kept beckoning to me, to me alone, waving her arms in a slowed-down version of the hitch-hiker dance, as I had first seen her do back in the goods wagon at Slew Hill, all those years before. Her movements were half a joke, half-seduction; and those two things combined were a fine and glorious spit in the face of death. So I gave in. Although, God knows, I am no dancer. I did my best, and was thankful when other people joined us on the floor. We were lost in the crowd. Greot danced with us, with her, with Eileen, colouring the air around her with dappled gold and vermilion, and sudden bursts of indigo. And then, yes, silver and rose-pink. My fancy, always drawing me on. Across the years the dust had travelled, binding me to my past, pushing me forwards. *Follow me, follow me!* Eileen's eyes sparkled under the lights. The music was visible as waves within the dust. Pulsations. Soft and sweet, and dreamlike.

Later we went onto the green to get some air. I suddenly remembered Tom Halfpenny and his mad dances outside the pub, his folk songs, and how he used to cadge for whatever was left in the bottom of beer glasses. The green was his favourite part of the town. In his end was my beginning, and so on, and so forth. But enough of such thoughts, for Eileen was dancing on the grass, lazily twirling in a circle. Her shoulders were bare. Denny spoke to me in a far-off whisper: *Go on, Joe. What are you waiting for?* I handed over my jacket, to keep her warm. Our eyes met. And that boy who had waited helplessly, hopelessly outside the girl's house so long ago was now taken over by the man of twenty-five years.

In the shadows of the war memorial, we kissed.

24

So this is a love story, then, and not just for people, but for ideas, and genres, and words, and writing, and learning, and most of all for science fiction, the endless possibilities of the impossible. These days I live in Blackheath, in London. The bookcase in my office contains a complete set of the works of G.K. Holbrook, the collected Orbit edition published in the 1990s. I also have a lot of his other books, those written under various pseudonyms. He never did finish that final book I saw him writing, the private eye story, *Moon Over Brendle*. That title stayed with me over the years, and whenever it popped into my head I would always remember my walk through the moonlit streets of Brendle on my way to the library, and my meeting with Spellcaster. And also, because, well... Tod Underhill did not know of Brendleshire to begin with, and then, by the story's end, he stood on the borderline of that realm. I remembered Holbrook telling me his imagined ending of the novel. I had been taken on the same journey, by the same man. Because of that the title remained as a constant temptation, but one I never dared to take as my own, not until...

Above the bookcase is a painting, *View From Brendle Pike*, a landscape, very, very abstract, but if you concentrate you can glimpse the dark hills, the vale, the towns battered by rain, and those poor sheep: thick splotches of grey. Sometimes I make out shadowy people amid the downpour, yet the next time I look, they are gone. Books and image, one above the other: my little shrine. Often, if I'm struggling with a chapter, I turn to gaze at the painting, and my eye always ends up on the artist's signature. I bought it at an auction a couple of years back. Margery Adams went on to have a successful career as an artist. She worked hard throughout the seventies and was rewarded well for it. The National Gallery has a fine example of her work in a side room, and just last year they had a retrospective at Tate Modern. I went to that show, and I bought the catalogue (foreword by Tracey Emin). The later paintings contain more obvious examples of those blurred figures, "the people of dust", as one critic dubbed them. Margery never gave up painting, but eventually she returned to her first love, music. She formed a jazz combo, the Margery Adams Quartet, and made a number of albums. Her compositions had two-word titles like "Split Second", "Razor Sharp", and "Third Eye". She had a minor hit record after her tune "Lone Dancer" was used in a Levi's advert. I went to see her perform at Ronnie Scott's club in Soho. I was married by then, with two young kids, one of them still a baby. So this was a rare night out, accompanied by my agent, Neil Clegg. I liked the way Margery mixed bluesy chords with classical twists and turns. My favourite bit was her rendition of Bartók's "Allegro Barbaro", jazzed up, broken apart, reshaped, broken again, as Margery's hands smashed at the keyboard with those five-pound hammer blows, sending splinters of music flying everywhere. *Slammm! Thuunk! Ping, pang ping pang! Jitter, skitter. Berang!* Glorious. It brought the house down.

Afterwards I went up to her at the bar and bought her a drink. This was 1986. She was fifty-two, I was closing in on thirty. She still had the slanted fringe, but greying now, which, along with the black polo-neck, gave her that long-coveted Bohemian air. The conversation was stilted. After all, we had only known each other for a number of weeks eighteen years before. But my God, this woman had helped me so much! I tried to tell her this, speaking of my A.J. Brooks pseudonym, my two published novels, and the numerous short stories in science fiction magazines, all to show her that my time at Pike View had been more than useful, in the long run. But she preferred to chat with the boys of the band. Her jokes were very blue. She was knocking back whiskeys. She would not speak of the man she had once lived with, nor her role as his amanuensis. Maybe her memories had been damaged by alcohol, I don't know. It can happen. It happened to my father in his later years. But as I said goodbye to Neil outside the club, Margery came up to me. We spoke in a shop doorway in Frith Street. It was spattering with rain.

"The Anti-Boredom Machine? Am I right?" Her voice was a little slurred.

I nodded. "That's right."

"And then… Let me think… *Helme's Threshold Inverted*?"

"*In Reverse.*"

"Right, right. The sheet of paper with the story on it, and the little bits of toilet paper."

"Please, don't remind me! And it was tissue paper, not toilet paper."

For a moment her eyes sparkled with golden dust as they used to; Koag was always attracted to her eyes. I looked as deeply as I could, hoping for a glimpse of the girl inside, Henrietta. But there was nothing.

She asked, "What was it George said about that story? I can't remember."

"Oh, I can. He hated it."

"He was probably jealous."

"Oh aye, because he'd never used toilet paper in his own work."

And we laughed then. It was a little awkward, a bit staged. But it felt good. "Here's the best bit." And I told her how I had rewritten "Helme's Threshold", as a proper story this time. "It was the first thing I ever sold. It started my career." As I spoke these words, I saw myself from above; a boy again, desperately trying to impress, to make sure that Margery knew my worth. It was pathetic. So, in a calmer voice, I added. "Despite everything, Holbrook made me work harder. You both did."

"It's a pity."

"What is?"

"He set such a high standard, he could never reach it himself."

"Is that a bad thing?"

She looked away from me. I think she was ashamed of what I might see in her face. Then she quietly said, "He *used* you, you do know that?"

"How do you mean?"

"He needed a youthful spirit, for his spell to work."

I was dumbfounded. But I rallied: "I was glad to be there. Truthfully."

She turned back towards me. Her gaze now had a hardness to it. "Georgie was never meant for this world." I wasn't sure how to respond. She went on, "But he wrote himself into life, as best he could."

And I suddenly remembered that the last time we had been together, dear Margery and I, truly together, we had both been crying, weeping our eyes out. Life. What can you do? It hurts, and then it doesn't hurt, and then it hurts, and then it doesn't hurt. And so on. You fight, and then you write a poem about the fighting. Nothing more could be said; nothing more can be said. Margery went back into the club and I made my way towards Charing Cross tube station. Her words echoed in my head.

He wrote himself into life.

Does that mean he wrote himself *out* of life, as well? I tried to remember the moment of his death, but the memories were silted up: too much dust. It gets in your eyes, it gets in your dreams. It covers the clock face, so much so that you don't even know the time has passed.

A couple of years ago my agent gave me a call. "We've had a rather unusual request."

"Hollywood wants to take out an option?"

He laughed. "If only. No, but you remember that woman we went to see that time, at Ronnie Scott's?"

He had lost me, for we went to a number of gigs together.

"It was years ago, when we first met. The eighties. You knew her from your youth, I think."

"Oh, right. Margery Adams."

"That's the one. Her assistant has been in touch. She wants to see you."

I was genuinely surprised. "Margery Adams? I thought she was... Well, that she was..."

"Dead? Apparently not."

I did a quick calculation. "She must be pushing ninety. What does she want to see me for?"

"No idea. Well, then, what shall I tell them?"

It took a moment's thought. Then I said, "Yes, I'll do it."

The address was a mews in Kensington. She had certainly done okay for herself. The street was leafy and secluded, with white-painted houses guarded by avant-garde sculptures and exotic-looking potted plants. Number 7 was a little unkempt compared to the neighbours, but still, a very nice piece of property. The door was opened by a well-spoken young lady who introduced herself as Margery's personal assistant. I was led to an inner doorway. "Go right on in." I really did not know what to expect. The room I entered was spacious, mostly empty, the few pieces of furniture set close to the walls. A high-walled garden was visible through the windows, a slightly overgrown paradise. The only dominant item was a piano, not the rickety upright job of Pike View fame, but a polished grand, a Steinway. Margery was sitting at a coffee table, hunched over, dressed in a black gown. Her only adornment was a pewter necklace of abstract design. She was skeletal thin.

"Come to me," she said, in a croaky voice.

I did so, bringing myself into her field of vision. But I'm not sure if she saw me, for her eyes, when revealed, were narrowed, and wet. Her skin was leathery. Her hands trembled. Her haircut was in the same style, entirely silver now, that severe bob hanging on no matter how her face aged. Yet despite these outward signs of decay, she was in good spirits. A ridiculous question came to me: was this old, old lady animated from within by a young girl, a ghost inhabiting the shell? The idea made me shiver. I tried not to show my discomfort.

"Is it you? Joe, is it?"

"That's right…" I almost called her *Miss*, as I had done upon our first meeting. That scene at the drystone wall, with Nipper biting at my legs. "Joe Sutter. You sent for me."

"Yes, yes. Sit with me, would you?"

I took a seat across the table from her, saying, "It's very good to see you again, Margery."

She smiled. I felt awkward. What was I doing here? She spoke, but too quietly to be heard. I leaned in, to make out her words.

"I can't remember why I asked you here."

What could I possibly say to that? Luckily, the assistant came in then, carrying a tray with tea things on it. In complete silence she set this down on the table and poured out two cups.

A pair of tiny fondant-covered cakes sat on a plate, one each, I presumed, less than a mouthful.

"Thank you, Samantha. Please, take the rest of the day off."

The young lady nodded and left us alone. I watched in silence as Margery ate her little cake with great delight, sipping her tea afterwards. I did the same.

"Tell me about yourself," she said.

I gave her a potted history, career, marriage, children, grandchildren, one of them a witness. A perfectly average life, as I related it. Yet she looked displeased, and a single word came to her lips in a whisper: *children*. I admit, I had looked her up on Wikipedia before coming here. *Margery Jane Adams, born 1934 (age 88), Bradford, Yorkshire. Visual artist and musician.* She had married, back in the early seventies, but it had not lasted long, and there were no offspring listed.

"I have something for you, Joe."

She indicated a shelf below the table. I reached down and pulled up a book. Whenever I had thought back to that day in the cellar of Pike View and the reading of the kestrel's egg, this book in memory was a massive leather-bound tome, very old, the pages crinkly and yellow. But as I now saw, it was just a large, somewhat fancy notebook, the kind sold at WH Smith's. But the contents were the same as I remembered, holding the same power: Holbrook's sightings through the Koag mask, all written out in Margery's fair hand.

"Joe, I'd like you to take this, for your own use."

"No, no, I couldn't–"

"You'll need it. Do you still have the mask George gave to you?"

"Yes."

"It is a living thing, that mask. And the more you use it..."

"I know. Slowly, the effect weakens. Perhaps that's why I haven't used it that much."

"It's your job to tell the story, Joe."

"I'm sorry?"

"The real story of what happened that final day in the woods, and everything that led up to it, complete and unadorned. People need to know what Georgie did for us, for all of us."

"Margery, what exactly did he do?"

"You will see."

"You said, *for all of us*?"

"Yes." She was getting irritated.

"Margery, what do you mean?"

She glared at me. "Will you promise?"

After a moment I answered her: "Of course. I promise."

She nodded at this. Then she stood up, and when I did the same she hooked her hand through my elbow and we walked across the room. It was a slow progress. She took a seat at the piano stool and waited as her breath came back. The room was very quiet. I stood close by in great anticipation. Her fingers began their separate journeys across the keys, left and right, creating from a complex web of notes a simple tender melody. It was vaguely known to me, in the way a pop record of your youth might be, but it took me a while to place it.

"Henrietta's tune," I said.

The music wound on as her hands explored stranger harmonies. "I would always turn it into a song by Delius, 'A Late Lark'." Her body swayed as the music took her over. Instantly I was back there, upon that summer's day, long lost, now recalled. But she did not sing this time. Instead she quietly spoke the words. *A late lark twitters from the quiet skies.* I could not move, nor would I want to. At the second verse her voice took on a melodious quality, half-singing, half-speaking. The high notes eluded her, her voice cracked. But it was lovely to hear. *The dust ascends in a rosy-and-golden haze. The spires shine, and are changed.* In response to the music, Koag rose from her body, the grains emerging from the silver of her hair, her veined neck and bony shoulders, her clothes, her hands, in many colours: turquoise, burnt sienna, jade green, dots of pink, ripples of ice blue. I now realised that the room had been arranged as a sort of theatre with a central stage area. Here the dust gathered. *In the valley shadows rise. The lark sings on.* Koag formed itself into a number of separate shapes, figures, very much like characters in a drama. Each note of music drew them more and more into life, until I could see them clearly: older, younger, male and female, half a dozen altogether, and a child among them, Henrietta Tudor herself, dressed in the same blue gown with the lace at the cuffs and neckline, ageless, exactly as she was when I had first glimpsed her at Pike View. And myself, now a man in his mid-sixties, a mortal soul. Over the years the girl had drawn fellow spirits into Margery's body, a new home. I whispered, *Koag, Koag, speak to me, help me.* The ghosts answered in words of dust that I understood perfectly, and misunderstood equally as well. Despite everything, and because of everything, and in praise of everything, the beautiful puzzle remains unsolved.

The music stopped. Margery's hands rested on the keys in the shape of the final chord, and then went to her lap. Her head was bowed; she might have been sleeping. I tried speaking with her, receiving no reply. When I looked again to the stage, the people of the dust were already fading away.

Margery Adams died a month later. On the day of her death, at the very moment of her death, the dust became visible to everyone in the country, crossing Helme's Threshold into a shared viewing. The phenomenon lasted for nine hours and thirteen minutes. We were all witnesses that day, all beholders. Last year, at exactly the same time, the same thing happened. We live in hope that it will take place a third time, this year, and from then on, every year the same.

The people have already given it a name: Specklesoft Day.

25

The house had changed. Flowery curtains, the roof repaired, window frames and door painted a nice shade of blue. No muddy Land Rover in the yard; a large people carrier had taken its place. In fact, no yard, but a neat front garden with a drive. The shed at the side had been converted into a double-doored garage. The name plate on the gatepost read not *Pike View*, but *Hillside Cottage*. I imagined a well-to-do family living there, the rooms brightly lit, kids laughing, dinner parties, the smell of fresh coffee.

"Was that the place?" Eileen asked.

"Yeah. Funny to look at it now."

We walked further up the slope to Brendle Pike. The tower was exactly the same, still bricked up, still guarding the land. There were a few other people, taking photos of each other on their phones. The two benches were occupied, so we stood and admired the view. These were the fields and lanes where I used to run wild, all the day long. As though reading my thoughts, Eileen asked how my knees were doing after the climb, and I told her they were holding up. Then she pointed out the four counties. "Lancashire, Cheshire, Derbyshire, Yorkshire. You see, I remember."

"Mrs Pierce taught us well."

"Mrs Pierce?"

"Our teacher at junior school."

"You remember her name?"

"Well, I've been writing the book, haven't I? It's all coming back to me."

"When will I get to read it?"

"Soon." (Eileen was always my first reader.) "I'm just finishing draft one."

"You've made some of it up, though?"

"A few elaborations. Other than that, it's real."

"The unvarnished truth, eh?"

"Sure. I have Chloe calling you a toffee-nosed cow."

She laughed. "Fair enough."

I pointed out the drystone wall, still intact (those things would last for centuries), where I used to hide, spying on the house with my binoculars. "I once shot you with a long-range sniper's rifle. Direct hit. Your head exploded."

"Nice. How had I offended you?"

"I thought you were stealing Denny away from me."

"Oh, Denny, Denny. Poor kid."

"I know."

We stood in silence for a moment, each with our own thoughts. Then a seat became vacant and we sat down before another couple could steal it.

Eileen asked, "How's Greot doing?"

"Greot is looking good. But lately, I've been calling it Koag."

"That was Denny's invention, wasn't it?"

I nodded. "Yeah. Because of the book, I've gotten used to it again."

"I remember now. You spelled it with a K."

"Well, it's much more magical that way."

"Oh, I agree."

There was a sly little smile on her face. I didn't mind. I described the highlights of Koag's local coagulations for her: where it was gathered over the towns in varied effects and colours, sparkling under the sunlight; how it still followed the line of Stubbs Canal. But some of the shapes and patterns were new; for instance, the horizontal layer of orange that used to hover above the cricket ground was now a stippling of violet and yellow dots. At least the spire of St Matilda's was still draped in Hendrix's purple haze: a constant holy ghost. It was a bright, crisp day in late May. The grass was fresh, a light breeze blew across the fields. Eileen pointed out a bird in the sky, a kestrel. I enjoyed the idea that it was a descendent of the one who had kept me company in 1968. The thought made me reappraise the view, seeing the things that had changed, or disappeared. For instance, Bradshaw's Mill was now a block of fancy apartments, and the wasteground next to it a supermarket. They say that Monty's caravan is still there, parked in the frozen food aisle. I might visit it at some point, I'm not sure yet. It doesn't feel right, to picture it in such a setting.

We were staying at the Barlow's family home in Cheshire. Eileen's father made his fortune in builder's supplies, and the company had half a dozen outlets dotted around the North West, although the firm was run these days by her brother. My mother remarried late in life, to Reg Saunders, a man in the motor trade. ("The Dreaded Reg", Chloe and I used to call him, when he first appeared on the scene.) Reg and Lily retired to the seaside town of Lytham St Annes. She is buried there, alongside her second husband. My father passed away at the age of 67 (my age now) of pulmonary thrombosis. We met a few times over the years. It was okay, it was fine.

My eyes travelled across to Brendle Woods, or what remained of it. A new housing estate had encroached upon it, leaving a smaller patch of trees, more a miniature nature park, complete with a picnic and play area. The old railway track was now a nature trail. For me, no matter how they change it, this area of land will always be associated with George Holbrook, his life, his death. It remains a place where love and sorrow touch and intermingle, each clinging to the other. He gave everything he had, in order that Henrietta Tudor might cross the border. Koag's story is not yet complete. I am happy to have played a small part in it, whatever it might lead to in the future.

In the meantime, I have given myself a project, following Margery's final instructions.

Task No.4
Construct a Time Machine

This novel is the first outcome of that endeavour, a way back, for myself, and a way forwards for the spirits of the people who aided me in that summer's adventures. I shall never forget them. They were the true warrior poets of this tale, the ones who fought every day of their lives, and who never stopped writing their poems of the fight. The fight might be an argument with a loved one, a spat at work, a mistake made, a crime committed, a joke that misfired, a punch, a rivalry, a battle, a war. Any of the many ways we as humans do harm to each other, and to ourselves, and how we survive despite all the knocks and scrapes and wounds. To never give up. And then to take that struggle and turn it into a poem, and by a poem meaning a joke, a tall tale, an anecdote, a juicy bit of gossip, a novel, a painting, a roar of defiance, the shake of a fist, a drunken singsong with your mates on a Friday night when everything else is lost. I believe this was Mr Holbrook's meaning in that final lesson at the tower, the one he never finished. Other artists, other writers, have also been an inspiration, but Holbrook and Adams were there at the beginning, the dust from which my stories were formed, crossing Helme's Threshold, becoming visible for the first time.

In the dust, in the dark, words are waiting.

Near to the edge of the new housing estate, I could see a faint shimmering in the air, a mirage. Red and lilac dust clouds were forming into the shapes of people, but with elongated forms. They looked like the figures L.S. Lowry used to include in his paintings, albeit seen through a haze of fog. I imagined they were residents of Brendleshire. I had read reports of sightings in the online witness forums. It was one of the reasons why I wanted to visit here, apart from any research value the trip might have for my novel in progress. I focussed my attention, but the more I looked, the less I saw. That was the trouble. It was so easy to be mistaken, even by beholders, which I am not, not by any stretch. I never achieved that status. I haven't moved the dust one quarter-inch since that summer.

"What have you seen?" Eileen asked.

"I'm not sure."

We were alone now, the other visitors having moved on further along the ridge. It was time. I reached into my knapsack and pulled out the linen bundle. Inside was the mask.

My wife said, "Go ahead, take as long as you like." She walked over to the tower.

I took off my glasses. No need for them; everything would be crystal clear. I brought the mask up to my face. It was true, what I'd said to Margery; I had worn it only a couple of times over the years, and always in places of limited interest, such as the spare room in our house, or a plain field of grass, locations that would not tax its powers too much. But this time would be different; this area of the world was the mask's birthplace, from here it drew its original magic. Once the material had settled itself to my face, I turned to look at the tower. Here was the written world.

I have read the skies, I have read the river.

In Brendleshire, naming and doing are not separate activities, so there is no difference at all between nouns and verbs. All is, all becomes. Accordingly, at first I saw only a swirling grey dust, without any of the distinctive colours that Koag prefers. But this greyness soon parted to reveal the tower in its truest form. The structure glowed with its own history. All the words and names for the various lookout posts and boundary markers of centuries past emerged out of the dust, and were superimposed over each other, forming a blur of meaning. There was so much history gathered here, it was actually quite painful to witness, especially the many words of blood and pain and anger shed in battle against the Romans, the Vikings, the Royalist forces in the Civil War.

I have read the birdsong, and the fall of leaves.

My wife's form wavered near to the tower, a dark figure speckled all over with sky-blue and ochre. I saw at once every single word related to her over the years of her life, and of her ancestors and her children – her work, her love for me, the arguments we had had, the year of separation, the reconciliation, her dreams and desires, her fears, each thought and feeling given a name, and then renamed, and renamed endlessly. I saw the shapes of her body as it changed over time, her thoughts now and forever in the past, the jokes she told herself and herself alone, her joys and sadnesses spelled out momentarily before they drifted away into the sky, only to be replaced by other words, a constant work in progress, every aspect of her life inscribed in the language of the dust, readable only in each moment passing, but fiercely present: the most complex book ever written. No wonder George Holbrook struggled so to express even one portion of this knowledge.

Sun bright, dreaming bright, dust of daylight dreaming lightly, woman walking darkly shadow walking slow around the tower high around the fields of falling shadow falling…

The bell of St Matilda's sounded in the distance, each soft *clang* a series of words that rolled in a wave of air towards me. I read them as they arrived, seeing in them the history of the bell and all it had tolled for over the years: births, deaths, marriages, the onset of war, the return of peace.

I stood up from the bench and gazed out over the landscape. Thanks to the mask, I saw not the fields and the towns, but the language used to describe those fields and towns throughout history: places names, descriptions from medieval atlases, lines of poetry, folk songs, street chants, and so on. Within this collective expression the people went about their lives, seen as patterns in the dust of England's pages, as brightly decorated as any illuminated manuscript. Koag was the ink, and the ink flowed freely. That shimmering mirage I had glimpsed near to the estate was in fact a group of children playing a counting game, and I felt I was viewing my own youth, even as their shapes were rewritten: now they were born, now they lived, now they grew old and died and were reborn as a new set of words, a story seeking a new expression.

I have read the blood, and the ploughing of the fields.

A movement in the sky caught my attention. It was the kestrel, or more accurately the idea of the kestrel as people have viewed it and written about it through the ages. It was a collection of words in flight, all of which coincided to make the kestrel into what it was, in the world. I saw the word *wind* and the word *feather*, the word *beak* and the word *prey*, and the word *wing* and the word *mate*, the word *hover* and the word *dive*, the word *glide* and the word *swoop* and the word *eye* and the word *claw* and the word *spoor* and the word *egg*, most of all the word *egg*, which contained all the others words in waiting within the word *shell* and the word *nest* and the word *hatch* and the word *song*, and so many other words as well, so many that I could never read them all, and all of these words fused together into the bird itself as it roamed the word *sky* seeking the word *cloud*, the word *distance*.

And then it was gone, off on its travels. I peeled the mask from my face as Eileen came up to me. She put her arm through mine and we walked back down the hill towards Weeping Cross Lane, and the little town of Ormsley Vale.

ACKNOWLEDGEMENTS

Like Joe Sutter, I was eleven years old in 1968. I lived in a town in Lancashire, in the North West of England. This story is inspired by my youthful days. It spins a fantasy from the things I experienced, the places I visited, and the people I knew – friends, teachers and family. That said, there is no intention to directly copy life, and the characters are not meant to represent real people. The town of Ormsley Vale is fictional, as are its residents.

I would like to thank everyone at Angry Robot Books, for believing in *Moon Over Brendle*, and for their work on the book, especially my editor Simon Spanton. As always, my agent Michelle Kass, and her team, have been a constant source of support over the years.

I have changed ever so slightly the poetry of William Blake and William Ernest Henley to include mentions of the dust. The real and the unreal overlap, I hope in interesting ways.

ABOUT THE AUTHOR

JEFF NOON is an award-winning British novelist, short story writer and playwright. He won the Arthur C. Clarke Award for *Vurt*, the Astounding Award for Best New Writer, and a Tinniswood Award for innovation in radio drama. He was trained in the visual arts, and was musically active on the Manchester punk scene before starting to write plays for the theatre. His Nyquist Mysteries series explores the interzone between crime fiction and SF.